WENDY MARKHAM

is a pseudonym for *New York Times* bestselling, award-winning novelist Wendy Corsi Staub, who has written more than sixty fiction and nonfiction books for adults and teenagers in various genres—among them contemporary and historical romance, suspense, mystery, television and movie tie-in and biography. She coauthored a hardcover mystery series with former New York City mayor Ed Koch and has ghostwritten books for various well-known personalities. A small-town girl at heart, she was born and raised in western New York on the shores of Lake Erie and in the heart of the notorious snow belt. By third grade, her heart was set on becoming a published author; a few years later, a school trip to Manhattan convinced her that she had to live there someday. At twenty-one, she moved alone to New York City and worked as an office temp, freelance copywriter, advertising account coordinator and book editor before selling her first novel, which went on to win a Romance Writers of America RITA® Award. She has since received numerous positive reviews and achieved bestseller status, most notably for the psychological suspense novels she writes under her own name. Her Red Dress Ink title, *Slightly Single*, was one of Waldenbooks' Best Books of 2002. Very happily married with two children, Wendy writes full-time and lives in a cozy old house in suburban New York, proving that childhood dreams really can come true. Visit her at www.wendymarkham.com.

Wendy Markham

Slightly Married

**RED
DRESS
I N K**
™

SLIGHTLY MARRIED

A Red Dress Ink novel

ISBN-13: 978-0-373-89538-0
ISBN-10:   0-373-89538-0

© 2007 by Wendy Corsi Staub.

www.RedDressInk.com

Printed in U.S.A.

Dedicated with love to my sons Morgan and Brody,
but most of all to my husband, Mark—
in some cosmic coincidence I finished writing the last page
of this book on our fifteenth wedding anniversary.

Cent'anni.

1

Meet Jack Candell, the man who bought a lifetime sub-
scription to TiVo without first trying it out, yet spent six
painstaking months in possession of an heirloom diamond
engagement ring and no clue how—or when—or, I suspect,
if—he should propose to me.

But all that excruciating will-he-or-won't-he suspense is
behind us now. Jack has finally committed to a lifetime sub-
scription to Tracey Spadolini, live-in girlfriend of two-plus
years.

What can be more romantic than getting engaged on
Valentine's Day?

I'll tell you: getting engaged on Valentine's Day on the
heels of your best friend's gay wedding while wearing a red-
and-black brocade bridesmaid's gown, your scalp coated with
sleet and the Aussie spritzed remnants of an elegant updo, as
your fiancé kneels in the slushy gutter on West Broadway.

Maybe you had to be there.

Well, I was, and believe me, hearing Jack's long-awaited, heartfelt proposal—and saying yes—was the most romantic, exhilarating event of my life.

The afterglow has lingered all the way uptown on the subway and throughout the short walk home from the Ninety-sixth Street station to our building. At this point, I'm bursting with joy, anxious to share the news and show off the ring. Too bad Jimmy, our favorite doorman, is off duty most Saturdays.

In his place tonight is Gecko, a dour old chatterbox who, if you say anything more than a polite hello in passing, will hold you captive in the lobby for hours with his ongoing monologue about his gout and diverticulitis, what he can and can't eat these days, and graphic detail about the effect on his various bodily functions if he disobeys the gastroenterologist's orders.

I wisely keep my hand in my pocket and afterglow to myself as we pass him.

But the glow resumes as Jack puts his arm around me on the journey up to our floor, even though we're sharing the elevator with a trio of yapping terriers and Quint, the effete neighborhood dog walker, clad in what looks suspiciously like lederhosen.

You know how some things in life can never quite live up to the anticipation? Like Christmas, losing your virginity and biting into your first Hostess Twinkie after a week on Atkins?

Well, for once, I'm not even slightly disappointed. I'm pleased to report that so far, being engaged is every bit as exhilarating as I thought it would be.

I walk on air toward the door to apartment 9K with a marquis-cut diamond newly twinkling on the fourth finger of my left hand and my future husband—*husband,* people!—by my side.

My mental string orchestra is launching into yet another lilting version of "Isn't It Romantic" when my beloved glances down, grimaces and informs me, "My feet are soaked. They're going to stink to high heaven when I take off these shoes."

Yeah, well, better stinky than cold, I think, undaunted, and my private orchestra plays a little louder to drown out any other unromantic proclamations Jack might be inclined to spout.

At least he hasn't informed me that he has to *piss like a racehorse*, which is a frequent mood-dampening line of his.

Jack retrieves his keys from the pocket of his overcoat as we cover the last few steps to our apartment. I do my best to focus on the afterglow lest my thoughts wander to his potentially stinky feet or my own throbbing ones crammed into fugly bridesmaid's shoes.

You're getting married! You're finally engaged!

Amazing. Does life get any better than this?

I imagine that from here on in, everything is going to be different. Food will taste more delicious, sex will be more fulfilling, plans of any sort will be more meaningful.

Watching my fiancé—I *so* can't wait to use that word out loud—literally unlock the door to our one-bedroom apartment, I can't help but feel as though he's figuratively opening it to our future together.

As we cross the threshold, I prepare to see our place in a whole new light.

Not that there *is* much actual light, this being a sleet-drenched February dusk.

Everywhere I look are signs that we raced out of here at the last minute this morning. My pajamas are in a heap on the floor in the doorway of the bedroom. The jelly and butter are still out on a crumb-littered countertop. On the small dinette table amid piles of sorted and unsorted mail and newspapers sit two untouched mugs of tea with the bags still in them.

Tea…for two…two…for tea, plays the jaunty orchestra in my head.

"Home sweet home," Jack announces with a contented sigh, tossing his keys on the table and throwing his sopping trench coat over the nearest chair.

"Uh-huh, we've got to move," I can't help but blurt in response.

This isn't an impulsive inspiration. It's something I've been thinking about for a while now.

Nor is this the first time I've shared the thought with Jack.

His gaze is promptly steeped with panic, same as it always is when I bring up trading our little love nest for something a little less—well, nesty.

Not that I have anything against nesting. Hell, I'm all for it. But I'd prefer a two-bedroom nest, at the very least. I'd love a heating system that isn't prone to clanging or wafting the aroma of other people's ethnic cooking. A view would be nice, too. Doesn't have to be of Central Park or the river, even—just something other than the ugly, claustrophobically close building next door.

Jack runs an agitated hand through his hair, which is normally the color of melted milk chocolate, but right now is more like dark baking chocolate because it's soaked with sleet. When we met, he wore it longer and it was kind of wavy. These days, it's really short and a little spiky on top, kind of retro-little-kid.

"Listen," I say reassuringly, "we don't have to move right away—"

"That's good, because one major life change per year is my quota."

Okay, this year's life change is obviously going to be marriage.

I can't help but wonder, though, what was last year's major life change? TiVo?

"But Jack," I proceed gingerly, unwilling to let it go yet determined to tread carefully in the wake of today's momentous occasion, "look at this place."

He does, quickly, before his brown eyes settle again—somewhat warily—on me. "What *about* this place? It's great."

"It's *tiny.*"

"I thought you said it was 'cozy.'"

I did, but that was back when I was trying to convince him that we were better off going for a one-bedroom in an Upper East Side doorman building than a more spacious Junior Four so far out in Queens that we'd have to take a bus to the subway.

"It *is* cozy," I agree, "but we've outgrown it."

Kind of like I've outgrown these dyed-to-match pointy red satin bridesmaid's pumps, which I kick into a corner of the living room. They collide with a heaping plastic basket of laundry that's been there for at least forty-eight hours. I wonder whether it's dirty, or clean and waiting to be folded, and note that I'm in no rush to find out.

"Yeah, well, this place is rent controlled." That's Jack, of course. Under the assumption that I may need to brush up on my New York real estate glossary, he adds, "Meaning, we can afford it."

"I know—" duh "—but I just got that raise with my promotion."

Yes, you read that right. As of a few weeks ago, I, Tracey Spadolini, former waitress and aspiring copywriter, am now account executive at Blaire Barnett Advertising.

I know, I have a hard time believing it myself. But I have the business cards and frequent stress headache to prove it.

"You haven't seen a penny of it yet, though," Jack points out re: my big raise.

"It should kick into my next paycheck. Or the one after that," say I, the eternal optimist. "And anyway, Carol said it would be retroactive."

Jack, who has been employed at Blaire Barnett since before I ever even started temping there, looks dubious.

It occurs to me that maybe he just doesn't want to face the fact that as an account exec for McMurray-White, a major packaged-goods client, I'll be making more than he does as a media supervisor. I read somewhere that some men are in-timidated by their wives out-earning them. But not Jack. He doesn't have a chauvinistic bone in his body, I assure myself.

Wife! I'm going to be Jack's wife!

"Come on, we're getting married," I remind him gently. "Don't you think it's time to get a real apartment? Maybe even *buy* a place?"

Jack doesn't answer for a moment.

That's because he's pretty much hyperventilating.

When he can speak, he chokes out, "Do you know what Manhattan real estate costs?"

"Who said anything about Manhattan? We can always look in the suburbs...or not," I add hastily, lest he hurtle himself out the nearest window.

"Come on, Trace, you were the one who convinced me that we had to live in Manhattan in the first place. I would have been more than happy to stay in Brooklyn—"

"You wanted to look in Queens."

"Or Queens," he says amenably. "But you had your heart set on the Upper East Side. Remember?"

"I do remember. But that was a long time ago, you know? I've changed my mind since then."

"About Queens?"

"Queens. Living there? No." I suppress a shudder.

It's not that I'm opposed to the outer boroughs in general. I'm the first one to hop on the subway to Yankee Stadium or the Staten Island Ferry for a weekend outing at my friend Brenda's.

Maybe not the first one. But I'm generally open to visiting the boroughs, with good reason, advance notice and nothing better to do.

I'm just not open to *moving* to a borough at this stage of the game. I mean, if I'm going to live in the city, it's going to be Manhattan. And if I'm priced out of the city...

"I can see us in the suburbs, can't you?" I ask Jack, who grimaces. "Like Westchester or Long Island, Jersey, maybe..."

For a second he just looks at me. Then his famous dimples reappear in his lower cheeks at long last as he laughs. Hard.

Maybe a little too hard.

Okay, maniacally.

When he stops, he says, "We've been engaged less than a half hour, and you've already got us buying a house in the suburbs, Trace."

"Or a condo." Two bedrooms, two baths and a permanent parking spot for the car we're going to get the second we move. Nothing fancy. Maybe a little sporty, but not red. Sleek and black might be nice....

"House, condo, whatever." Jack shakes his head. "Why are you suddenly worrying about moving?"

"Because not only are we running out of room here, but things keep breaking down on a daily basis."

"That's an exaggeration."

"Not really."

"Name one thing that broke down today."

You, I think, *when you decided to pop the question at last.*

Bwa-hahahahahahaha...that's one quip meant for my personal amusement only. No need to remind Jack that he dragged his feet all the way to the fateful waterlogged gutter where he finally proposed.

"The toaster."

Jack blinks. "The toaster?"

"It refused to pop after I shoved it down this morning. I scorched three pieces of bread."

"But the toaster isn't part of the apartment. That's ours. Let's just buy a new one. It'll be cheaper than a colonial in Scarsdale by, like, one point four mil and change."

I crack a smile, but also point out, "The toaster wouldn't be on the blink if there weren't something wrong with the wiring in the kitchen outlet."

"Who are you, Bob Vila? How do you know that?"

"I just know. Come on, Jack. There's a lot of stuff that needs to be fixed around this place, and every time something crashes, we have to wait for other people to do something about it. Wouldn't you rather have a place of our own?"

He tilts his head. "You mean, would I rather be the one calling the electrician and paying him than the one calling the guy who calls the electrician and pays him? Or, better yet, would I rather be the one who gets a bad shock trying to figure out if an electrician is necessary in the first place?"

"You don't have to be so negative. You've never gotten a shock in your life."

"I've gotten plenty, since I meant you."

His tone is light and I can't help but grin. "You mean the little lightning bolts of passion, right?"

"Definitely." He grins and kisses my forehead affectionately. "Whoa. Sparks."

I make a face at him.

"Come on, Trace. Do we have to discuss this right now? Don't you think you should try and live in the moment a little? You know…bask in the glow?"

"I'm glowing," I protest. "Sparking, too. Remember?"

"Maybe on the outside. Inside, you're fast-forwarding, scheming real-estate strategies…"

"*Scheming* makes it sound like I'm doing something wrong."

"Planning, then. Is planning better?"

"Much. And I can't help it. I'm excited."

"So am I. Let's just enjoy it for a while. This is the only time in our lives we're going to get engaged. So tonight, let's bask, dammit." The Candell dimples deepen charmingly.

"I'm basking. I'm definitely basking," I say with a laugh, feeling a little sheepish. "Basking, glowing, sparking..."

"Good." Jack gives me a squeeze, kisses my forehead again and opens the fridge.

What I don't dare admit aloud is that in my heart, I've been engaged to him for months—ever since his mother, Wilma, told me he had the heirloom ring in his possession.

We...will raise...a fa-mily...a boy...for you...a girl...for me...

See, I like to be proactive. Not only have I got our entire future mapped out, but I already picked a wedding date. Which reminds me...

"While we're basking," I say to Jack, "what do you think of the third Saturday in October?"

"For what?"

He didn't really say that, I tell myself, watching him grab an Amstel Light, then head to the living room to fish the remote from beneath the toppled stack of magazines on the coffee table.

What he really said was, *I would love to marry you on the third Saturday in October, darling.*

And he isn't really turning on the television and flipping the channel to ESPN.

No, in reality, he's heading for the shower to wash his stinky feet for the romantic candlelight dinner we're going to have tonight to celebrate our engagement.

Except, he's not.

"Jack—" I am incredulous, watching him bend over to unlace his dress shoes, one eye on the television "—are you watching TV?"

His gaze flicks in my direction.

"Yes?" he says tentatively. "Why?"

"It's just—" I break off and try to think of a way to phrase it. A delicate way. Or at least a way that doesn't involve any four-letter words.

I settle on, "I thought we were basking."

"We are. I just wanted to check a couple of scores."

"But…" The mind boggles. "We just got engaged, remember? For the only time in our lives. Don't you think we should…celebrate? And maybe…talk about the wedding?"

"You mean, *plan* it?" he asks, wearing the same expression he might have if I asked him to knock over the Bank of New York branch on the corner to prove his love for me.

"Not the whole thing right this second, but we definitely need to set a date."

"Okay, the third Saturday in October. That sounds good." He pries his shoe off his foot, then peels off his black dress sock and sniffs it.

Watching him, I have to remind myself that I am head over heels in love with him. So what if he behaves, on occasion, like a caged primate at the Bronx Zoo?

You find him endearing, faults and all. You really do.

You have to, because the moment his little quirks cease to be endearing, it all goes to hell in a handcart.

"I told you my feet were going to stink," he tells me before tossing the sock in the general vicinity of the laundry in the corner, which I hope to God is dirty.

I smile to show that I have absolutely no problem with stinky feet. No problem at all.

I'm in love, dammit.

"About the wedding…" I say as he bends over his other shoe.

"Yeah?" The other shoe comes off and he's sniffing that sock now.

Okay, I'm sorry, but he just crossed the line from endearing to freakish.

"Jack…cut it out."

"What?"

"Please stop smelling your sock."

"I'm just seeing if it stinks."

"The other one did. What are the odds that this one doesn't?"

He makes a face and it sails through the air after its partner. "Zero."

Mental Note: you are in love with this man. Quirks others might find unappealing—disgusting, even—are charming to you. Going to hell in a handcart is not an option.

I allow myself a moment to get back into a romantic frame of mind before saying again, "If we do go with the third Saturday in October—"

"I thought we just agreed on it."

"It's not that simple."

"Why not?"

"The number-one place we'd want to have it at is booked all the other Saturdays in October, actually, and by now it's probably booked that day, too. There aren't that many other decent places to choose from, so…"

Oops.

I said too much, starting with the word *booked*.

But instead of asking the obvious—*how can you possibly know that, if we've been engaged less than an hour and we've spent every moment of that time together?*—Jack asks, "What number-one place is that?"

"Shorewood Country Club. In Brookside," I add at his blank look.

"We want to have our wedding in *Brookside?*"

"My hometown," I clarify, realizing there must be a crack enclave in the South Bronx also called Brookside. No wonder he's mixed up and wearing that *are-you-out-of-your-mind?* expression.

"We never said that," Jack informs me as he sneaks another glance at the television, where an ESPN reporter is animatedly recapping some game.

"I know we didn't say that. We never said *anything* because we never talked about it before," I point out.

I neglect to add, *That's because you once said something along the lines of "getting married is for assholes."*

Pardon his French.

"I just assumed we'd get married in Brookside," I say instead.

"Why?"

Realizing a crash course in Nuptials 101 is in order, I patiently explain, "Because weddings are usually held in the bride's hometown. Kate and Billy's was in Mobile, remember?"

To Jack's credit, he doesn't point out that there's a tremendous difference between a charming Gulf Coast city and a tiny blue-collar town south of Buffalo on Lake Erie.

To his discredit, he says instead, "Well, since we happen to live in New York, where there are millions of decent places to have a wedding, why wouldn't we just get married here?"

I'll admit this gives me pause.

Because, when you come right down to it…he has a point.

Why *not* just get married here?

Back when I was certain I would eventually marry my ex-boyfriend, Will McCraw—which, unbeknownst to me, Will McCraw never once considered—I assumed the wedding would be right here in New York.

That's because Will didn't like Brookside. He didn't like my family, either, I suspect, although he never said it. What he did say, frequently, and in their presence, was that he didn't like Brookside. Pretty much in those words.

Just one of the many reasons I suspect that all those novenas my mother sent my way for years were probably her pious Catholic answer to voodoo. If there's any truth to the power of prayer, my messy breakup with Will can be attributed to Connie Spadolini's direct pipeline to God. Imagine what she could accomplish if she converted all that maternal energy to global causes.

"Well?"

Oh, yeah. Jack is still wondering why we shouldn't just get married here in New York.

"Cost, for one thing," I say. "Do you know how much we'd pay for a sit-down dinner for three hundred in Manhattan?"

"Three hundred?"

I have his full attention now—and he certainly has mine, because it looks as though I may have to administer CPR any second.

"Tracey, you're not serious about that, are you?"

"A sit-down dinner? Well, we can look into a buffet, but sometimes it's more cost effective to—"

"No, I'm talking about the head count. Come on. Three *hundred?*"

"I have a huge family, Jack. And then there's your family, and all our co-workers, and our friends from New York, and our high-school friends, and college roommates…"

"And don't forget my old Cub Scout den leader or Jimmy the doorman," he says dryly.

I decide this is probably not a good time to mention that Jimmy the doorman was on my initial guest list—the one I pared down from just under five hundred to the aforementioned three, and with considerable angst over every cut.

"Hey," he says suddenly, "if we had it here in New York, I bet a lot of your family wouldn't come."

I bristle at that. "So we want to have the wedding in the most inconvenient place as possible? Is that your point?"

"No. That was definitely not my point. Forget I said anything."

"Listen, Jack…we don't have to decide all of these details right now. We're supposed to be basking in the moment, remember?"

"I was basking," he says defensively, and gulps some beer. "You're the one who's scheming."

"Not scheming. Planning."

"Planning to turn our simple little wedding into an extravaganza."

Our *simple little* wedding?

Correct me if I'm wrong, but did I ever say anything about simple? Or little?

Granted, the guest list is somewhat negotiable…to a certain point.

But if there's anything I learned from my six months of

reading *Modern Bride* on the sly, it's that weddings are anything but simple.

However—how could I have forgotten?—if there's anything I learned in the last few years of living with Jack, it's that you don't just spring things on him.

He has always needed time to get used to new ideas—like, say, ordering brown rice instead of white with Chinese food. Or setting the alarm clock to radio instead of that annoying high-pitch bleating sound.

He's not going to instantly embrace the notion of a gala event for three hundred as opposed to a "simple little wedding."

The trick is to let an idea seep in and simmer for a while. If I'm lucky, and I let enough time go by, he'll wind up thinking he came up with it himself.

"Let's just back-burner the wedding discussion for tonight," I suggest. "We can talk about it tomorrow."

"Tomorrow?"

"Not tomorrow?"

"I was thinking in a few days," he says. "Or maybe, I don't know, next weekend? We can schedule a time when we can sit down and discuss it."

"You make it sound like a client meeting," I say, only half amused and not the least bit surprised.

As I said, he's not the most spontaneous guy in the world, unless you're talking about home-entertainment technology.

Then again, a lifetime commitment to TiVo doesn't involve a public religious ceremony, a wide circle of witnesses or exotic canapés.

In any case, I decide to let Jack off the hook tonight. Between Raphael's wedding and the engagement, we've experienced enough drama for one day.

I go over to the couch, plop down beside him, sling my legs across his lap and my arms around his neck, and ask, "So how do you think we should celebrate our engagement?"

"And Valentine's Day," he reminds me.

"Right. I almost forgot." I have a card and a gift-wrapped sweater for him hidden under the bed. I bought the sweater on winter clearance at Bloomingdale's.

Had my raise already kicked in—or had I suspected I'd be getting a delightful diamond ring today—I probably would have sprung for a nice shirt from Ralph Lauren's spring collection for men.

But I had no idea this was the big day. How could I? Even Jack didn't realize it.

So I guess he can be spontaneous after all. I mean, the man got down on his knee in the streaming gutter on the spur of the moment.

Then again, how spontaneous is a proposal after six agonizing—at least, for me—months of his having the ring in his possession?

Not that he has any idea that I already knew about the ring, thanks to his mother's inability to keep a secret. He'll never know that I had actually laid eyes on it once already, when I stumbled across it while rummaging through his suitcase during our Caribbean vacation last month.

No, I wasn't shamelessly snooping around for the diamond. I'm not *that* sneaky.

I only wanted to borrow his sweatshirt and stumbled across the ring box accidentally.

Yes, I opened it and snuck a peek.

Yes, I am that sneaky.

Anyway, I was genuinely surprised by his proposal today. So surprised he'll never suspect that I've been waiting for him to do it since Labor Day weekend; that every gift-giving occasion since then has had me anticipating a diamond, and being crushed with disappointment.

Sweetest Day brought a Chia Pet; Christmas, a Gore-Tex Mountain Guide Gold parka…

Need I say more?

Like I said, though, that's all behind us now.

"Listen, I made reservations a few days ago for a nice dinner tonight," he informs me, putting his arm around me as I snuggle close to him on the couch. "Do you still want to do that?"

"Sure." I'm relieved that he at least had a plan for Valentine's Day. A plan that doesn't involve a zip-out fleece lining or a creepy, living green Afro. "Where are we going?"

"To that new bistro you wanted to check out on West Fourth Street. I heard the French onion soup is amazing."

"That sounds great."

"Hey! Maybe we can have it at our wedding!" he suggests enthusiastically.

"Maybe we can!" I say just as enthusiastically, but I'm thinking there's no way in hell I'm going to surround myself by three hundred people with onion breath at our once-in-a-lifetime event.

"So what time are those reservations?" I ask Jack.

"Eight-thirty. Why? Are you hungry now?"

"Not really. I'm sure I will be by then, though."

"Yeah, I can think of a great way to work up an appetite," he says suggestively, and in a swift, smooth move, flips me onto my back.

He nuzzles my neck with his stubble-studded face. "Your hair is sticky."

"That's hair spray."

"And it's all pinned together."

"That's my fancy hairdo from the wedding. Don't you like it?"

"No. I like it better down. Don't wear it like this for our wedding, okay? It doesn't feel…normal."

I laugh, thinking this is one of the things I really love about him.

You know, that he's such a…typical *guy*. That, aside from sock sniffing, he's unabashedly into sex, and sports, and beer, and me…unlike the late thinks-he's-great Will the Metrosexual.

I really have come a long way from that one-sided relationship with a man—and I use the term loosely—who was head over heels in love with somebody else. Not another woman. Not even another man. No, Will McCraw was deeply in love with himself. That's the only thing we ever had in common. It just took me a couple of years and a whole lot of heartache to figure that out.

Jack Candell, however, is indisputably in love with me. Only me. And he's promised to love me forever.

I am definitely basking now.

So much so that I'm positive we'll be able to agree on the details of our wedding.

What counts more than anything is that we love each other, and we're going to spend the rest of our lives together.

Nothing else matters.

2

Okay, so I take back what I said last night.

Other things *do* matter.

Things like head counts and menus and which end of New York State gets to host the big event—and that it will, indeed, be a big event.

So no, this getting-married thing isn't just about being in love.

I figure that out the moment I awaken on my first Sunday morning as a fiancée to realize that A) I've got about eight months to plan my dream wedding, and B) the afterglow-basking must come to an abrupt end if I'm going to get this show on the road.

I slip out of bed quietly so that I don't disturb Jack, who's sleeping soundly at last. He was up and down for most of the night, blaming the hour delay in getting our reserved table at the bistro and the rich pasta dish he scarfed down after a fried-cheese appetizer.

I, however, suspect that last night's extreme case of *agita* could be attributed to the cause célèbre for our dinner, rather than the food itself, or the hour.

This, after all, is a man who regularly comes home from late nights at the office to unwind with family serving–size Chef Boyardee beef ravioli—often gobbled cold from the can—topped off by an entire row of Double Stuf Oreos.

There was a time when I, too, could have chowed through that midnight spread, and more—and followed by a Salem Lights chaser.

Thank goodness my days of binging-without-purging are long behind me. My stint as a human chimney is more recent history, but after a couple of false starts I ultimately kicked that habit, too. I know I definitely won't go back now because there's something unsettling about envisioning myself as a bride with a cigarette butt hanging out of her mouth.

Somehow Jack, who never smoked, has always managed to avoid both a weight problem and indigestion despite his lousy late-night eating habits.

So like I said, I think his upset stomach last night was due to the shock of actually being engaged.

Oh, well. I'm sure he'll eventually get over it. And while he's lingering in the recovery stage, I really do need to get busy with the planning stage.

I open the closet and swiftly pull my lilac-colored velour robe over my comfy red-plaid flannel pajamas, then slip my bridesmaid-blistered feet into a cushy pair of green terry-cloth scuffies.

Yes, I clash. Who cares? I'm a fiancée.

And Jack—unlike Will McCraw—cares about who I am, not what I'm wearing.

You know, I can't believe there was ever a time when I thought it was normal to have your boyfriend offer fashion pointers—or that I dutifully followed Will's.

Wait until he hears I'm engaged. I can't wait to tell him.

For that matter, I can't wait to tell *someone*. Anyone.

Too bad Raphael is currently winging his way toward Africa and his safari honeymoon.

I wonder if it's too early to call Kate. She likes to sleep in. Who cares?

This is big news. I close the bedroom door behind me, grab the phone and quickly dial her number.

"Is Kate there?" I ask excitedly when Billy answers on the third ring.

"She's throwing up."

Oh. Right. Morning sickness. I forgot all about Kate's new pregnancy. She's due in late September…which means we'll have to increase the guest list to three hundred and one. Two, if she insists on bringing a nanny. Three with an accompanying wet nurse, which, knowing Kate, isn't all that far-fetched.

"Can you have her give me a call when she's done?" I ask Billy, who mumbles something that might be an agreement.

To be sure, I say, "Can you tell her it's urgent?"

"Yup." Billy hangs up.

You'd think he might at least have asked me if everything is okay.

No, you wouldn't think that. Not if you knew Billy, anyway.

Don't get me wrong, it isn't that I can't stand him—although sometimes I really can't. But that's just because he can be an arrogant, prejudiced, elitist prick.

When he's not being an arrogant, prejudiced, elitist prick, he's fine. More or less. He's just not my kind of person. We simply have nothing in common other than his being married to my best girlfriend.

Anyway, I really should be glad he didn't inquire about the urgent nature of my call, because I might have been tempted to blurt it out.

And I really don't want Billy, of all people, to be the first to hear the big news.

I consider calling Buckley O'Hanlon, my best straight guy friend. Then I remember that after Raphael's wedding, he and his fiancée, Sonja, were heading out to spend the remainder of Valentine's Day weekend at some romantic inn in the Hamptons. They won't be back until tomorrow.

I could call Brenda, Latisha or Yvonne, but I'll see them at the office first thing in the morning. It will be much more satisfying to stick out my hand and *show* them.

But I have to tell someone, and soon.

I'll just wait for Kate to call back. I'm sure it won't be long. How long does it take to barf, brush your teeth and dial the phone?

In the kitchen, I brew a big pot of coffee, throw on a Frank Sinatra CD—and promptly find myself homesick.

Between the fragrant hazelnut grounds and Frankie baby singing "My Kinda Town," I could close my eyes and imagine I'm sitting at a vinyl-covered chair in my parents' kitchen. No, it's not in Frankie baby's Chicago.

It's in Brookside, New York, just south and west of Buffalo—which might as well be in the Midwest. My father frequently plays Frank Sinatra on Sunday mornings as we lounge around in our robes with coffee. The only thing that's missing is the aroma of something frying. Bacon or pork sausage, pancakes or eggs in butter, onions and hash browns in olive oil—there's always something frying in my parents' house.

Suddenly, I'm desperate to share my big news with them—the news I told Jack just last night should wait until we see our families in person.

Since my future mother-in-law lives a short train ride away, in Westchester County, we can tell her anytime. Wilma is the one who gave Jack the heirloom diamond in the first place, so she's not likely to be very surprised.

My parents, on the other hand, gave up any hope of my getting married the day I moved in with Jack. That's because, as everybody knows, people—namely, men—don't buy cows who give milk for free. At least, everyone in Brookside knows that. Probably because Connie Spadolini told them.

What my mother never did understand is that in Manhattan, where cows are as scarce as affordable apartments and a gallon of milk is as expensive as a gallon of gasoline, living together is a prelude to marriage, not an alternative.

I can't wait to see the look on her face when she sees my ring and witnesses the end of the shameful era she refers to as *Tracey Lives In Sin*. It was only slightly less traumatic for my family than the previous eras known as *Tracey Turns Her Back on Her Family* (i.e., Relocates to New York) and *Tracey Falls in Love With a Flaming Homosexual*.

Not that Will actually was. Gay, I mean.

But as far as my father and brothers are concerned, if you're going to wear black turtlenecks and expensive cologne and have an affinity for show tunes and fresh herbs, you'd damn well better be a middle-aged Italian man. Or have a vagina.

Poor Waspy Will, sans vagina, obviously had to be closeted, according to the macho macho men in my family.

Anyhoo, the only thing Team Spadolini would find more disturbing than my living with—and not marrying—Jack, would be my marrying Will McCraw.

No danger of that. Will never was the marrying type. He told me that right from the start. I just chose not to hear him. I didn't stick my fingers into my ears and sing "Love and Marriage" at the top of my lungs whenever he opened his mouth, but I might as well have.

If Jack had told me from the start that he wasn't the marrying type, I wouldn't have believed him, either…but not because I was delusional. I've just never had any real doubt that Jack loved me and would marry me sooner or later.

Okay, I may have had *some* doubt.

And all right, at one point, I may have suspected him of having a secret girlfriend in Brooklyn to whom he was planning to give the ring.

But like I said, that's all behind me now.

The diamond is on my finger. Mine.

I'm a fiancée, tra la!

Amazing what a difference a day makes.

You know, if I thought there was any chance I'd find my mother at home right now, I'd call her and tell her my news if for no other reason than to ease her worries about my eternal salvation.

But a glance at the clock ensures me that my parents are currently at their regular Sunday-morning mass at Most Precious Mother. My mother is probably praying for me and my sins at this very moment. I know she does that every week because she likes to keep me apprised of her religious intentions.

The sooner I tell my mother the news, the sooner she can resume praying for something more relevant, like world peace, or a price break in imported almond paste.

Last night, I suggested to Jack that we try to get a cheap Jet Blue flight to Buffalo for next weekend, and he agreed.

What I strategically neglected to tell him is that while we're up there, we can also find a caterer, talk to the priest, choose a band or DJ and start the paperwork with the florist, videographer and photographer.

Over the next few days, I'm positive Jack will come to realize that we should absolutely get married in Brookside, in which case firming up our plans while we're there will be an added bonus of the trip.

I pour my coffee, grab a notepad and sit down on the couch to get the basics on paper.

Fortunately, I'm really good at organizing details.

Or maybe a better way to put it is, *A control freak.*

Whatever. The important thing is to approach this wedding with a cohesive plan of action.

That's why I immediately decide to use a technique I learned back in junior high when I started writing for the school paper. As I recall, the key to researching a solid article is answering the five W's: Who, What, When, Where and Why.

Can the same formula be applied to a wedding plan?

Why, I believe it can.

In this case, **Who** would be the guest list.

Oh, and the bridal party—though I've already picked out my eight attendants. Yes, eight. You don't expect me to leave anyone out after the way they've all stood by me, do you?

My sister, Mary Beth, will be my matron of honor, of course. Then there's my sister-in-law, Sara; Jack's sister Rachel, and my friends Raphael, Kate, Brenda, Latisha and Yvonne. I've even matched them up with the guys Jack will be having. Not that he's ever said who his groomsmen would be, but I have a good idea. So I jot down their names on the list, opposite each of my bridesmaids—or bridesman, as the case may be.

I'm careful not to match up Raphael with any of my homophobic brothers or Jack's old frat brother, Jeff, whom Raphael once insisted is a closeted gay man. I shudder, remembering how he attempted to give Jeff a lap dance in an effort to prove the point.

I strategically link Raphael with Buckley, who is as comfortable with his sexuality as he is with Raphael's. The only possible hitch would be if Jack protested to having Buckley as an usher, but I doubt he will. Buckley might have started out as my friend, but now he's a pal of Jack's, too. We hang out together a lot as couples.

Not that I've got any intention of having Buckley's fiancée as one of my bridesmaids. It isn't that I dislike Sonja, or that I'm jealous, which would be so *My Best Friend's Wedding.*

Really, my relationship with Buckley is strictly platonic and always has been.

Except that we kissed a few times. Passionately. But that was over two years ago.

And yes, I may have, on occasion, wondered if Buckley and I were falling in love.

But that speculation ended the moment Jack came along.

Okay, maybe not *the moment*.

But definitely within a few weeks.

Naturally, I ended it because of Jack.

Naturally, Jack will never know that I had an unplatonic era with Buckley while I was embarking on a relationship with him. Presumably, Sonja is equally clueless.

And I like her. I really do. There might just be a part of her that's secretly, instinctively jealous of my entirely platonic-these days friendship with her fiancé. Or maybe on some subconscious level she suspects that there might have been something between us at one time.

Whatever it is seems to keep Sonja from ever entirely opening up to me—not that I want her to, because then I'd have to.

I'll admit it: there might be a teensy part of *me* that wonders if Buckley and I might have wound up together if the timing had been different. If Jack hadn't come along just as Buckley and I were starting to notice each other in a different way.

None of that matters now.

Because we're both in love with other people.

We're both about to get married.

And what happened between us wasn't exactly unresolved.

Not really.

Faced with the choice between Buckley and Jack, I chose

Jack. Buckley handled it just fine, and went back to Sonja shortly afterward anyway.

In any case, that's all ancient history. And I'm sure Jack will want Buckley to be in our wedding party, as long as he doesn't find out that we kissed.

More about that later. Now is not the time to be dwelling on past loves. Not that Buckley was ever my "love..."

Oh, let's drop it.

Next on the list is **What**. This one will have to wait for Jack, but I do make some notes. Afternoon or evening reception? Sit-down dinner or buffet? Black-tie optional or out of the question?

When? I can answer that right now: the third Saturday in October, if at all possible. I've had my heart set on an autumn wedding since before I ever laid eyes on Jack, so as far as I'm concerned, the timing is nonnegotiable, provided we can find a place. The last time I checked, Shorewood Country Club in my hometown was available that particular day, but that was a few months ago. I'm sure it's since been booked.

Which leads me to...

Where? I write *Brookside* and underline it three times. Then, in case Jack wants to read my notes, I add an obligatory question mark. Then, to be fair, I put down *NYC* and, of course, follow it with a question mark. A few of them, actually, to reflect my imaginary doubts about that particular locale.

And now we've arrived at...

Why?

What the hell kind of question is that?

Since I'm asking myself, I guess I can't complain.

Okay, so why are Jack and I getting married?

The answer is obvious: because we love each other. Because we want to spend the rest of our lives together.

Nothing else really matters, I remind myself with a guilty glance at the pad in my hand.

Not *who, what, when or where.*

Nothing but the *why.*

The phone rings as I'm contemplating that profoundness.

I grab it, and it's Kate, of course.

"Where have you been?" I ask, glancing at the clock.

Good thing I wasn't bleeding to death and calling on her to save my life.

Not that I ever would, because she's not good with blood, or heroics. She's the kind of person who runs screaming from the room if there's an insect, loud noise or the slightest hint of gore....

Which makes childbirth an interesting prospect for Kate, to say the least.

"I was throwing up, Tracey." She always pronounces my name "Trice-ee." Today, her Alabama accent is laced with misery.

"For an entire half hour?"

"Pretty much. I can't do this."

"You can't do what?"

"Be pregnant."

"I hate to tell you this, Kate...but it's kind of too late to change your mind."

She's silent.

Ominously so.

"Kate, you're not considering—"

"No!" she says indignantly. "Of course not. I didn't say I'm not going to do this, I just said that I *can't*," she says as if that makes the slightest bit of sense.

"Sure you can."

"I really don't think so. It's horrible. All of it. My boobs are huge…"

No, *my* boobs are huge. They've always been huge, regardless of my weight fluctuations. I inherited my grandmother's famous Bullet Boobs, and I shudder to imagine what will happen to them when I find myself pregnant someday. They'll be instantly transformed into dangerous Missile Boobs, I'm sure.

Kate's boobs, however, went from twin chest freckles to twin mosquito bites, if that. I know, because she insisted on showing me her new "cleavage" when we were having our final bridesmaid-gown fitting for Raphael's wedding.

"I hate feeling sick all the time, too," she grouses on. "And I hate getting so big and fat—"

Mind you, as of Friday night, she was still zipping her size zero jeans, and you could have stuck the Manhattan White Pages between her belly button and the snap.

"Plus, I'm so tired all I want to do is sleep."

I should probably point out that the last issue isn't necessarily a huge problem since all she has to do, really, is sleep. She's a stay-at-home wife thanks to her family's money and Billy's Wall Street salary with staggering bonuses. She has always spent a lot of time sleeping.

"I know how hard this is for you, Kate."

I say that because I'm a good, loyal friend.

I also say it because it's the truth.

But mostly I say it because I'm anxious to move on to my news.

As always, however, Kate is the main topic of conversation and she isn't eager to relinquish that role.

"Do you know what makes me throw up in the mornings, Tracey?"

No, and I really don't want to.

But I daresay that doesn't matter, because I bet Kate is going to tell me.

"Everything."

See?

I murmur my sympathy, glad that at least she didn't elaborate.

"Billy's breath is the worst," she says then, and it takes me a moment to realize we're still talking about morningsickness triggers and haven't moved on to a new topic, i.e., *Billy Has Halitosis*, in which case I'd be more comfortable changing the subject to my engagement.

"I make him get up and brush his teeth the second the alarm goes off every morning. And I make him open the refrigerator whenever I need something because the smell of it just does me in."

"Good idea," I say, rather enjoying the image of arrogant Billy as foul-breathed refrigerator doorman at Kate's beck and call.

"And then there's the thought of meat—any meat... Oh, God, Tracey, I feel like I'm going to hurl just talking about it."

"Then let's change the subject," I say quickly. "I've got news for you."

"What is it?" she asks feebly.

Realizing she's fading fast, I blurt, "Jack and I got engaged last night."

"Oh my gosh! I'm so happy for y'all!"

I have no doubt that Kate means that from the bottom of her heart...even though she follows it up with a horrible gagging sound and throws down the receiver with a clatter.

I hang on, hoping she'll return momentarily so that I can regale her with the romantic saga of Jack on his knees in the gutter.

But it's Billy who a good minute later picks up the receiver and asks, "Hello? Tracey?"

"Yeah...?"

"Listen, Kate's got her head in the toilet again. She told me to tell you congratulations and she wants to take you out to lunch next weekend to celebrate."

"Okay...thanks. And be sure to tell her the wedding won't be until after she has the baby, so not to worry."

"What wedding?"

"Mine and Jack's," I say, miffed that Billy would offer secondhand congratulations without even asking Kate the reason.

"Oh, that's great," he says in exactly the same fake-enthusiastic tone he might use if somebody's six-year-old niece gave him an ugly crayon drawing.

"Well, see ya." Billy hangs up.

Wow. First time I get to make my big announcement, and one audience member pukes, and the other doesn't give a damn. Where do we go from here? I just hope it isn't an omen of some sort.

I can't help but feel sorry for poor Kate.

I also can't help but feel the distinct need to share my news with somebody who won't be dismissive. Or vomit.

But there's nobody to tell, unless Jimmy the doorman is on duty…and I'm not dressed for the lobby at the moment.

Talk about anticlimactic.

Maybe I was wrong last night about getting engaged at last being different from Christmas, or losing your virginity, or eating a post-diet Twinkie.

Maybe there is just a hint of letdown after all….

Or maybe I'm just experiencing a momentary lapse, because when I hear Jack stirring in the bedroom, my heart does an excited little flip-flop.

I go in to find him lying on his back, stretching. He was staring at the ceiling but his eyes flick immediately to me, and he smiles and pats the mattress by his hip.

It looks like he's over his panic-infused gastric attack.

"Hey, good morning," I say, and sit on the edge of the bed beside him, one leg curled underneath me. "Want to get up? I've got coffee made, and I think we've got a couple of eggs I can scramble…"

"In a few minutes, maybe. Or you could just come back to bed…"

He pulls me down and kisses me.

I kiss him back, but I'm thinking of all the wedding details I need to get moving on; the plane tickets that need to be bought; the shower I should be taking…

"I don't know," I hedge.

"Come on…it's Sunday morning…"

Then Jack kisses me again, and I decide that everything can be put off a little longer. What's another hour when I waited six months to get engaged, and we've got a lifetime in front of us?

3

My friend Brenda materializes by my desk the moment I sit down in my office Monday morning.

Yes, my *office*. Not my tiny cube down the corridor, where I spent the first few years of my advertising career. My own office, not spacious but definitely less tiny than the cube, with my own window. So what if it's just on the seventh floor and overlooks a solid brick wall across a narrow alleyway occupied by a Dumpster?

It beats cube life, as I'm sure Brenda would attest if you asked her.

I wouldn't. Ask her about cube life these days, that is. Ever since I got promoted a few weeks ago, I've found myself feeling oddly guilty and undeserving. Kind of like that guy who escaped the *Titanic* wearing a dress.

"Well?" Brenda asks. "How was it?"

For a second, I think she's talking about my engagement

and wonder who could have possibly spilled the beans. Did Jack, that rascal, tell my co-workers we would be getting engaged on Valentine's Day?

No, he did not, because he didn't know himself, remember? Brenda is obviously talking about something else.

Because I seem to have developed Alzheimer's regarding recent events other than my engagement, I say, "Huh?"

"The wedding! How was it?"

Um, should I be worried that I'm still drawing a complete blank?

"Tracey! Don't tell me you forgot about Raphael's wedding already?"

"Of course I didn't forget! It was a beautiful wedding." And it was. However, it wasn't *my* wedding, and I can't wait to tell Brenda that I'll be having one.

But before I can thrust my ring finger at her, my supervisor, Carol, says, "Tracey? Good, you're here."

I look up to see her round face poking around the doorway, framed by her perfectly curled-under pageboy that I'm sure is all the rage—in, say, Lincoln, Nebraska. Or some foreign land where people dance in clogs.

Here in Manhattan, not so much. Yet despite her hairdo, Carol worked her way up to management rep here at Blaire Barnett. And I will be forever indebted to her for promoting me to account executive on McMurray-White's All-Week-Long Deodorant and Abate Laxative accounts.

All right, so it's not the junior copywriter position I've been coveting all my career, but it's definitely a stepping stone.

"The Client thought our Abate meeting was at ten instead

of two today, so they're on their way over!" Carol informs me, obviously alarmed.

"What?" I blurt, instantly alarmed, as well.

It seems that alarm is a frequent state of mind here in Account Exec Land, where people frequently exclaim—and sometimes even shout and curse. Here in Account Exec Land, Client is always spelled with a capital C, deodorant and laxatives are life-sustaining products and the Client is always, always, always right. Even when they're wrong. Which they often are.

So naturally, I don't suggest to Carol that we simply call the Client and tell them the Abate meeting is at two, not ten, as one might in any other—sane—industry.

I just bellow, "Oh my God!" like someone who has just witnessed a violent explosion.

"I know! We've got to get our tushies up to eight and go over the presentation with the Creatives right now!" Carol shrieks like a fire warden evacuating the floor after the violent explosion.

"Oh my God!" I shout again and bolt from my seat, grabbing my presentation folder with my right hand and pretty much shoving Brenda out of the way with my left…

Which she seizes. "Oh my God!" she screams, and not because the Client is on their way to a premature laxative-planning meeting.

"Tracey! When did *this* happen?"

"What? What happened?" Carol demands frantically.

"What's going on?" Adrian Smedly, the director of our account group, has come out of the woodwork. In his custom suit and tie, as impeccably stylish as, well, as Carol is not, Adrian is poised just outside my office, waiting for a reply.

"I got engaged," I explain as dispassionately as possible, because of course Adrian is putting a damper on the whole damn thing.

Brenda, still clutching my freshly manicured ring finger, squeals and hugs me.

"Congratulations!" Carol hugs me, as well. "That's wonderful news!"

"Thanks." My mouth is muffled by hair: Carol's brown mushroom do and Brenda's teased, sprayed one.

"When did he pop the question, Tracey?" Brenda wants to know, bouncing up and down, still wearing her white commuting Reebocks with her suit and stockings.

"Valentine's Day!"

"At Raphael's wedding?"

"No, but right after, when we...were..." Having caught sight of Adrian's lethal expression, I trail off into sheepish silence.

I think it's safe to assume that our group director won't be gushing over my ring or asking me where I've registered.

"Ladies?" is all he has to say, and Carol and I snap to it.

The three of us scurry to the elevator, where a bike messenger is waiting for a down elevator. Susan, my friend Latisha's boss and a fellow account executive on the Abate account, is already there, on her way to the same meeting we are.

I loathe her.

All right, *loathe* is a strong word, especially on this joyful post-engagement day, when I am basically loving the world.

But Susan, whom Yvonne calls Miss Prim among other less charitable nicknames, is hard to love: all buttoned up in her gray suit and black pumps with tasteful makeup and no jewelry other than a gi-normous engagement ring.

We all—meaning all of us gossipy office underlings—noticed that it appeared over Christmas, but nobody wants to ask Susan about it because, frankly, she's cold and dull and staid and nobody really cares who's marrying her. We're just surprised someone wants to.

I guess that goes to show you that there's someone for everyone.

Anyway, Susan sucks up to Adrian with a big cheery hello, and offers a slightly less stellar one to Carol. Me, she ignores.

To my satisfaction, Adrian all but ignores Susan. He jabs the Up button repeatedly and glares at the messenger, obviously holding him personally responsible when a lobby-bound car is the first to stop.

As that elevator departs, Adrian turns to Carol. I fully expect him to order her to do something about the elevator situation.

He just asks, "Did John tell you they're having a fat-trimming meeting over on the Choc-Chewy-O's account tomorrow?"

"No. I thought they were going to let that go for now."

She looks disappointed. Well, judging by her figure, she's not exactly one to watch her weight.

On the contrary, I notice that Susan has absorbed this news and looks pleased.

Secretly, I am, too. I love Choc-Chewy-O's—this great cereal that tastes like Twix bars. But at ten grams of fat per half-cup serving, I never let myself eat them. Which is a shame because my friend Julie, who's an administrative assistant in that account group, furnishes all of us with free boxes from the Choc-Chewy-O's supply closet.

Hey, now that it'll be lower in fat, I can actually eat it, not just watch Jack dig in.

Ho-hum.

Still no elevator.

We wait, collectively on edge. I'm sure the three of them are thinking about the meeting. I'm thinking about Choc-Chewy-O's, wondering if the low-fat version will be out anytime soon, because I want to lose a little more weight before the wedding, especially if we decide to go to some fabulous beach resort for our honeymoon.

Actually, I've already decided we should. And I mentioned it to Jack last night as we were watching a commercial for some luxury hotel in the Carribbean. You know, the kind of commercial where they show clear aqua water, sumptuous food, tropical foliage and a buff couple strolling hand in hand on the beach, contemplating their future amid steel-drum music.

"Doesn't that look amazing?" I asked Jack, who had once mentioned something about his family's cottage up in the Catskills being the perfect spot for a honeymoon. He needs to be reprogrammed ASAP, as far as I'm concerned.

"It looks expensive," Jack replied maddeningly, barely looking up from the *TV Guide*, and I knew I'd better drop the subject before he vetoed it altogether.

"Tracey, did you remember to bring our task force notes?" Carol asks me now, interrupting the steel-drum music in my head.

"Right here." I wave the folder in my right hand. My left,

which has become so happily conspicuous these past few days, is now wedged unhappily into the pocket of my black blazer. I have no desire to flash it around in front of buzz-kill Adrian and that pill Miss Prim.

"What about the pork ribs nutritional data?" Carol asks me.

"Got it."

"Good." She nods with approval.

Miss Prim primly stares into space.

I sneak a peek at Adrian to make sure he knows that I'm not all about my wedding. No sirree Bob, I'm entirely on board with the upcoming summer campaign for Abate laxatives.

We're going after the barbecue crowd in a big, aggressive way. All that meat, very little fiber…well, it's a natural target audience for our product.

Unfortunately, Adrian is too busy glaring at the closed elevator bank to appreciate my uberefficiency.

An upward-bound elevator finally arrives and the four of us stride on board, where we ride in stony silence to the eighth floor.

Well, Adrian and Susan are stony. Carol is stony by association.

Me, I'm just pondering my bridal bouquet, wondering if I should go for a circular nosegay–type arrangement, or more of a cascade.

Either way, I'll need roses. Lots of them. In red. Or maybe off-white. But not yellow, because my Sicilian grandmother says yellow roses are bad luck.

The elevator stops, dings, and we step out onto the eighth floor.

I used to think it was my imagination that the Creative

Department's offices were bigger and better than ours down-stairs. I also thought Jack was just being paranoid when he claimed that the Media Department's space two floors below—which is where he works—is dingy and small compared to the other departments.

Guess what? All true.

How do I know, you might ask?

Because my friend Latisha and I went out to Duane Reade for a tape measure one day when we were bored. We snuck around wearing our trench coats, measuring offices, taking notes, cracking ourselves up with our spy routine.

None of our underling peers—except Jack—was amused when we told them what we'd done. In addition to being amused, Jack was all, "I told you so."

On the Creative floor, which occupies all of eight, the paint is a fresh and soothing shade of off-white. Ceilings are lofty and higher than on other floors, and most of the window offices face Lexington Avenue or the side street, where there's a partial view of the Empire State Building.

In direct contrast: the media floor, which is all the way down on five and shares space with an architectural firm. There, the offices are painted phlegm yellow, a few square feet smaller with drop ceilings, and even some of the super-visors don't have windows. Those who do have windows overlook views that are even more dismal than mine.

If you were going to compare the agency heirarchy to, let's say, jeans: the Creative group would be your 7 for all mankind, the Account group would be Ralph Lauren, and Media would be Wranglers.

Wait, do they still make Wranglers?

See? That's exactly what I mean. Media is definitely Wranglers. They exist (I'm pretty sure), and they're functional, but nobody really notices them.

Mental note: share clever jeans/agency department analogy with Jack, who will appreciate it.

On the eighth floor, we Account people rush to the sleek and subtly lit exposed-brick and glass-walled conference room where the Creatives are waiting.

I am struck with a familiar longing to be on their side of the room. I resist the urge to sidle up to them and whisper, "I'm really one of you."

Because technically, I'm not.

Not on the outside, anyway.

The women are collectively thin, black-clad and attractive, with sleek short haircuts, most in trendy glasses that make them look erudite and chic.

The men—most of them good-looking with longish hair—are carelessly stylish in jeans and turtlenecks with blazers. They tend to remind me of my friend Buckley, who also happens to be a freelance copywriter. They have that quick-witted, funny-sexy-smart thing going on, just like Buckley.

Jack has it, too, but in a quieter, more subtle way.

Jack. My fiancé.

Hallelujah! I actually have a fiancé!

Yet as we take our seats around the conference table, I sneak my left hand out of my pocket for a quick glimpse of my ring, just to make sure it's really there and I didn't imagine the whole thing.

Nope, the diamond's there, all right—and Adrian just caught me staring lovingly at it.

Oops.

I ingeniously pretend there's a bug crawling on my knuckle and slap at it with my right hand, saying loudly, "Ouch!"

Everyone stops talking and moving chairs to look over at me.

"Mosquito," I explain, scratching as if I've just been bitten. Then I wave the air in front of my face for added authenticity. Then I remember that it's February in a Manhattan office building.

Then I note that if I don't stop this charade right now, I might as well keep on waving…goodbye to my brilliant advertising career.

Adrian is watching me with this expression that's…well, I guess you'd describe it as a fascinated frown. Not in a good way.

"Tracey?" Carol interjects, looking from our boss to me. "Do you have that nutritional data for pork ribs that we'd like to add to the presentation?"

What she is really saying is, *"I'm saving your ass. Now prove that it's worth saving and show us what you've got."*

Good old mushroom-headed Carol.

"I have it right here," I inform her and the rest of the group, some of whom—*cough, Susan, cough*—look vaguely disappointed at my efficiency. They were probably hoping to watch me slide slowly into madness. It happens all the time in this industry. I'm sure it starts with slapping at imaginary bugs, frequently on Monday mornings.

But it doesn't happen to me.

No, I, Tracey Spadolini, account executive extraordinaire, am hell-bent on maintaining my sanity.

I whip out my manila folder and open it briskly, scanning the top document. "Pork ribs…pork ribs…pork ribs…"

…are available at Shorewood Country Club with a smoked hickory or honey-mango barbecue sauce for the cocktail hour, not the main course, at an added $5 per head.

Oops.

I stare at the reception catering menu I printed off the Internet last night, then slowly lift my head to find a roomful of expectant faces.

"Wrong folder," I say in a small voice, pushing back my chair. "I'll just run back down and get the right one."

Then I bolt for the elevator, clutching the folder whose tab is labeled Wedding and decorated with lopsided red-Sharpie-drawn hearts.

It's a little anticlimactic to walk into Tequila Murray's that night just as two-for-one margarita happy hour is ending, where Yvonne, Brenda and Latisha are waiting to toast my engagement.

The four of us have been working at Blaire Barnett together for a few years now. Well, actually, Yvonne—who is well past retirement age—has been there a few decades, working as Adrian's secretary. Before that—well before that, I'm sure—she was a Rockette. She still has a dancer's lithe body and has been known to demonstrate a few kickline moves when pressed…and smashed.

I slide into the fourth chair at our regular table before hanging my bag over the back. The chair would tip over without me in it to counterbalance the weight in the black leather tote. It's jammed with stuff—some of it work related, but most of it wedding related. *Modern Bride* alone is like lugging a brick doorstop around on your shoulder.

"I'm so glad you guys didn't leave," I tell the three of them.

"No, you're so lucky we didn't leave." Brenda checks her watch. "I've got fifteen minutes, tops, to hang out, and Paulie said the baby is already sound asleep. I missed his bedtime nursing for the second night in a row—last night was my cousin's baby shower and I didn't get home till eleven. Poor little Jordan's going to wonder where his mommy is."

"I hate to say it," I tell her, "but Carol and Adrian are still at the office now, making a gazillion changes to the campaign, and we have to present it again on Thursday… You're probably all going to be working late all week."

"Paulie might as well grow a tit," is Yvonne's predictably dry take on the situation before she downs the last swallow in her martini glass. She doesn't go for "girlie drinks" like margaritas and cosmopolitan.

"Well, Susan knows I've got to leave early tomorrow for Keera's teacher conference," Latisha says firmly. She's fiercely devoted to Keera, the now-teenage daughter she raised as a single mother before she met and married her husband, Derek. They have a child together, too, a boy Latisha the New York Yankees fanatic named after her favorite player, Bernie Williams.

Latisha has her hands full these days. Poor Keera was just diagnosed with dyslexia. Latisha has been absorbed with trying to get the right services for her while constantly doing battle with Bernie, who is a terrible two now.

"I hate to be the bearer of bad news, but I wouldn't count on Susan letting you go early," I tell her reluctantly. "Adrian's on the warpath and everyone's going to be going nuts. It's going to be all hands on deck until the Client approves this thing."

Is it my imagination, or is there suddenly tension in the air?

I can't help but suddenly find myself all too aware that I'm now privy to information that isn't readily available to the three of them, with their administrative jobs and joint cubicles down the hall.

They must be aware of it, too. But trust me, when I was promoted last month, nobody was more thrilled for me than they were.

Well, maybe Jack was—since he not only loves me but gets to reap the salary benefits.

But these three were the ones who encouraged me to ask for a promotion, and they were the ones who took me to Tequila Murray's to celebrate the moment it came through.

Just as they insisted on taking me out tonight after Brenda shared the big news about me and Jack. I haven't seen the others yet, thanks to the ongoing Client meeting from hell, and it was a little disappointing that I didn't get to tell them in person. I didn't even have time to ask Brenda to save the news for me to share—let alone time to revel in her thrilled reaction.

But I was touched when I returned to my office at last to find a bunch of congratulatory e-mails from the girls and orders to meet them here for happy hour.

"Well, anyway, I'm really sorry I'm so late," I say apologetically, reaching for a broken-off tortilla chip from the nearly empty basket on the table and dredging it through what's left of the salsa. "If I'd have known I was going to be stuck there this late, I would have said we should celebrate another night."

"It's okay… Here, we ordered you your raspberry margarita." Brenda hands it over. "Actually we ordered one when we first got here, but we had to drink that. This is your freebie second. It's a little melted."

It's pure liquid, but who cares? I take a sip and the tepid tequila burns its way down to my empty stomach. Pure heaven after a hellacious day in Account Exec Land.

"Come on, come on, give it over." Latisha snaps her fingers and beckons for me to show her my left ring finger. "Let's see what Jack did."

I grin and thrust out my hand, wiggling my fingers and admiring the way the marquis-cut diamond catches the red and green neon light reflecting from the Tequila Murray's Semi-Kosher Mexican Restaurant sign in the nearby window.

"Mmm, mmm, mmm. Look at you!" is Latisha's satisfyingly appreciative response. "Girlfriend, that is some serious bling."

Yvonne lifts a raspberry-colored eyebrow—tinted to match her raspberry-colored hair, which just so happens to match my melted raspberry margarita—to indicate her approval.

"Did I not tell you it was go-aw-jus?" Brenda asks in her Jersey accent, which always becomes more pronounced after a margarita or two.

"You even got a manicure," Yvonne observes, knowing my fingernails are usually a mess.

"Don't look too closely." I withdraw my hand. "I did it myself last night. And I messed up a few nails trying to type while they were wet."

"Typing?" Latisha shakes her cornrows in dismay. "Please don't say you were working on a Sunday night."

"I wasn't working, I was online looking up wedding stuff." I reach into the black tote bag and rifle around for the manila folder that *doesn't* contain statistics geared toward constipated barbecue-goers.

"When are you going shopping for your dress?" Brenda asks. "Because I can come with you, if you want."

"I already found my dress." I pull out a dog-eared, months-old clipping from *Modern Bride*. "What do you think?"

Two agree that it's beautiful, the other—guess who?—declares it go-aw-jus.

"The ad lists stores that carry it and there's one on Madison, so I'm going to go up there as soon as I can and order it so it'll be in on time."

I'm about to tell them that I've also picked out the brides-maids' dresses—navy velvet sheaths—but first, I have to of-ficially ask them to be in the wedding.

Before I can do that, Brenda asks, "Did you set a date yet?"

"Honey, she set a date last year," Yvonne comments.

Which is true.

Still…

"Jack and I are thinking the third Saturday in October would be good."

Rather, I'm certain the third Saturday in October is when we're getting married, because I called Shorewood on the sly yesterday. I didn't even give my name, because I don't want the news of my engagement to leak back to my family through the small-town grapevine.

Although the banquet manager, Charles, wasn't in, the waitress who answered the phone checked the book for me and said it looked like the date had been booked by someone else then crossed out. I was supposed to call Charles back today to check, but of course, I never had time.

So, yes, I'm fairly certain that we're getting married on the third Saturday in October.

I tried to discuss the details with Jack a few times yesterday, but got nowhere. Still in the basking mode, he kept asking why we had to worry about details now.

Let me tell you, it's a relief to be able to discuss the details with someone, even if it isn't the actual groom.

"This is where I want to have the wedding," I say, passing around a photo I printed off Shorewood's Web site last night. "It's a country club up in my hometown, right on the lake."

"Lake Tahoe?" Yvonne asks cluelessly.

"No. Lake Erie," I say. "Lake Tahoe is out West somewhere. California. Anyway—"

"It's in Nevada," Latisha cuts in. "I know because Derek wanted us to elope there at one point."

"No, it's in California," Yvonne rasps, holding somebody's margarita straw like a cigarette. I can tell she's itching for a smoke. Who isn't at this point?

Brenda starts to protest. "No, it's in—"

"California!" Yvonne cuts in. "I was there once, a long time ago, and the only time I was ever in Nevada was when I was a showgirl in Vegas."

"You were a showgirl in Vegas?" Brenda asks incredulously. "I thought you were a showgirl in New York. A Rockette."

"Well, I was a showgirl in Vegas, too. Just for a few months," she adds ominously, and I gather that stint didn't have a happy ending.

"Well, you were also in Nevada more than once," Latisha informs her, "because that's where Lake Tahoe is."

"Maybe it's in both states," Brenda interjects. "Like the Grand Canyon."

"The Grand Canyon isn't in California and Nevada!" I protest, wondering why we're talking about western geography in the first place. I use it to segue neatly into eastern geography with, "Getting back to Lake Erie, though—"

"No, I know, the Grand Canyon's in Arizona and Utah," Brenda cuts in. "Jeez, I'm not as dumb as I look. What I meant was, it's in two states, and maybe Lake Tahoe—"

"I don't know…is the Grand Canyon really in Utah?" Latisha asks. "I'm trying to picture it on the map. I don't think it's in Utah."

"Paulie went out there to hike the canyon a few years ago with his buddies right before we got married," Brenda says, "and I know he said they were going to Utah because I remember I told him not to let those polygamists out there give him any ideas."

"Oh, for the love of God." Yvonne pulls out a cigarette and her lighter and heads for the door.

"What?" Brenda asks with an innocent little frown.

"Come on, baby girl…" Latisha shakes her head. "Do you really think Utah is swarming with polygamists who want to brainwash a bunch of hiking cops from New York?"

Who cares about any of this? is what I want to scream.

"Speaking of New York cops, Paulie's on the night shift, so I've got to get home." Brenda throws down a couple of twenties and pushes her chair back. "That covers me and my share of Tracey's."

"Thanks," I say, "but you don't have to—"

"I want to." Brenda stands over me and gives me a big squeeze. "This is your engagement celebration, remember?"

Yeah.

Only I forgot.

"Hey, wait, Brenda—"

She turns around, en route to the door. "Yeah?"

"I want you to be a bridesmaid. Will you?"

She grins broadly. "Of co-awse. It would be an hon-ah."

Left alone at the table with temporarily abandoned Yvonne's coat and purse and Latisha, I hastily add, "You, too. Will you be my bridesmaid?"

"Hell, yes," she says, and hugs me hard.

I catch her checking her watch as she releases my shoulders.

"You should go," I say, checking my own. "It's getting late. Go tuck your kids in."

"Ha, you think Keera lets me do that these days?" She shakes her head. "I've been hangin' out here until it's safe to go home. Which it isn't until I know Bernie's in bed and sound asleep. Because if he's still awake and he hears me come in, he gets all wound up and he's awake for another two hours, wanting to climb all over me."

"Jack is kind of the same way," I say with a sly smirk.

"Yeah, that won't last."

"What do you mean?"

"Once you're married, everything gets to be old hat. And I mean *everything*. Trust me on that."

"You mean...?"

"I do." Latisha shakes her head. "Me and Derek used to have some big ol' sparks goin' on, morning, noon and especially night. Now all I want to do when I get into bed at night is sleep."

She reaches out and pats my engagement ring. "But don't worry, those days are way down the road for you. You just have fun planning your wedding."

With that, she's gone, and I'm left wondering when the fun is going to begin.

4

My cell phone rings as I'm striding down Lexington Avenue on Wednesday afternoon, headed to Sushi Lucy's for lunch.

I bet my next paycheck that it's Carol, wondering where I am. Everyone's going crazy getting ready to present to McMurray-White again tomorrow.

I snuck away while Carol was on the phone with the Client, who have made it abundantly clear that they don't believe we Account people need meals, sleep or natural light.

Checking caller ID, I see that it's not Carol; it's Will McCraw.

I was just kidding about my next paycheck—you knew that, right?

"Tracey, how's it going?"

Yes, I answer the call. I've been waiting for this moment for years now.

"Funny you should ask that, Will, because it's going particularly well, as a matter of fact. I—"

"That's great. I just wanted to call and thank you for the Valentine—"

Yes, I sent him a Valentine, but it's not what you think. It was a funny Shoebox one and I only sent it as an excuse to tuck in my new Tracey Spadolini, Account Executive, business card. Which apparently he didn't notice, because he says nothing about the promotion.

"—and I couldn't wait to tell you I got a lead in a European touring-company production of *La Cage Aux Folles!*"

Will starring as a gay man?

"Wow, I'd love to see that," I say truthfully. "Listen, I have news—"

But he's talking over me— "Yeah, it's going to be great"— at least, that's what I think he said. It might have actually been "I'm going to be great," knowing Will, but I'll give him the benefit of the doubt.

"I'm sure it will be," I say, "and I've got something to—"

"I leave for Transylvania next week—"

"Will, I have to tell—wait, did you say *Transylvania?*"

"Right."

Huh. I didn't even realize Transylvania is a real place. Had I known it was a real place, I would imagine it filled with dark, brooding types and, yes, vampires—not musical-theater buffs. You learn something new every day.

"Will," I jump in, realizing there's been a lull, "I'm engaged."

Dead silence.

"Hello?" That explains the lull; we must have gotten disconnected.

Nope. He's still on the line.

"That's great," he says slowly, for once having been struck momentarily speechless. Ah, life is good. "Congratulations."

"Thanks." I beam.

"When's the wedding?"

"October, I think. We have to—"

"October, I should be back by then."

Okay, *back?*

Does he actually think he's going to be invited to my wedding?

I really want to say, "You don't know Jack."

How I longed to tell Will McCraw, after he pretty much threw me away, that he was utterly clueless. About me. About life.

But now, strangely, I don't feel as though I have anything to prove to him.

My work here is done.

"Well," he says, "good luck with the planning and everything."

"Thanks. Good luck to you, too."

Doing gay musical theater in Transylvania.

For once, I think as I hang up the phone, both Will and I have simultaneously gotten exactly what we deserve.

I get to Sushi Lucy's and hang around in the small mirrored vestibule, trying to diagnose the painful bump on my nose. Yup. It's a newly erupting zit, all right. It's been ages since I've had one, but I know they're brought on by stress.

I bet I've escaped this problem until now because I could always rely on cigarettes to blow off steam. Now that I'm no longer smoking, all that tension is pent-up inside me, just waiting to erupt.

Is it any wonder that my reflection reveals a big, ugly red blemish, thanks to the living hell that is Abate's Summer Barbecue campaign?

Mental note: stop for cigarettes—I mean, Clearasil—on way home later.

There's some in the medicine cabinet at home, but I noticed when I was rummaging around in there the other day that it expired in '03.

I know, you're wondering why I don't just toss it.

Because it's Jack's, that's why. The last time I got rid of one of his decrepit belongings—a single stray gray-white nubby gym sock that had been kicking around various surfaces in the bedroom for ages—he was annoyed.

No, I don't know why. But I decided on the spot that he would be responsible for disposing his own useless crap from there on in.

And I've noticed he never does, even when I call his attention to stuff like expired medication, single socks and aging takeout leftovers he never should have saved in the first place.

Magazines are the worst. Thanks to his media job on consumer electronics and men's personal-care products, he gets comp subscriptions to just about everything but *Modern Bride.* There are towering stacks everywhere. I wouldn't be surprised if, near the bottom, there are cover stories on the pope's passing, the Red Sox World Series or Nick and Jessica's divorce. Their wedding, too, probably.

Oh, well, that's a fault I can live with, in the grand scheme of things. Nobody's perfect.

Nor, to my dismay, is my complexion.

That's a big fat ugly zit on my nose, all right.

But I'm not here at Sushi Lucy's strictly for pimple verification. I'm actually waiting for my friend Buckley to meet me for lunch so I can finally share my big news. I wanted to do it yesterday, but it was such a zoo at the office that I couldn't get away.

Today is a zoo, too. I shouldn't be here, I should be working.

But I want to tell Buckley about my engagement in person before he hears it from someone else because…

Well, partly because I still haven't been able to relish the pleasure of telling anyone in person. That will happen when we meet Jack's mom and sisters for dinner tomorrow night, I'm sure, and when Raphael comes home from his honeymoon, and again when we fly up to Buffalo in a few weeks to tell my family—the soonest we could get an affordable flight.

But I'm dying to share my news in person right away with someone who will appreciate it. And I'm sure Buckley will, because he's my friend.…

Except…

Part of the reason I want to tell him in person is that maybe there's a lingering teensy, tiny shred of something other than friendship in our relationship.

Did I mention that Buckley and I almost hooked up a few years ago? And that it overlapped with me and Jack, but not really with him and Sonja…?

Oh, right. I did mention it.

I guess I've just been thinking about that a lot lately for some reason.

Ever since I got engaged.

I wonder why.

Maybe because when you're engaged, you realize that you will never ever kiss anyone else ever again. Not just kiss, but…fool around with.

I mean, you'll fool around with your fiancé, of course— and you will go on fooling around with him after he becomes your husband…

(Unless you listen to Latisha, and I've chosen not to. The next time she starts in about the postmarital lack of sparks, I'm going to stick my fingers in my ears and sing "Love and Marriage" at the top of my lungs.)

Anyway, being an engaged woman, you can't help but wonder about what you might be missing from here on in.

I can't help but wonder that, anyway.

But just about Buckley. No one else.

Probably because Buckley is the last person I kissed before Jack, and because it never went any further with him than that, physically. Emotionally, yes. He's the only other guy I've ever felt really connected to, unless you count Will (which I don't because that was all an illusion on my part—make that a delusion) or Raphael (which I don't, because I guess I kind of think of him as a girlfriend).

So I guess I kind of think of Buckley as the One Who Slipped Away.

And something tells me he kind of thinks of me that way, too…even though he's never said it. I mean, he and Sonja have been engaged since last fall.

I still remember exactly how and where he broke the news to me.

Not that it had to be *broken*, like bad news. Because it

wasn't. I mean, isn't everyone happy to learn that a good friend is getting married?

It's just that I was a little surprised, that's all. Buckley and Sonja had already broken up because she had given him an ultimatum and he didn't want to get married. Then he changed his mind.

And I guess I'll always wonder whether...

Nah. Never mind. Forget I said anything about that, or about there being a lingering shred of anything other than friendship between us. Really, the only reason I'm so determined to tell Buckley my news in person is because he'll be thrilled for me.

For us.

Maybe I should have included Jack today. But he was having lunch with a print rep anyway.

Then there's Sonja, who is a production editor at some publishing house. She happens to work just a few blocks away and is usually free for lunch. Hmm, maybe I should have asked her to come, too.

Then again, if Buckley wanted her to be here, he'd have asked her himself, right? I mean, it's not like he knows we're having lunch together for a specific reason today. I just e-mailed him this morning to set it up. We do that all the time. Still...

Mental note: Set up celebratory dinner that includes both Jack and Sonja.

We were right here at Sushi Lucy's when Buckley told me he'd realized that if he didn't step up to the plate, he was going to lose Sonja. He said it in those words. Then he said he had gotten engaged to her the night before, in the middle of watching the World Series.

At the time, I'll admit, I was a little taken aback. Maybe even a little upset. Not jealous, definitely. Just...I don't know. Maybe wistful.

But that was ages ago, and I'm sure that it will be no big deal to tell him Jack and I are getting married in October. (Did I mention that I found out—still, without giving my name—that Shorewood is definitely available that third Saturday in October? No? Well, I haven't mentioned it to Jack yet, either, but I plan to, so we can book it ASAP.)

The second I spot Buckley's familiar long-legged stride heading toward the restaurant door, my stomach does an uneasy little somersault for no reason whatsoever.

After all, it's just Buckley. Familiar, solid Buckley. He's got on his worn brown leather jacket with a scarf tied around his neck and manages to look effortlessly fashionable, as usual.

Oh, and it really *is* effortless. That's one of the things I liked about him when I met him. He's just a regular, casual, good-looking guy. He—like Jack—doesn't have a metrosexual bone in his body. *Unlike* Will.

I met Buckley right around the time that Will was leaving me for summer stock, never to return...to me, anyway. Will came back to New York with Esme, his new girlfriend, in tow, after I spent the summer reinventing myself so that he would find me more desirable. Yes, I know that sounds pathetic.

And it was.

But who, at one point or another, hasn't had her pathetic moments where some guy is concerned?

In the end, my reinvention was also a reawakening. Or maybe just a long-overdue awakening. For the first time, I was able to see who I am and to see Will for who he really is. More importantly, for who he isn't.

But it took awhile for that to happen. If I hadn't been so wrapped up in him when I met Buckley, who knows what might have happened between us? By the time I came to my senses, Buckley was involved with Sonja. When they broke up, I was involved with Jack.

So pretty much, Buckley and I have never been simultaneously romantically available.

But I've got this terminal case of wondering what if.

What if I'd met Buckley after I fell out of infatuation with Will?

What if I'd been on time meeting him the night he met Sonja, who started chatting with him in some bar while he was waiting for me?

What if, when I found myself in Buckley's arms the December after Will dumped me—and right after I met Jack—I hadn't decided that I was kissing Buckley by default, and we were meant to be platonic?

Who knows what might have happened?

We probably would have hooked up, the relationship would have run its course because it wasn't meant to be, and we would have gone our separate ways.

Or maybe we would have hooked up and stayed together. Who knows?

I don't like to think about it, and I usually don't let myself. So why now?

Mental note: JACK. Remember Jack? Do not forget about Jack. Your fiancé.

I take a fortifying look at my engagement ring, then find

myself swept into Buckley's familiar, platonic embrace. His face is cold against mine.

"Hey!" he says, smelling like cold air and Big Red. "Sorry I'm late. You could have sat down."

"I didn't want to sit alone. You know I hate that."

"I know you do."

Jack knows, too, that I'm self-conscious about being alone in a restaurant even if someone is meeting me. It's one of my little quirks.

Jack knows pretty much everything there is to know about me, just as Buckley does. And I know pretty much everything there is to know about Buckley, too.

Except, of course, for the intimate stuff.

Of course.

Anyway...

We sit down and tell the waiter we're going to order right away. I have to because I've got to get back to work. Adrian has been treating me differently ever since he caught me showing off my new engagement ring to Brenda and Carol the other day. I can't help but sense an undercurrent of disdain whenever I have contact with him.

And I've had a lot of it because we're working on the new presentation.

"Hungry?" Buckley asks as we open our menus.

"Starved."

"Me, too. Want to share an app?"

We do that a lot, me and Buckley—especially when we go out for Japanese. We'll order a maki appetizer to split, and eat it with chopsticks off a platter between us.

We've done that dozens of times.

But suddenly, there's something unnervingly intimate about the idea of it.

"No, thanks," I say quickly. "I'm not *that* hungry."

"You just said you were starved."

"Did I? I meant for soup. What I really want is soup. And sashimi. No appetizer."

I shift my weight and find myself involuntarily playing footsie with Buckley under the table.

"Sorry," I say.

"It's okay. I don't need an appetizer, either, I guess."

I open my mouth to tell him I meant that I was sorry about my foot rubbing against his shin, but that seems awkward, so I close my mouth again and pretend to study the menu, but of course I've already told him what I'm ordering: soup and sashimi.

Sneaking a peak around the room, I've noticed that they've reconfigured the dining room since we were last here, to get more tables in. So that's it. We're at a newly installed table for two by the window. It's close quarters, which is why my stocking-clad legs keep bumping up against Buckley's jean-clad knees no matter how I position myself.

"Oops, sorry," I say again as I try to change position only to find myself all but intertwined with him under the table.

"It's okay," he murmurs, focused on the menu, which is good.

That way, he can't see the alpine zit on my nose.

Or how rattled I am, for no good reason.

Normally, this physical contact with Buckley wouldn't faze me…much less make me acutely aware of how good-looking he is.

"Hey," I say a little loudly, because Buckley flinches a little and looks up. "How was your weekend at the bed-and-breakfast in the Hamptons?"

"Oh…we didn't stay the whole weekend."

"Why not?"

"Sonja didn't really like it so we left Sunday morning."

A bed-and-breakfast in the Hamptons…what's not to like? If you ask me, she's unnecessarily picky.

But Buckley didn't ask me, and the waiter is back with tea, so I keep my opinion of Sonja to myself.

"How's work going now that you're the big cheese?" Buckley asks me after the waiter leaves us alone to sip from steaming, handleless teacups.

"Work? Oh, God, it's crazy, actually. But—"

"Don't tell me the promotion is turning out to be one of those *be careful what you wish for* things?" he cuts in.

No, I find myself thinking, *but* this *might be.*

And, dammit, yes, I'm looking right at my engagement ring when I think it.

Why would I think such a thing, even in passing?

What the hell is wrong with me?

I'm in love with Jack.

I'm not *in love with* Buckley, by any means.

Because I'm *in love with Jack.* I'm marrying Jack.

You can't be *in love with* two guys at the same time.

And when you're *in love with* someone, you shouldn't be attracted to someone else. So I'm not.

"No, I'm definitely not regretting anything," I tell Buckley firmly—and I'm not just talking about the promotion at work.

"Good. Because you deserve it, Tracey. And I'm really happy for you. You've got a great future ahead of you."

I know he's not talking about being Jack's wife, but I pretend that he is. It makes it that much easier to stick my left hand across the table and say, "Guess what?"

He looks down, removing his chopsticks from their red paper sleeve.

I wait for him to look up…

But he doesn't.

Not right away, anyway.

And when he does, his crinkly Irish green eyes aren't wearing the ultra-ecstatic expression you'd expect.

Well, the one I would expect, anyway, especially since I dutifully wore it for him when he announced he was engaged.

"You're engaged?" he asks, wide-eyed and, dare I say…

No, I don't dare say it.

But I do dare think it.

Dismayed.

That's what he seems to be.

"Yes!" I say with gusto. "I'm engaged! Yes! See? Yes!"

All right already with the gusto.

"Jack proposed?"

I nod vigorously and repeat my new favorite word, "Yes!"

I add, "On Valentine's Day, after the wedding!"

Then I add, "So you didn't know he was going to?"

I add this part because I want to remind myself—and him—that he and Jack are friends.

Maybe Buckley and I were friends first, but he and Jack are definitely friends now. Not that the two of them pal around together without me so much, come to think of it, the way they both do with their other friends.

I'm the common denominator in their relationship with each other. Which is fine. It's not as if I hang out doing girl things with Buckley's wife-to-be, either. He's my primary friend; she a friend by default. I'm sure that's how she thinks of me, too.

"No," Buckley says, having broken apart his chopsticks.

Huh? The conversational thread seems to have snapped as well—at least, for me.

"No…what?" I ask him blankly.

"No…I didn't know Jack was going to propose. In fact…"

He begins rubbing his chopsticks against each other to remove the splinters.

"In fact what?"

"No, it's just…" He's rubbing those chopsticks so hard I'm expecting them to ignite any second now. "I was thinking he wasn't going to."

"Propose? Did he say that?" I ask, wondering if Buckley knows something I don't know about Jack after all.

"No! He never said that. I just thought that if he hadn't done it by now, he wasn't going to."

"Why did you think that? You took your sweet time proposing to Sonja." I mean it as a quip, but it comes out more as an accusation.

Buckley reacts with a defensive, "That's different."

"How?"

"Because I wasn't sure."

"About wanting to get married?"

"About anything," he says cryptically, and the waiter arrives with two steaming miso soups.

When he leaves a second later, I wait for Buckley to elaborate on what else, exactly, he wasn't sure about.

He merely eats a spoonful of soup.

"Buckley."

"Yeah?" He looks up, spoon halfway to his mouth again.

"You were saying…?"

He blinks. "What?"

"What were you saying? About not being sure you wanted to get married?" I add helpfully. *And about anything else?*

"Oh. Right. I mean, you know better than anyone—well, except Sonja—that I wasn't sure about it."

It, I want to ask, or *her?*

Because that's what we're talking about here, folks. And it's the first time in ages that Buckley has said anything the least bit ambivalent about his relationship.

"I think it's just a guy thing," he concludes. "You know…cold feet."

I want to ask him if that's really all it is, but I'm afraid Buckley would think I'm not rooting for him and Sonja to live happily ever after. And believe me, no one wants that for them more than I do.

Okay, well maybe Sonja wants it more than I do. And I'm sure her family, who adore Buckley, want it more than I do. I'm way down on the list of people rooting for their happily-ever-after, I'm sure.

What about Buckley, though?

Does he want happily-ever-after with Sonja?

I honestly thought he did.

I think *he* honestly thought he did, too.

But maybe he doesn't anymore. Maybe he needs to talk about this with a good friend.

A good platonic friend who has no personal agenda where he's concerned.

That would be me, I tell myself…except that it wouldn't be me. Because after hearing that Buckley may not be gung ho about marrying Sonja after all, I can't help but be… well…not all that disappointed.

Wait a minute.

Did I really hear that Buckley may not be gung ho about marrying Sonja?

I mean, I know that's what I *heard*…but did he really say it?

No. He didn't. What he said was that he wasn't sure "about anything," including getting married.

What else is there?

There's being in love with the person you're marrying.

Forgive me if I'm jumping to conclusions here, but…

Well, hasn't it seemed all along as though Buckley wasn't a hundred percent on board the Sonja train? It's like he jumped on when he realized it was about to leave the station without him, and he's enjoying the ride, more or less…but now he might not want to take it all the way to its final destination. And he wishes he could jump off.

Okay, I really am very clever with my analogies lately.

Too bad I can't channel all this creativity into a Creative job at the agency.

Too bad I can't even tell Buckley what I'm thinking.…

But I can't, because that would open the door to trouble. Exactly what kind of trouble, I don't know. I just sense that

I should keep my verbal speculation on the apparent state of his relationship to a minimum.

What I *can* do, however, is ask him how things are going with Sonja and the wedding plans.

So I do.

"Not great," he replies.

"Uh-oh." I swear to God I'm psychic. "What's wrong?"

"Remember how we were going to get married a year from this summer so that Sonja would have time to plan the wedding?"

"Yes."

"Well, now she wants to expedite things."

"How much?"

"A year. She wants us to get married in July."

"*This* July? But that's only a few months away."

"I know." He shakes his head, looking at me.

I shake my head, looking back at him.

Okay, this is going to sound crazy, but remember that old movie *Dead Man Walking?* The one where Sean Penn is on death row and Susan Sarandon is the nun who tries to save him?

The vibe between us is exactly like that right now.

Then again...

Buckley didn't kill anyone, and he isn't sentenced to death. And I'm not a nun. Far from it.

So maybe this vibe isn't *exactly* like that.

"Well," I say, "I guess since you're getting married anyway, it doesn't matter when."

Yes, that came from the girl who had her heart set on an October wedding before she ever had a fiancé.

"Yeah, but this July is just so soon…"

"You're right," I tell him. "If Sonja has her heart set on her dream wedding, it will probably take much longer than that to plan it anyway. Trust me, she'll figure that out when she starts trying to pull something together."

I sure as hell did.

"That's the thing. She says she doesn't care about the wedding anymore. She just wants us to be married. The sooner the better, she says."

Aha!

Does my pimply nose smell a desperate bride?

"Did you tell her you'd rather wait until next summer, like you planned?" I ask him, reaching out and putting a hand on his lower arm, all Sister Prejean again.

Or maybe it's more *My Best Friend's Wedding* than *Dead Man Walking*.

"Yeah, I told her. Well, I tried. But she wanted to know why we should wait. Then she accused me of not wanting to marry her."

"At all?"

He nods.

See? What'd I tell you? Desperate bride.

But I refuse to play Julia Roberts to Sonja's Cameron Diaz. Truly, I don't want to disrupt Buckley's wedding plans so that I can steal him away for myself. I'm just his friend, looking out for his best interests. I have a fiancé and a wedding-in-progress of my own.

Buckley sighs and shakes his head, pushing his soup bowl away. I think he's so upset that he's lost his appetite until I look down and see that the bowl is empty.

I dip my spoon into my own bowl and fish around half-heartedly for a floating ribbon of seaweed.

Maybe I'm the one who's lost my appetite.

This just isn't going the way I imagined it would.

I push away my own soup, which I was supposedly craving so desperately, and do my best not to ask the million-dollar question that I'm sure is on both of our minds.

Unfortunately, my best isn't good enough, and I hear myself ask, "So is Sonja right about you not wanting to marry her at all?"

I wait for Buckley to tell me of course she's not right.

But some small part of me hopes he'll tell me that she *is* right, and he doesn't want to marry her after all.

Why am I hoping that? Good question. I have no business hoping that.

"Forget I said anything." Buckley heaves a two-ton sigh as the too-damn-efficient waiter pops up to whisk our soup bowls away.

He simultaneously replaces them with two sashimi deluxe lunches.

And I try to forget Buckley said anything. Really I do.

I pour soy sauce into the little square saucer beside my plate and I try to forget, because an otherwise engaged woman has no business having a vested interest in the romantic status of an otherwise engaged man.

I jab the tips of my chopsticks into the blob of green wasabi paste and transfer a hunk into the saucer, ferociously mixing it with the soy.

I mean, we're friends, Buckley and me. Aside from anything that ever happened between us—or didn't—in the past, friends is all we are and it's all we're ever meant to be.

If we were meant to be anything more, we wouldn't both be in love with other people.

Well, I can't speak for Buckley but *I'm* definitely in love with someone else.

Jack and I clicked from the start. He's everything I ever wanted—smart, loyal, kind, loving, a good person. A *great* person. My family and friends have welcomed him with open arms, and his family has done the same with me. We belong together and we're going to have a great life together.

There isn't a doubt in my mind about that, or about marrying him.

Not when I'm actually *with* him, anyway.

Not any other time, for that matter, aside from right now, today, when I'm with Buckley.

I guess any lingering feelings I might have subconsciously been harboring for him just aren't going away as quickly as I expected them to, now that I'm engaged.

Then again, is that any surprise? It's not as if a person can just turn feelings on and off depending on her marital status.

It's not as if someone puts a ring on your finger and bam!—you've turned off every bit of attraction you've ever felt for anyone else in your life.

Too bad, because wouldn't that be convenient?

As I pinch a slab of raw pink tuna between my chopsticks and dredge it through the soy-wasabe concoction, I find myself envisioning a bunch of levers in my back, behind my heart. They're all labeled with names: Jack, Buckley, Will.

The Jack one, of course, is full-throttle up. The Will one is entirely turned off—and it's about time, don't you think?

The Buckley one is hovering in the halfway zone, like a light switch on a dimmer. I imagine giving it a firm yank and clicking it off altogether, but it seems to be kind of sticking somewhere in the middle, flickering.

"Wow, I'm a shitty friend," Buckley announces abruptly.

I look up in surprise. "What?"

"You just got engaged. We should be celebrating. You celebrated with me when I got engaged."

Yes. But not wholeheartedly.

Only he doesn't know that.

"Here I am dumping my problems on you when we should be toasting your engagement." He scowls. "What's wrong with me?"

"It's okay."

"No, it's not. We need...we need champagne. That's what we need."

"They don't have it here," I say as he spots the waiter and raises his hand. "I tried to order it that day we were here when you got engaged, remember?"

No, he doesn't remember. He was too caught up in his newly engaged elation to have noticed anything that day.

"Well," he says now, "let's finish eating and go down to the Bubble Lounge for a toast."

"Can't. That's way downtown. I've got to get back to work."

Not to mention, I'm afraid of what might happen if Buckley and I started drinking champagne together, given the state of his relationship and my frayed nerves.

"We'll stay in midtown, then."

Tempting, but… "Can't. Really. You have no idea how crazy it is at work with this presentation coming up."

"How about after work, then? I don't have any plans. Do you? We can have dinner."

"No, I'll have to work late—" I *soooo* am not looking forward to that "—and Jack has a focus group or something anyway, so…"

"Oh, right. Jack should come. That would be great," he says, but he doesn't look all that convinced.

"Listen," I say, "let's set up a dinner with Jack and Sonja so that we can all go out together. To celebrate. With, you know, champagne and everything." And everyone.

Jack and Sonja.

Buckley and me.

I mean, Jack and me.

Buckley and Sonja.

"That would be good, going out, the four of us," Buckley agrees. "We'll have to do that."

We'll *have* to…

He says it just like that, as if it's a requirement.

And I guess maybe it should be, from here on in.

You know, maybe I shouldn't be spending time alone with Buckley now that I'm an engaged woman.

Come on, Tracey…what is this, Victorian England?

Of course I'll go on spending time alone with Buckley, just as I always did.

Our friendship isn't going to change just because we're getting married to other people.

Well, *I'm* getting married, anyway.

Buckley doesn't seem so sure about himself anymore, dammit.

If he seemed sure he was getting married, I wouldn't be having this conversation with myself in the first place. I would just go on assuming he's madly in love with Sonja...

Now that I think about it, though...did he ever really seem madly in love?

He'd hemmed and hawed an awful lot right from the beginning. And I can't help but note that every time he and Sonja took their relationship a step further—exclusively dating each other, moving in together, getting engaged—it was entirely her idea. Buckley had dragged his feet from day one.

Maybe not from day *one*. I was there on day one—or rather, night one. I watched Buckley fall all over Sonja, with her long curly dark hair, white-white-white smile and one of those impossible figures that is svelte with big, perky boobs.

Don't get me wrong, I'm not lacking in that department. Especially not when I'm less-than-svelte.

But whenever I lose weight, I lose it all over and things immediately start to sag. A good push-up bra takes care of it.

Sonja doesn't rely on underwire, though. She goes braless every now and then—very obviously—and I happen to know that the only thing pushing up her boobs is good fortune and a good gene pool.

Anyway, this isn't about boobs and bras—or lack thereof— it's about Buckley's feelings for Sonja. He was definitely into her the night they met, and immediately thereafter.

So what changed that for him?

Her constant pushing for a commitment.

I pushed Jack for a commitment, too.

What if he changes his mind about me? asks a small voice in my head—the voice that belongs to Inner Tracey, who is frequently insecure.

I haven't heard from her in quite a while.

I didn't miss her.

He won't change his mind, I assure Inner Tracey, irritated. *Don't worry.*

After all, Jack might have been slow to commit, but now that he's in, he's in. That's just how he is. He takes his time making up his mind to do something so that he's absolutely sure it's the right choice.

Trust me. I've been shopping with the man for everything from suits to groceries. It's a painstaking process.

I, on the other hand...

Well, I've been known to make an impulse purchase on occasion. My closet—and our kitchen cupboards—are full of proof:

A pair of scary, dressy wool shorts—remember when dressy wool shorts were all the rage? (Me, neither: I'm sure the rage lasted all of a week after some frivolous starlet wore them to an awards show. I, of course, must have had the misfortune to go shopping that week and the greater misfortune of thinking they'd look hot with a blazer and heels.)

A tin of canned salmon (in the cupboard, not the closet) because I thought I would learn to make croquettes, which must also have been all the rage at the moment.

Back to the closet: a pair of perennially trendy spike-heeled boots that couldn't safely and steadily transport me across the shoe department floor, let alone anywhere else.

A can of steel-cut Irish oats—probably bug-infested by

now—that are supposed to be good for you but take forever to cook (cupboard again, and I really should toss them).

A pair of marked-down Levi's in my size that should have fit but didn't, which I would have realized had I tried them on, but I didn't feel like it.

I could go on, but I won't.

The point is…

Wait, what is the point?

Well, one point is that *dressy shorts* is an oxymoron.

Another point is, who buys jeans without trying them on? Not Jack.

What that has to do with anything is unclear to me at the moment because my head is spinning—without benefit of champagne.

Maybe I never should have thought that an engagement ring—not to mention a promotion—would solve anything.

Now I'm starting to wonder if my problems have just begun.

5

If the first three days of the week were bad at work, Thursday is absolutely atrocious.

The presentation didn't go well. The Client hated it—and us.

That's what I tell Latisha when she sticks her head into my office just after six-thirty to see how it went.

"They hated *you?*" she echoes dubiously, catching me with a pocket mirror examining the latest stress-generated blemish on my face.

"Yup," I say, nodding vigorously and snapping the mirror closed.

"They hated you personally."

"All of us."

Latisha smirks. "What did they do? Push you down and call you names?"

"Don't laugh. They might as well have." Sitting in my desk

chair, I wedge my poor aching, swollen feet from the evil yet *très* fashionable high-heeled shoes I wore all day.

"So what happened?"

"It was a horrible presentation." I reach into my bottom desk drawer and grab a pair of antique black flats for my crosstown walk to meet Jack and his family.

Not cool vintage indy-actress antique.

Scuffed old somebody's-cleaning-lady antique. Aerosoles that are *très* ugly but feel like slippers. Ah, bliss.

"Thank God this week is almost over," I tell Latisha, flexing my grateful toes. "Thank God at least this *day* is over."

"Yeah, everyone else is already gone. I didn't realize you were even still here until I saw your light on. Come on or we'll be late."

I look up from putting my brand-new issue of *Modern Bride*, with its tantilizing "Exotic Honeymoon Destinations" cover story, into my bag.

"We'll be late?" I echo. "Late for what?" Last I knew, she wasn't coming along to dinner with the Candell clan and me.

"For Julie's thing."

"What thing?" Julie is one of the administrative assistants on the cereal account down the hall. She's a sweetheart. I love her.

"You know…her goodbye party."

"What?" I am completely nonplussed.

"Her goodbye party," Latisha repeats, but with less conviction this time. In fact, it almost sounds like a question.

And, I've got one of my own. Two, actually: "Julie's *leaving?*" and "What party?"

Is it my imagination, or is Latisha actually squirming?

"You didn't know Julie was leaving?"

Yup. She's squirming all right.

"No. She quit?"

"She was laid off. Today's her last day."

No, I did not know that.

"She's having a party?" I ask, because I did not know that, either.

"It's not that big a deal. She just asked if a bunch of us wanted to go out for drinks at the Royalton to help drown her sorrows. Not that she's all that sorrowful because they all got great severance packages and she's paying for everyone's drinks."

Except mine, of course. Because I won't be there. Because I wasn't invited.

Wow.

"*They all* got great severance packages?" I echo. "Who is *they all?*"

"Don't you mean who 'are' they all?"

I fix Latisha with a hairy eyeball. Since when is she the queen of good grammar?

"You know what I meant."

She shrugs. "Yeah. A couple of other people got let go from that account. Two of the executive VPs in Creative, an assistant A.E. and a few people in production, I heard. The media group will be reassigned to other accounts."

Glad Jack isn't on the Choc-Chewy-O's account, I watch Latisha sneak a peek at her watch.

"Go ahead." I bleakly shove a folder filled with notes from the meeting into my already jammed black bag and reach for my coat on the back of the door. "Looks like you're late."

"Do you want to come?"

"To the party?" *To which I was not invited?*

"It's not really a party," Latisha backpedals with unchar-
acteristic and unappealing reticence. "It's just, you know,
a...thing. But you should come."

"Don't you think I'd feel a little funny?"

"Why? It's just Julie, and, you know...everyone."

I thought I was a part of *everyone*. Apparently not.

"I really thought you knew about it," Latisha—not prone
to mumbling—mumbles. "I mean, I figured you probably
hear stuff now that you're up there."

"Up where?"

"You know...out of the cubes with the rest of us, into the
room with a view."

"Yeah. Well...I didn't know." I shrug, feeling uncomfortable.

"So you want to come or not?"

"That's okay. I've got plans tonight with Jack anyway. We
have a seven o'clock reservation at Gallagher's with his family."

"Cool." She looks relieved. "Well...have fun."

"You, t—" I smack my forehead. "Oh my God."

"What?"

"I just realized something."

"What?"

Adrian mentioned the other day that the Choc-Chewy-
O's account group would be meeting to talk about trimming
the fat...and, being naturally food-and-weight-obsessed, I
took it literally.

Trimming the fat...they were talking about layoffs.

Duh.

"What, Tracey?"

"Nothing, I just... I think Adrian might have mentioned

something about layoffs on that account, but at the time, I...you know..."

"Didn't think you should say anything?" she supplies.

"Right," I say, because it's more appealing than *didn't get it*.

Hmm. So what do you know? Maybe I do hear things now that I'm up here with a view. I just don't know what those things mean.

Idiot.

"Listen, tell Julie I said...uh, good luck. Okay?"

"You have her number, right?" Latisha seems a little terse. "Call her tomorrow and tell her yourself."

I sigh inwardly, watching Latisha walk away.

Maybe it's been years since middle school, but suddenly I'm right back in the thick of it, a pimple-faced loser in comfortable shoes, being dissed by the popular girls.

You are not, I tell myself. *You're a glowing, newly promoted bride-to-be*.

With zits.

Wearing Aerosoles.

Not invited to the party.

I glumly shove the pointy pumps into my bag along with everything else, and throw the strap over my shoulder.

Damn, it's heavy. Mostly due to *Modern Bride*, of course. By the time I actually become one, I'm going to need an exotic-honeymoon package that throws in a masseuse and a chiropractor.

I reach over to turn out the desk light, then hesitate. I should probably wait a few minutes. I don't want to ride down the elevator with Latisha and whoever else is on the way to Julie's "goodbye thing" to which I wasn't invited.

Really, what's up with that? Since when do they go out together without me?

Could I possibly have done something to upset Julie? Or someone?

Nothing that I can think of.

Hurt, I linger a few more minutes in my office until the coast is clear.

Out on the street, swept into the familiar throng of rushing commuters, I breathe some cold, fresh February night air to clear my head.

Maybe I should have point-blank asked Latisha why they left me out.

Then again...she probably doesn't know why. She didn't even realize I wasn't invited in the first place. She assumed I was.

Well, of course she did. Why wouldn't she? I was there when we all went out for Chinese to celebrate Julie's birthday after New Year's. And I was there when—

My thoughts are interrupted by my ringing cell phone.

Maybe it's Julie, calling to say it was an oversight and that I should get my butt over to the Royalton.

I pull the phone out of my pocket and check caller ID.

Jack.

Middle school again, and who cares about the popular girls? A cute boy is calling me.

"Hey, cute boy," I say into the phone, feeling better instantly.

"Cute boy? Huh?"

"Where are you?" I ask, deciding against telling Jack I'll be calling him Cute Boy from now on.

"I'm just leaving Penn Station." He had to take the train

to Jersey for a meeting this afternoon and is just getting back into town. "The uptown subway isn't running so it's an absolute madhouse over here. I'll have to walk up."

I don't bother to ask him about a cab. As any New Yorker knows, you can stroll to Long Island in the time it would take to snag a rush-hour cab from Penn Station when the subway isn't running.

"Where are *you?*" Jack asks.

"Heading across Forty-eighth Street toward Gallagher's." Which is just a few blocks northwest of the oh-so-hip, monochromatic lobby bar where the entire cubicle population of Blaire Barnett Middle School is enjoying flavored mojitos.

"I'll be at Gallagher's in about ten minutes," I tell Jack.

"You'll beat me, then. The reservation's under Candell. Go ahead and sit down. Tell Mom I'm on my way. And don't tell her or my sisters the news until I get there."

As if. We've been looking forward to this for days. We still haven't had a chance to tell anyone about our engagement in person.

Not together, anyway.

Last night before bed, I nonchalantly mentioned to Jack that I'd had lunch with Buckley and shared our news with him. He wanted to know what Buckley had to say about it.

He asked me that question in the most casual way, not even looking up from his iPod, which he was programming with a couple of Springsteen albums for today's train trip out to Jersey.

I, of course, answered the casual question in the most casual way. "He said congratulations." *And that he isn't sure he wants to marry Sonja.* "Oh, and he said the four of us should go out. He wants to celebrate with us."

"Really?"

Not really…but that's what *I* want. Actually, it's what I should want. I *should* want all of us to go on being a happy little foursome. Maybe we can all move to the same suburb and have babies and, I don't know, play bridge or whatever it is that old married suburban foursomes do together.

At the very least, Buckley should stand up in our wedding. Which I plan to mention to Jack the first chance I get.

I spent the rest of the walk to the restaurant dwelling on that strange lunch Buckley and I had shared. He definitely seemed unusually quiet as we finished our sashimi, and I was relieved when it was time for me to hurry back to the office.

I haven't heard from him since, not that it's surprising. It's not like Buckley and I connect every single day. I rarely give it much advance thought, but now I've been wondering when and where I'm going to see him again, and what he's going to say about Sonja.

I push them both firmly out of my mind now, because tonight is the night I've been looking forward to all week.

The West Side is teeming with a pretheater crowd, and so is Gallagher's.

I pause a few feet from the door to balance on one foot at a time while wedging my feet into the excruciating-but-to-die-for heels again.

Jack's sister Emily is really into shoes. I know she'll notice and approve. I also know she'll notice—and disapprove of—Aerosoles.

I shouldn't care what Jack's sister thinks of me, and maybe I won't, once I'm officially part of the family. But for now,

I still want to put my best foot forward, and I don't want it to be wearing an Aerosole.

Wilma is waiting right inside the entrance. She's looking very Hepburnesque as usual this evening. (Audrey, not Katharine.) She's wearing an adorable nubby wool coat and hat over a chic black dress with coordinating velvet pumps and pearls.

With Jack's mom are three of his four sisters: Emily, Rachel and Jeannie.

Emily, who works for a fashion showroom and is built like a model, has on jeans, boots and a leather jacket. So does Rachel, but Emily's jeans are more fashionably cut, her boots have high, thin heels, and her leather is black, not brown.

"Ooh, Tracey, great shoes," Emily says, first thing. What did I tell you?

"Thanks," I say. "How's everything going?"

"Great," Emily replies, and adds somewhat cheerfully, "Although I broke up with Giancarlo."

"Oh, no." I could have sworn her boyfriend's name was Dale. I guess he was the one before Giancarlo. Emily changes boyfriends as often as she changes sweaters. But I ask sympathetically, "What happened?"

"No one specific thing. He's just a pompous ass."

"I'd say that's pretty specific," is Jeannie's typically dry comment.

Plainer than her sisters and a little on the chunky side, she probably came straight from her court-reporter job. She's wearing a plain crepe navy dress and low-heeled pumps, a long charcoal winter dress coat slung over her arm.

Of course, Jack's father, who wasn't invited, is conspicuously absent. The decision not to include him was Jack's call.

The Candells are fairly recently, and not so amicably, divorced. I guess Jack figured his father's presence might put a damper on any optimistic, marriage-related toasts.

I immediately notice that Jack's sister Kathleen, who *was* invited, is also conspicuously absent.

I ask Wilma if Kathleen is running late.

"Oh, she's not coming. Poor thing was just too exhausted to think about getting on a train at this time of day."

I should point out that Poor Thing, who is married and lives in Westchester not far from her mother, perpetually claims debilitating exhaustion at any time of day. I recently suggested to her that she get a blood test to check for mono, Epstein-Barr, Lyme or some other disease that might cause a pampered stay-at-home mom to sleep in until eleven every morning of the week. (She also requires daily naps, nightly bubble baths, frequent hot-stone massages and regular spa stays.)

Jack kicked me under the table when I suggested the blood test because Kathleen is also a notorious hypochondriac. In fact, she's kind of an all-around drag.

Still, I tell Wilma, "I'm sorry she couldn't make it," which is the truth because I know Jack really wanted all the women on Team Candell to be here tonight.

"Well, you know how hard it is for her, with the twins," Wilma says.

Yes, but it's not as though she just last week birthed a pair of colicky babies and is nursing them both around the clock. Ashley and Beatrice turned five in December, go to full-time preschool and have a full-time live-in nanny.

"Come on, Mom, everything is always hard for Kathleen and we all know it has nothing to do with the twins,"

Rachel pipes up. Did I mention that she's Jack's favorite sister? And mine?

She's eighteen months older than Jack, and shares not just his lanky wholesome, brown-haired good looks and tailored, classic clothing style, but also his sense of humor and his pragmatic, no-bullshit outlook on their family situation. Come to think of it, she, too, is Hepburnesque-only it's confident Katharine, not dainty Audrey.

I really want to ask Rachel to be a bridesmaid, but I can't do that in front of her sisters. Too bad I can't have both her and Jeannie, whom I really adore, as well. But I'm sure that would make Emily feel left out.

Well, what if I had Emily, too? I mean, is there any rule regarding how many bridesmaids are too many? It's my wedding, right? Who says I can't have...

Eight, nine...ten?

Ten.

That's kind of a lot.

And anyway, I can't have three of Jack's sisters without the fourth, even if Kathleen really is a tremendous pain in the butt to everyone but her mother.

"Rachel, your sister is overwhelmed," Wilma chides. "You know Kathleen's got a lot on her plate."

Yeah. Kathleen's got about as much on her plate—figuratively speaking—as I literally had on mine the summer I lost fifty pounds.

"She doesn't have any more on her plate than the rest of us have," sandy-haired Jeannie mutters, rolling her brown eyes. She's married and lives in the suburbs, too. No kids yet, but she's working two jobs to put her husband, Greg, through law school. Plus, they're remodeling their new house, a falling-apart fixer-upper, doing all the work themselves because they can't afford to hire help.

Yet here she is, in typical Jeannie fashion, willing to go the extra mile—rather, thirty-some extra miles—when summoned.

Yeah, I really wish I could have her in the wedding party.

"Is Jack on his way, Tracey?" Wilma asks, pointedly changing the subject.

"Yeah, but the subway isn't running. He should be here in a few minutes. He said we should go ahead and grab our table."

"Oh, that wouldn't be polite. Let's just wait for him."

Honey-haired Emily, the baby of the family—in every way—protests, "I'm starved. Why do we have to wait for Jack? Can't we just sit down and order something?"

Maybe it isn't a whine, exactly. But somehow, a lot of things she says come out kind of…well, whiny.

Maybe it's just the naturally high-pitched tone of her voice.

"We should wait for your brother," Wilma says again.

"But I haven't eaten anything since breakfast! If I don't get something into my stomach right away I'm going to drop right here and cause a big scene."

Funny how Emily and Kathleen are so different from the three middle siblings. Jack, Rachel and Jeannie are all so easygoing, more like Wilma. The others are more like their dad. Jack's father is about as easygoing as Donald Trump, and almost as rich.

Okay, maybe not *that* rich.

But rich. He made a fortune as an advertising executive

back in the boom years of the eighties. The Candells are a whole lot wealthier than anyone back in Brookside.

For the first time, I allow myself to consider a definite downside to having the wedding in my hometown: the snob factor. Not just Jack's father, but Billy, and maybe even Kate.

The thing is, anyone who's accustomed to glitzy society-type weddings is probably going to be taken aback by a non-glitzy, Spadolini-type wedding. I shouldn't care what anyone thinks, but I can't stomach the thought of my future father-in-law being pulled into a tarantella line by my shrillest cousin, Allegra.

Then again, my wedding is already going to be a notch more fancy than all the others in our family simply because it won't be held in the church hall at Most Precious Mother, where my parents and siblings all got married. Nothing against the church hall, but...I just don't want crepe-paper-festooned basketball hoops and paper tablecloths. And really, who can blame me?

I still haven't had a chance to discuss Shorewood with Jack, but I'll need to before someone steals that October date out from under us. The banquet manager said he did indeed just have a cancellation for the third Saturday, but he expects it to be snatched up by someone else right away. Charles also reminded me that he can't hold it without a hefty deposit— another thing Jack and I will need to discuss, pronto.

I'm thinking that if we can somehow scrape together the deposit using whatever my parents can afford to give us plus cash advances on our credit cards that aren't maxed out, we can go on an austerity budget between now and October and come up with the rest.

Hopefully tonight's official revelation and celebration will get the ball rolling. I bet Jack will be psyched about planning the wedding once his mother and sisters are involved.

By the time Jack comes breezing in, Emily and Wilma have resumed bickering about whether or not we should be seated, and I could really use a drink and a hug.

He promptly offers the latter, and I feel better already.

"You look wiped out," he says, brushing a clump of hair back from my cheek. "Rough day?"

"Very." I pull the clump of hair forward again. I was using it to camouflage yet another burgeoning blemish from the peaches-and-cream Candell females.

Watching my fiancé give his mom a big hug and kiss, I am reminded of the old saying that you can tell what kind of husband a man is going to be based on how he treats his mother. I hope that's true, because Jack adores Wilma. He's crazy about his sisters, too—even Kathleen.

The only family member I've never heard him mention with affection—let alone warmly interact with—is his dad. Having met Jack's father, I have to say he's not the greatest guy in the world.

I'm not prone to understatements, but that definitely is one.

I guess I'd be more rattled if I thought there was the slightest possibility Jack might turn out to be the same kind of husband and father Jack Senior was: a controlling, arrogant workaholic.

Not a chance of that, though, thank God. There are some things you just *know* about a person's character. Jack simply doesn't have it in him to change that drastically.

Now that he's here, we're quickly seated at a red-check-ered-cloth-covered table in one of the vast dining rooms.

"What a wonderful place," Wilma says, looking around appreciatively, though I suspect she would probably be more at home breakfasting at Tiffany's.

But Jack and I love Gallagher's, with its high ceilings, wooden floors and walls lined with framed photos of celebrities who've dined here. I'm glad I was too busy today at work to eat lunch because I'm famished, and a thick steak will really hit the spot.

Jack waits until we've ordered our food, including a bunch of side dishes to share and a bottle of red wine.

Then he lifts his filled glass. "I want to make a toast," he announces, cutting into his mother and sisters' chatty conversation.

Naturally, everyone lifts her glass and waits expectantly, wondering what's going on.

Or not.

I can't help but notice that everyone seems to anticipate what's coming, because I catch all four of them, Jack's mother and sisters, trying to catch a glimpse of my left hand. Which I'm sitting on.

Bummer—they obviously know we're engaged. Or at least, they suspect it.

Then again, why wouldn't they? Wilma gave Jack the diamond last summer. She even confided to me that she ran it by Emily and Rachel first, to make sure they didn't want her to save it for one of them when the time came.

She probably asked Jeannie and Kathleen to green-light it, too, even though they were both already married by the time Wilma's ring—which was from her failed marriage— became available.

So presumably, the four other women in Jack's life have

spent the last six months the same way I have: wondering when he was going to propose.

You might imagine, then, that it would be a tad anticlimactic when Jack announces, "Here's to Tracey, my future wife."

But somehow, it's not anticlimactic at all.

Wilma, sitting next to me, gives me a big hug and says, "Welcome to the family!" To Jack, she says, "It's about time!" and he shrugs sheepishly.

"Of course I'll want to help you with the wedding," Wilma says mostly to me.

"That would be great!" I smile, feeling relieved, and wondering what she means by "help." Does she mean help pay for it? Or help plan it? Or both?

Jack's sisters congratulate us and want to see the ring.

Everyone agrees that it's gorgeous, and we toast to mine and Jack's future.

The middle-aged couple at the next table, who have overheard, add their congratulations and inform us that they're here celebrating their thirty-fifth anniversary.

"That's wonderful!" Wilma says a little wistfully. "What's your secret?"

"The first words out of our mouths every morning and every night are 'I love you,'" the wife says.

"Afternoons, too. And we mean it," adds the husband, reaching out to brush a crumb of bread from her cheek.

Aw, how sweet.

This is turning out to be a good night. A really, really good night. At last, I feel like a giddy bride-to-be as I sip my wine contentedly.

"Ouch!" the woman at the next table blurts.

"What?" her husband asks. "What's wrong with you?"

"My eye! You poked me in the eye!"

"Well, can you still see?"

Pause. "Yes...thank God."

Thank God, I think. A little selfishly, I'll admit: paramedics would ruin the ambience.

Jack catches my eye as the waiter arrives with our salads. His smile is like hot cocoa on a cold night; sweet and welcome. Warmed by it, I reach for his hand under the table and give it a squeeze.

You know what? Sometimes, you just don't need words. I have to remember that the next time I'm wishing Jack would be more vocal about his feelings.

You know what else? I was wrong yesterday when I thought that getting engaged had opened the door on a whole new set of problems. Maybe that's the case with my promotion at work, but not with this.

Jack and I belong together. I must have been crazy to think I could possibly regret never again kissing anyone else in this world—Buckley included.

"You two will have to come up to Westchester this weekend," Wilma muses as the waiter grinds pepper over her salad, "so that we can get busy."

"Busy with what?" Jack asks.

His mother sends me a good-natured eye-roll. *Men!* "Busy with wedding plans," she tells Jack. "What else?"

"Why do we have to come up to Westchester for that?" Jack wants to know...which is exactly the question that's on my mind, but I don't dare voice it because I suspect I know the answer.

"So that we can start looking at places for your reception," Wilma informs us.

Ah. I was right.

Jack's sisters are nodding. But of course. The reception. In Westchester.

"Actually," I say when Jack doesn't jump in immediately—or thereafter, "we're not sure where we want to get married yet."

That's not a lie because officially, *we* aren't sure.

Privately, however, *I'm* sure.

"So you were thinking of the city?" Emily asks, brightening. "Because we did an awesome shoot last summer at this gorgeous loft space downtown. I think it would be perfect for your wedding."

"Really? Because I thought you said it would be perfect for *your* wedding," Rachel says dryly.

"Yeah, well, it looks like I'm not having one anytime soon, so…" Emily shrugs and grandly informs me and Jack, "The loft is all yours."

"Gee, thanks."

Missing Jack's sarcasm, Emily adds, "I have to warn you, though—you'll pay a fortune to have it there."

"I bet Westchester is a lot cheaper," Jeannie comments.

"Not necessarily," Rachel points out.

"Well, Greg and I had our reception over in Yorktown Heights, and it wasn't as bad as Bedford, or the city."

I wait for Jack to speak up and mention that upstate in Brookside, everything is much more affordable than Yorktown Heights or anywhere around here. But he says nothing at all. He's just chomping away frantically at his mixed greens like a furtive rabbit determined to get back under the fence before the farmer shows up.

"If Jack and Tracey want a wedding in Bedford or the city, they should have it," Wilma declares, and still, Jack is maddeningly silent. "They should have their wedding wherever they want. After all, you only get married once."

Coming from her, those last five words seem to land in our midst like a bucket of rocks. Thud. Silence.

We all know how Wilma's one shot at marriage turned out. And that Wilma makes no secret of the fact that she wouldn't be opposed to finding someone new, should the opportunity arise.

Starting to feel more bummed than bridal, I look at Jack. He's still intent on his salad.

I look harder at him—glaring, if you will. I'm just trying to send him a signal. But I get the distinct impression that he's deliberately ignoring me.

You know, now is really not the best time for Wilma's ironic statement to remind me that sometimes weddings don't lead to happily ever after.

Yes, I'm crazy about Jack. Yes, I'm optimistic about our future.

But you know what? Sometimes, you *do* need words. I can't help but wonder why my soon-to-be husband is less involved in this conversation than everyone else, including the formerly giddy couple seated at the next table—who, I notice, seem to have run out of things to say to each other and are now eavesdropping while toying with their crab cake and shrimp cocktail.

Is it all that surprising that their conversation has stalled?

Really, what is there to say to someone after thirty-five years together?

My own parents have been married about thirty-eight now, and their dinner conversation is pretty much limited to "Hey, how come you shut the window? It's a thousand degrees in here," and "Are you sure this is really imported Asiago? Because it tastes like domestic Romano." That sort of thing.

Is that how it's going to turn out for me and Jack?

Does it happen to everyone?

If you're lucky enough to make it to thirty-five years and beyond, does the spark die a natural death? Are you reduced to just coexisting?

I look at Jack. He's thoughtfully eating a piece of tomato and doesn't see me. Or maybe he's just pretending he doesn't.

I turn my attention back to the morning-noon-and-night-I-love-you anniversary couple next to us.

The husband is leaning over to taste the wife's food.

Aw, how sweet. See?

Wait, the wife's swatting the husband's fork away, hoarding her crab cake.

Oh.

Well, at least they're still together, and so are my parents, which is more than you can say for Jack's.

I wonder if his being the product of a broken home has any bearing on our chances for making it to our own thirty-fifth anniversary and beyond.

Well, it's not as if Jack actually grew up in a broken home. I mean, the home wasn't broken until long after he moved out.

Not officially, anyway.

But Jack has mentioned that his parents always fought a

lot. They were, reportedly, just waiting until their nest was empty before they made the official split.

As soon as Emily graduated from college, his father was gone.

I try to imagine how I would feel if my parents got divorced at this late date.

Devastated. Sorrowful. Shocked.

But of course, there's no chance of that happening. Not only is divorce out of the question when you're a Vatican-obeying novena queen, but my parents really do love each other. I'd say equally so, although my mother confided to me, back in the days when I was trying to get over Will, that my father was the one who fell first, and much harder. She said he didn't make her heart crazy, and that she had to learn to love him.

What, exactly, were Connie Spadolini's words of wisdom? "Marry someone who loves you more than you love him, because he'll always treat you like gold."

Something like that.

Hmm.

Does Jack love me more than I love him?

Somehow, I would find that hard to believe. Then again, he does treat me…

Well, not like gold. I mean, it's not like he bows to my every whim…and seriously, would I want him to? That would be pretty scary.

Jack treats me with love and respect, though. And he wants to spend the rest of his life with me.

What more do I want or need from him?

Well, sometimes, words.

"I'll call Reverend Devern about performing your

ceremony as soon as I get home." Wilma has ominously popped back into the conversation like crazy Glenn Close rising from Michael Douglas's bathtub.

I look at Jack, screaming a silent *Help!!*

He pokes obliviously through his salad, on a determined hunt for another tomato.

You know, it's a really good thing my life isn't in danger, the way he's been ignoring my telepathic messages.

Or maybe he just plain doesn't get it. Which is hard to believe, since he's read my mind plenty of times in the past. Usually when I'm thinking something I don't want him to know.

"He's going to be so happy to hear you're getting married, Jack," Wilma goes on.

Reverend Devern—who is affectionately referred to as Rev Dev on the rare occasions Jack has reason to mention him—is the clergyman at the Candells' Presbytarian church in Bedford. It's a beautiful two-hundred year-old white-clap-board building with a steeple and stained-glass windows...

And somebody really should mention to Wilma that Jack and I are not getting married there before she books the place and sends out invitations.

"You know, Mom, Tracey's Catholic, so she probably wants to have a priest do their wedding."

No, that's not my noble groom coming to my rescue. It's his sister Rachel, God love her.

"Oh! I didn't even think..." Wilma turns to me. "Tracey, I didn't mean to jump the gun. Did you want a priest instead?"

"I..." Might as well set things straight right from the start,

I decide. "Yes," I say firmly. "I want a priest. No offense to Reverend Devern. I'm sure he's great."

"Oh, he is great. He baptized Kathleen's twins."

"That's nice," I murmur, thinking that a priest probably would have better served their needs, since Rev Dev probably isn't trained to perform exorcisms.

Oh my God, did I really just think that?

Talk about inappropriate. I mean, Ashley and Beatrice are going to become my nieces. I shouldn't think such negative thoughts about them...even if they are evil little devil children.

"You know, I'm sure that if your priest wanted to fly down and perform the ceremony with Reverend Devern, he wouldn't have a problem with that," Wilma tells me unexpectedly. "Fortunately, the rules of our church are pretty flexible."

"Unfortunately, the rules of ours aren't," I say, as if that's news to anyone. "I don't think Father Stefan will go for our not getting married in the Catholic church. And my parents definitely wouldn't, either."

Silence.

Then Wilma smiles and says brightly, "You know, I really can't wait to meet them, Tracey. I hope they'll be able to come down for the engagement party."

"Engagement party?"

"We'll wait until the weather warms up so we can have it outside," Wilma decides. "That's what we did for the girls."

"Uh...Mom? My engagement party was in January," Jeannie contradicts.

"She's right, it was, because I wore those Ralph Lauren boots Daddy got me for Christmas," Emily points out helpfully.

"*Was* it January?" Wilma muses. "Huh. I must be thinking of Kathleen's."

"Hers was in June. I remember because I had on that black Armani strapless dress," says Emily. In case you haven't noticed, she tends to recall special occasions strictly by her choice of personal attire.

"Well, we can have your party in June, too," Wilma tells me and Jack. "What do you think?"

"Sure," Jack says with a shrug. "Whatever. That sounds good."

"You really don't have to throw us an engagement party, Wilma." I can't help but shudder a bit at the thought of my family traipsing down to Westchester to meet the Candells.

For one thing, my parents are hardly world travelers. Their last actual trip was to Schenectady on a church bus trip to some shrine around there somewhere. I remember it because they got me a T-shirt that reads Schenectady: The City That Lights and Hauls the World, which is some ambitious motto, don't you think?

Needless to say, Mom and Pop haven't visited me in New York since I moved here after college. Did I mention that they were absolutely crushed when I left Brookside? No one else in my family ever has. I'm sure they're still thinking I'll get over it and go back home where I belong.

Of course, now that I'm marrying Jack, they'll probably suspect that I might actually be here to stay…but that doesn't mean they'll approve. Or visit.

What if Wilma goes to all the trouble of throwing an engagement party and my parents refuse to come?

"Really," I tell her, "it's not necessary."

"Don't be ridiculous, Tracey. Of course I'm going to throw you an engagement party," she says as if it's all settled. "I just wish we still had the house so we could have it there."

The sprawling family home in Bedford was sold after the divorce. Now Wilma lives in a condo community.

"You really can't host a big party at your place, Mom," Jeannie points out.

"I know, no worries, we'll just have it at a restaurant," she says briskly. "I've got it all under control."

Well, better that than the wedding itself, I tell myself.

I'll just have to try and convince my parents to get on a plane to New York in June—then make excuses to my future in-laws when they refuse.

Meanwhile, Jack and I have to have a conversation about our actual wedding plans before his mother takes over.

It's ironic for me to even consider that possibility, because Wilma never struck me as the overbearing mother-in-law type.

Not that she's overstepped her bounds…yet. I mean, she's probably just excited, wanting to help, like she said.

But the sooner Jack lets her know that we'll be getting married at Most Precious Mother in Brookside with a reception at Shorewood afterward, the better.

Mental note: Let Jack know ASAP that we'll be getting married at Most Precious Mother in Brookside with a reception at Shorewood afterward.

"You know," Wilma is saying fondly, "I still remember what fun I had planning my wedding all those years ago. This is such a wonderful time in your lives. Enjoy every minute of it."

"We will," I assure her, and Jack leans over and kisses her on the cheek.

"Thanks, Mom."

She's a little shiny-eyed all of a sudden, I notice. Well, he's her son. And being single, she depends on him for things a husband might otherwise do—like helping her move heavy furniture and keeping track of investments.

It can't be easy for her to realize that another woman is going to come first in his heart from now on. Maybe she feels as if she's losing him. It's kind of amazing that she's been so supportive of me right from the start, never showing the slightest bit of jealousy or resentment.

Then I think about how my own mother still adores and babies my brothers, and how she frequently criticizes their wives for what she considers inadequate laundry, parenting and, especially, cooking skills.

She only complains to me and my sister, Mary Beth, of course. And only behind my sister-in-laws' backs. To their faces, she treats them…

Well, as lovingly as Wilma treats me.

Hmm.

Thinking back to when my brothers got married, I remember that my mother definitely put her two cents' into every decision. She even reduced my most laid-back sister-in-law, my brother Joey's wife, Sara, to tears at her own rehearsal dinner. Somehow, my mother had it in her head that Sara's mother would be wearing navy blue to the wedding the next day, so she had bought a powder-blue dress for herself. It turned out Sara's mother would also be wearing powder blue—and had been planning to all along—and my mother flipped out.

She wound up wearing the royal-blue dress she'd worn for

my sister Mary Beth's wedding, which had taken place so long ago that we convinced her nobody would remember it. Then we rushed around telling each arriving guest to compliment her on the dress as if they had never seen it before.

A year later, when Mary Beth caught her husband, Vinnie, cheating and her marriage hit the skids, my mother decided the dress was cursed. She's been worried about Joey and Sara ever since.

And, of course, she complains every chance she gets that Joey's too thin, and we all know she thinks it's because he can't eat Sara's cooking.

Mothers-in-law.

Watching my future one affectionately ruffle her only son's hair, I uneasily tell myself that at least I'm not marrying my brother.

Then, remembering that my mother has three sons, and Wilma only one, I reach for my wine and chug the rest.

6

One would think there would be plenty of opportunities over the course of a stormy February weekend to have a serious conversation with your live-in fiancé.

But it's Sunday night already, and I still haven't had a chance to pin down Jack to talk Wedding.

Friday: I came home from work stressed after eleven straight hours of avoiding all my friends there, who may very well have been avoiding me in return. I still have no idea why I wasn't invited to Julie's goodbye party. All I know is that by the time Friday night rolled around, my window office felt like solitary confinement.

I crave carbs when I'm upset about something, so I whipped up a great pasta with everything we had on hand in the cupboard: olive oil, canned tomatoes, capers, black olives, mushrooms.

It was surprisingly good but I wound up eating it alone because Jack worked until after midnight.

Saturday: Jack slept till noon while I killed the better part of the morning reading *Modern Bride* from cover to cover, an incredibly enlightening experience.

Who knew that bustles would be all the rage in wedding gowns by next fall? Who knew that aromatherapists were now creating bridal bouquets meant to evoke a specific mood in the nuptial couple and their guests? Who knew that one could rent a Tahitian honeymoon hut—not waterfront, but right *in* the water, perched in the sea on stilts?

Still waiting for Jack to awaken so that I could regale him with the marvels of modern matrimony, I began pricing honeymoon packages online.

Still no Jack, so I conveniently laid out all our possible honeymoon destinations on a Microsoft Excel spreadsheet that would appeal to Jack's media-planner sensibility. I used smaller type for the cost column, but the amounts were still daunting. I could only hope that Jack would be as enchanted as I was by the prospect of Tahiti, Paris, Nevis...

Pricey? You bet your white silk bustle. But it would be a once-in-a-lifetime event, so why not go all out?

By the time Jack woke up, though, there was no time for honeymoon talk. I was leaving to meet Kate at Ruby Foo's for our engagement-celebration lunch.

She gave me a gorgeous white silk peignoir from Saks as an engagement gift. When I asked her to be a bridesmaid, she told me she'd love to—if she survives childbirth. There seems to be some doubt in her mind about that. She then spent the entire hour and a half either complaining that she felt like she was going to throw up, or in the bathroom actually throwing up, while I gorged myself on maki and saki. Cheers.

She was supposed to come with me to the wedding boutique afterward but said she was sure I didn't want her to get puke all over the pristine white gowns. She was absolutely right about that.

So I spent the remainder of the afternoon solo, trying on one silk confection after another even though I had always known the dress I wanted from the start. I had coveted it for months in every bridal magazine. In the end, that's the one I ordered—the simple white gown with a square neckline, elbow-length sleeves, minimal lace and no bustle. Elegant, sophisticated, figure flattering.

Seeing myself in it at last, I got a little misty—and homesick. I have rarely regretted moving away from Brookside, but this was one of those times that I wished my mother were readily available. I remember when we both went with my sister to get her wedding gown, years ago. There was a lot of crying, laughing and hugging. I was just a teenager and of course I kept envisioning the day my own turn would come.

Now here I was, in an ethereal white gown, and there was no one to see me but me. Oh, and a saleswoman named Milagros who spoke broken English but said *Bee-you-tee-ful* several dozen times. I bet she says it to all the brides, but it made me feel good.

When I got home afterward, Jack's friend, Mitch, was parked on the couch watching a college basketball game with him. He stuck around for takeout Italian and more, more,

more college basketball, during which I dozed in a chair before finally going off to bed alone.

Sunday: we woke up to a flood in the kitchen. Everything nonmetal or plastic that we keep under the sink—a box of garbage bags, another of SOS soap pads, the newspaper-recycling bin—was thoroughly sodden.

Jack had to track down the super, who in turn had to track down a plumber—not easy on a snowy Sunday. By the time the pipes were fixed, we realized we were starved and the cupboards and fridge were empty, so we went down the block to our favorite diner.

I thought we might be able to discuss the wedding over lunch, but we ran into a couple of guys who live in our building. They sat with us and talked sports with Jack while I toyed with my moussaka and daydreamed idly about aromatherapy-inspired bouquets and five-star-resort honeymoons.

Now here we are, home again.

It's sleeting outside but cozy in here. I just changed into sweats and put the teakettle on high. Things are looking up already. I'm in the mood to curl up on the couch and watch *60 Minutes* with a mug of hot tea. I heard that they're doing some kind of feature on weddings in America.

In the kitchen, I glance at the jumble of waterlogged stuff I pulled out from under the sink earlier, and wonder if I dare put it back yet. The plumber claimed the leak was fixed, but the pipe joint looks suspiciously wet to me.

After deciding to keep the space under the sink empty for now, I open a cupboard door to take out the box of tea—and the knob comes off in my hand. Again.

Frustrated, I break off the tip of a wooden toothpick,

shove it into the screw hole and turn the knob on again. It holds…but I know from experience that it won't be for long.

Have I mentioned that it seems like every time I turn around, something needs fixing around here?

I go into the living room, where Jack's settling onto the couch, *TV Guide* in hand.

Uh-oh. Should I remind him that *60 Minutes* is starting in about ten minutes? Somehow, I don't think that's on his viewing schedule. He's probably planning to watch *Caddyshack* for the hundredth time and laugh as hard as he did the first: one of his favorite ways to spend a lazy Sunday evening. He calls it Couch Time.

"Sweetie?" I call him that whenever I'm about to break something to him, and he knows it.

He looks up suspiciously. "Yeah?"

"The knob came off the cupboard door again."

He sighs. "Which one?"

"The tall one where we keep the cereal and stuff."

"I'll fix it with a wooden match later."

"I already did, with a toothpick, but I don't think it's going to hold."

He sighs again.

"Want a cup of tea?" I ask strategically.

"That sounds good." He aims the remote at the television.

"Wait, Jack, before you turn that on…"

He looks up wearing an *uh-oh* expression. "What?"

"I think we need to sit down and talk."

"I knew you were going to say that." He lowers the remote and leans his head back, staring at the ceiling, clearly brimming with enthusiasm about the conversation ahead.

"Come on, Jack, we have to do this now. Otherwise, we might as well just put everything off for a year or two."

"That's exactly what I want to do."

I stare at him. "But...I thought you agreed that we're going to get married this year."

"Oh...you want to talk about the wedding!" Eye contact at last, his expression sheer relief.

"What did you think I was going to say?"

"Never mind."

"No...what?"

"I thought after the plumbing thing this morning and now the cupboard knob, you were going to bring up moving to the suburbs again."

"Oh...well, now that you mention it—"

"Forget I did. What kind of wedding details do you need to talk about?"

I hesitate. The suburbs discussion is tempting, since he's the one who brought it up and it has been in the back of my mind.

But by the time we hash out all that, he won't be in the mood to discuss the wedding.

As if he is now, I think, watching his itchy trigger thumb on the television remote.

Still, the door has been opened at last, so I decide to barge right through it.

"We've got to figure out when and where we're going to have it, what kind of wedding it's going to be..." Stuff I've already worked out in my head, basically. But I need his official approval before we can move ahead.

"Relax, it's only February, Trace," he says as I reach into

the drawer of the end table for the honeymoon spreadsheet printout I stashed there yesterday. "I thought you wanted a fall wedding."

"I do, but it's not 'only' February! It's already February! Weddings take ages to plan if you do it right. We're running out of time."

"Okay. Well...when were you thinking for a date? Third Saturday in October, didn't you say?"

"I did." And I'm pleasantly surprised he remembered.

"Good. So we know *when*." He ticks that off on his finger and looks at me. "What else?"

"*Where*," I say, starting to unfold the spreadsheet. "And luckily, Shorewood is available!"

Good, we're just breezing along here. At this rate, we'll be booked into a private Tahitian hut with time to spare before *60 Minutes*.

I ask Jack, who has yet to react, "So what do you think?"

"I think it sounds like you don't need to know what I think."

"Of course I need to know." I perch on the arm of the couch, feet propped on the cushion beside him. "So...what *do* you think?"

"Honestly?"

I nod.

"I think we should take our time and look at a bunch of places before we make a snap decision where to have the wedding."

Take our time? Is he kidding?

"Like my mother said," he goes on, dead serious, "there are plenty of places up in Westchester or in the city."

Okay, I really wish I hadn't asked him, because he was right the first time. I don't need to know what he thinks. Basically, I just need him to agree with what *I* think so that I can forge ahead with the fun stuff like the flowers, the food, the music.

But I try to sound accommodating as I point out, "Shopping around would be a good idea...except that places around here will cost us a fortune."

"Not if we have a small wedding for just family and a few friends, though."

Aside from the fact that it would still cost a fortune...

"We both have big families and a ton of friends, Jack. We can't leave people out."

"Well, we'll just have to keep the list limited to immediate family and the closest friends."

"That's still going to be a lot of people. And expensive around here."

"Well, Shorewood can't be *that* cheap," he says disagreeably. "It's a country club, isn't it?"

"Yeah, a country club, Brookside-style. It's nothing like a Westchester country club and nowhere near what we'd pay here."

"Well, what about some other place in Brookside? Why does it have to be there?"

"Because that's the only place in town that can hold as many people as we want to have." *Aside from the Most Precious Mother church hall, which is out of the question, and the Loyal Order of the Beaver Club, also out of the question.*

My father and brothers are all Beaver Club members. They have a big, no-frills clubhouse where they hold events like their weekly spaghetti dinner, and, yes, weddings.

But like I said...

You are cordially invited to the nuptials of Tracey and Jack at the Beaver Club?

Uh-uh. Out of the question.

"So what do you think?" I ask Jack again, trying hard to be diplomatic.

"It sounds like you've already made up your mind, Trace. What do you need me for?"

"Don't be ridiculous, Jack. I need you for…well, for everything. It's *our* wedding. Not just mine."

He shrugs, watching the TV—which, by the way, isn't even on.

I sigh, folding the spreadsheet again, thinking now is not the time to bring it up.

He flicks a glance my way. "What's wrong?"

"Just—come on, Jack."

"Come on, what?"

"I just feel like I'm the only one who cares about any of this," I hear myself say.

Definitely not a good idea.

He flicks a dark gaze at me. "Well, if I honestly thought I had any say in how this goes down, I'd probably care a little more."

How this *goes down?* Are we plotting to knock over a casino?

Somehow, I bite back the sarcasm. "You have equal say."

"Okay. Good."

Silence.

"So what *do* you have to say?" I ask through gritted teeth.

He shrugs, maddeningly casual. "I say we have French onion soup at our reception."

"Which will be held…where?"

"I think we need to shop around a little for a place."

"But *where?*"

"You know…everywhere."

"Like…?"

"Like…" Clearly, he is racking his brain for possibilities. "For one thing, we can check out that loft my sister was talking about."

"She said it would cost us a fortune. I mean, even with my raise…we're pretty much broke, Jack. It's not like my parents are going to be able to pay to give us a lavish Manhattan wedding and a great honeymoon."

"What about *my* parents?"

Hmm. That gives me pause. What about them?

"They're going to want to help," Jack says. "My mother said so."

"Help pay for it? Or help plan it?"

"Probably both."

Which, I have to admit, would only be fair.

"Can you ask her what she has in mind?" I ask Jack. "Moneywise, I mean."

"I'd feel funny doing that. You can ask, though."

"You think I wouldn't feel funny asking your mother how much cash we can count her in for?"

"Well, the thing is, she's not the one with the cash. That's my father's department. And I'm sure he'll want to help."

Hmm. What if Jack's rich father wants to throw us a lavish Manhattan wedding?

I picture myself pulling up to Saint Patrick's Cathedral on Fifth Avenue in a rose-bedecked horse-drawn carriage—or better yet, one of those vintage limos. I'm in a designer wedding gown, of course. No bustle, latest style be damned. I mean, who wants added padding there?

"Did you talk to him about it yet?" I ask Jack, wondering if the Rainbow Room does weddings and if it's available on the third Saturday in October. If not, there's always Tavern on the Green, or—

"My father? He doesn't even know we're engaged," Jack reminds me. "And when he finds out that my mother knew before he did…"

"Well, why didn't you invite him to come out with us the other night?" As if I didn't know.

"Because he's a miserable human being and I didn't want him to put a damper on our celebration."

Right…albeit a miserable human being with a big fat checkbook, I want to point out, but I just say, "Oh, yeah."

Still…wow. This is a whole new ball game. I mean, usually the bride's parents pay for the wedding, but given my parents' financial state, I just assumed Jack and I would have to cover the bulk of it ourselves.

"Maybe we should go up to Bedford and visit your dad to tell him the news," I suggest tactfully, once again unfolding my honeymoon spreadsheet. "You know…so he won't feel left out."

"Yeah, we'll do that." I'm about to get my coat when Jack adds, "Eventually."

Damn.

But we can't make wedding and honeymoon plans until we know if your father's helping to pay for it, I want to remind him.

"I don't think we should keep your father in the dark for

very long," I tell Jack. "I mean, I think he deserves to know what's going on. Don't you? It's not fair that your mother knows and he doesn't."

"Why not? Your parents don't know."

"But they will when we go up there."

"Well, after we tell your parents, we'll tell my father."

I'm shaking my head before he's even finished speaking. "Nope. That won't work."

"Why not?"

"Because we need to know before we go up to Brookside whether we're having the wedding there. And if your father actually wants to get involved in it, we might decide to have it here."

"You know, on second thought, I really don't think I want my father to be involved in this," Jack says. "I'd rather have a small wedding that we can afford ourselves, wherever that may be, and leave him out of it."

Poof—there go the cathedral and vintage limo, designer wedding gown and Rainbow Room reception, not to mention that tropical honeymoon hut of my dreams.

"Do you really think that's fair?" I ask Jack. "Leaving your poor father out?"

"My 'poor father'?"

"You just said he might want to help us."

"If we take his money, we have to let him take control."

"How much control?" I ask, even though I'm well aware that if it wasn't for his father financing his education, Jack would have become a chef—his dream job—and not an ad agency guy—his father's dream job for him.

"He'd take total control, Trace. Trust me. There's no

one more domineering than my father. We don't want him involved."

"But I thought you said—"

"Forget what I said. It was a moment of insanity. We can't let him help pay for it." Jack is adamant. "I don't care if we have to have the wedding at the charbroil in Brookside, we're not getting him involved."

Back to square one. Well, square two, if square one is the charbroil.

Trying to remain optimistic, I say, "I should call Shorewood and tell them we want it for that Saturday in October, then. Right?"

"I guess so. If it's that important to you."

Yes! Mental high five.

"It is that important."

"Okay. Reserve it." Then Jack adds, "For now. We can always change our minds." He picks up the remote again and aims it at the television.

"The thing is, Jack…"

He looks up at me wearing a *now what?* expression.

"It's not that simple. If we want to reserve Shorewood, we have to put down a deposit."

"How much?"

"I'm not sure exactly, but it would probably be…" I hem. I haw. I distract myself momentarily by wondering what, exactly, hemming is and what hawing is.

Then, when I can no longer put it off, I force myself to blurt the ugly numerical truth: a dollar amount that's roughly three times our monthly rent budget.

Jack gapes. "Are you kidding me? That much? Just for the deposit?"

"Unfortunately, no. Not kidding."

"That's sick."

I shrug.

I felt the same way when I first discovered the deposit requirement last fall when I was furtively making wedding arrangements, sans fiancé. By now, I've had plenty of time to grow accustomed to the financial logistics of wedding planning. I'm sure Jack will get used to it, too, eventually. For now, I'll just have to let him sit there looking as though he was just given a retroactive pay cut equal to ninety-nine-point-nine percent of his salary.

"How are we supposed to come up with that kind of money?"

"We can do cash advances on our credit cards—"

"No. No way." He looks even more horrified than he did when I told him how much the deposit would be.

"Why not?"

"Do you know what the interest rate is? There's no way we're doing that. You're pretty much maxed out as it is."

This is true. He's not, but—

"Listen, I have an idea," he says then, surprising me, because who knew the wheels were actually turning behind that horrified expression?

"Great. Let's hear it."

"Let's just sublet an empty studio apartment in New York in October and have it there. It would be a hell of a lot cheaper. Think about it."

I do think about it. And I laugh.

Jack does not.

"What, you think I'm kidding about this?"

"You're not?" Then, in the kitchen, we hear a sudden, clattering, escalating hum.

For a moment, I think something's about to explode—and I'm not all that surprised, mind you. Then I remember the teakettle.

"You must be kidding about this," I tell Jack as I jump off the arm of the couch, "because there's no way you honestly think we should have our wedding in some empty studio apartment."

"Why not?"

I shove the honeymoon spreadsheet back into the drawer. The teakettle is swiftly building into a full-blown whistle.

"Because it's depressing!" I say over my shoulder as I hurry into the kitchen, feeling as if I, too, am about to explode.

"How is that depressing?" Jack calls after me.

"It just is!"

To my surprise, Jack follows me. I honestly thought he'd turn on the television in my absence, but he pops up behind me as I fill two mugs with boiling water.

"Listen, Tracey, I don't want to argue about this for the next eight months. Whatever you want to do about the wedding is fine with me, because how it happens is obviously much more important to you than it is to me."

I nod.

"I just don't know how we're going to come up with such a huge chunk of change anytime soon," he says heavily.

"Selling stuff on eBay?" I suggest impulsively, setting the hot kettle carefully back on the burner.

"What kind of stuff?"

"Whatever we don't need. I've got some clothes I don't wear..."

"Yeah, I'm sure those snazzy wool dress shorts of yours will fetch a few hundred at least."

Ha.

"Look, Jack," I say, my back still turned because I can't bear to let him see that I'm about to cry, "we're going to have to figure this out because we can't book a reception place without a deposit."

"I know."

"I guess we could wait to get married until we can save up enough money to give ourselves a decent wedding," I suggest reluctantly, bulging my eyes so that the tears won't start falling. "By this time next year, we could probably—"

"No. We don't want to wait." Standing behind me, Jack puts his hands on my shoulders. "If worse comes to worst, I can always sell my stock. I'd get eight or ten thousand, at least, if I did that."

Stock?!

"What stock?" I turn slowly to look at him.

"I've got some Disney shares my grandmother gave me for my birthday when I was a kid."

Wow. My grandmother gave me hand-crocheted sweaters. Ugly wasabi-green ones. I still have them, tucked away in a drawer.

Back then, I don't think I'd have appreciated stock any more than I did the sweaters. At least I knew she'd spent all that time on making a special gift. Handing a kid a stock certificate seems so...impersonal.

From the perspective of an adult bride-to-be, though...
brilliant move. Gotta love Jack's grandmother, God rest her soul.

"I didn't know you had Disney stock," I tell him, wondering what else I don't know about him. My tears seem to
have subsided. "Are you sure you'd actually want to sell it?"

No. He isn't sure.

I can tell by the look on his face, even as he nods.

"I can sell it."

He *can*. But he doesn't want to.

"Well, don't do that yet," I say, feeling guilty. "Maybe we
can come up with another idea."

"Like what?"

"Like...I'm sure my parents will help us with the wedding."

But they'll have visions of crepe-paper-festooned basketball hoops and candied almonds in fluted paper cups. I know
it. Maybe they'll ask Grandma to crochet me a veil.

"I guess we should just wait to make any decisions until
after we've talked to my parents," I tell Jack, dismally dunking
my tea bag in and out of the steaming water.

"That's what I think."

"And I'm sure nobody will book Shorewood for that
October date between now and next month."

My tone is laced with sarcasm.

At least, I thought it was.

But it must not have come out that way, because Jack leans
over and kisses me tenderly on the cheek. "I love you."

I look up in surprise. "What was that for?"

"I honestly thought you were going to make a big stink
about not having a place yet..."

He honestly thought right.

"But you're being very mature about this."

He sounds pleasantly surprised.

Like I'm not very mature about most things?

Turning away, I reach up for the cupboard to put away the box of tea bags. Naturally, the wooden knob comes off in my hand.

I curse.

Jack reaches around and takes the knob from me. "Here. Let me fix it."

"I did fix it."

"You need to use a wooden match. A toothpick is too thin to give it enough traction." He opens a drawer, rifles through it. Pulls out a limp, nearly empty book of matches from some restaurant we haven't been to in years. "Is this all we have? Where are the box matches?"

I shrug. "We probably don't have any."

He jerks open another drawer—the one where we keep the silverware. I take a cautious sip of my tea and let him conduct a fruitless search for box matches among the spoons and forks. He slams the drawer shut and grumbles, "How can we not have any?"

We might have some if you hadn't made me give up smoking, I want to point out crankily. But I refrain, because I never lit my cigarettes with box matches anyway.

And because, to be entirely fair, he didn't really make me quit—that was my decision.

And because ninety-nine percent of the time, I'm glad I gave up smoking.

The other one percent of the time, I'm ridiculously stressed and would positively kill for a cigarette.

Like right now.

Since that's out of the question, I leave Jack to fix the knob and retire to the living room with my mug of tea, the television tuned to *60 Minutes*.

Ah. That's better.

Sometimes, you just have to take your pleasure wherever you can find it.

One would assume that pleasure, for an engaged woman, wouldn't prove to be quite so elusive.

You know that *Weddings in America* feature I was so psyched to watch? Turns out it's one of those hidden-camera exposés on wedding planners. Apparently, the industry is filled with predators out to rip off engaged couples and their parents.

Who knew?

I'm glad Jack is still puttering around in the kitchen. He doesn't need to hear any wedding horror stories right now.

In the midst of an interview with a pair of sobbing newly broke newlyweds, the phone rings.

I grab the remote and freeze the screen, courtesy of TiVo, on the groom's stricken, tear-soaked face.

"Tracey, is that you? Guess who's back in town?"

Well, if it isn't the happy honeymooner himself. Things are looking up at last.

"Raphael!" I set down my mug and sit up on the couch, heartsick newlyweds and wedding planner con men immediately forgotten. "How was your safari?"

"Hot and wild," he replies. "And, Tracey, don't think I'm talking about the jungle."

Oh, I wouldn't.

I've known Raphael long enough to realize that nothing is sacred.

Why am I surprised, then, when he spends fifteen minutes regaling me with intimate newlywed escapades?

In the midst of it all, Jack appears in the doorway wearing a jacket, and mouths, "I'm going down to the hardware store."

I nod and wave.

Raphael goes on to tell me about the bush lodge in Botswana and the luxurious bed in the bush lodge in Botswana and exactly what he and Donatello *did* in the luxurious bed in the bush lodge in Botswana.

I cut him off abruptly. "That sounds romantic, Raphael…"

Well, no, actually, it doesn't. It sounds perverse. But who am I to judge?

"And speaking of romantic," I scurry on, "I've got some news for you!"

Nice segue, huh?

"Tracey! Romantic news? Don't tell me…you met someone!"

"What?"

"Did you meet someone?" he asks excitedly.

"Um, no." Nonplussed, I say, "I've got Jack, remember?"

"Right. I thought maybe…"

"Maybe…?" When he doesn't elaborate, I have to ask point-blank, "You thought maybe what?"

"I thought maybe you two had gone your separate ways and you'd met someone."

Where to begin?

Frequently faced with that dilemma in the midst of a bizarre Raphael conversation, I choose the obvious question, and manage to pose it evenly: "Why would Jack and I go our separate ways?"

"Because, Tracey, he doesn't want to commit," Raphael says with exaggerated patience. "And I don't blame you one bit for moving on. Nobody deserves to find happiness more than you do. Well, I did, but I've found it, so it's your turn."

"I've found happiness, Raphael."

"I knew it!" he gloats. "So…what's his name?"

Rolling my eyes, I say patiently, "It's *Jack.*"

"His name is Jack, *too?* What are the odds of that?"

Grrrrrrrr.

No joy in mudville today, I swear.

I glare at the teary-eyed, victimized sap still frozen on my television screen.

"Raphael, there is only one J—"

"Hang on a second." Raphael covers up the mouthpiece and says, loudly and clearly, "No, Donna, I meant the other one. With the G-string. Right…that's the one."

I cringe.

"Who's Donna?" I ask when he gets back on the line.

"Tracey! My husband! How would you like it if I asked who Jack is?"

"You pretty much just did," I grumble, and wonder when Donatello allowed his name to be shortened. I thought he was a real stickler about nicknames.

Of course, that was probably because Kate's husband, Billy, insisted on introducing him and Raphael as "Don" and

"Ralph" one night when we were all out and ran into a bunch of his colleagues.

We all had a hearty laugh about that later…minus Billy and Kate.

"Raphael," I repeat succinctly now, "I have news for you."

"You quit your job?"

Again, I stumble. "Why would I quit my job?"

"Because it just seems like it's going to be overwhelming, Tracey."

That might be true, but…

"I did not quit my job and it wouldn't be good news if I did because I'm broke," I tell him. "I do have good news, though—and don't guess what it is. I'll just tell you. Okay?"

Silence.

"Raphael?"

More silence.

"Hello?"

Then I hear him in the background, talking to Donatello. "Right. I know. No, I don't think the gold lamé one makes your skin tone look sallow. It makes you look tawny, like a glorious lion."

Oh, for God's sake.

I hang up the phone moodily.

It rings a few seconds later.

Caller ID: Raphael.

"Are you ready to listen?" I bark into the receiver.

"Sorry, Tracey," he says breezily. "We were just going through our souvenirs from the trip. So what's your good news?"

"I'm getting married!"

"To Jack?" he asks in disbelief…but not disappointed disbelief. He sounds genuinely happy for me when he says, "Oh, Tracey, that's great news!"

"I know!" Naturally, I've bounced right back.

"Do you love the ring?"

"I love it!"

"When did he propose?"

"On the way home from your wedding!"

"How inspiring! I'll admit I thought it was a bad omen when you didn't catch the bouquet, Tracey…"

"Which is only because one of your annoying friends shoved me out of the way to grab it. I swear he had wings, the way he flew through the air."

"Oh, that was Edward. I don't blame you for being upset. He can be a pushy little bugger. Donatello and I can't stand him."

"You don't like him? Then why did you invite him?"

"Tracey! We invited everyone," Raphael tells me, as if that explains it.

Facing a growing guest list of my own, I've already concluded we might have to cut people we adore. Definitely no room on the list for people we can't stand.

"So when's the big event?" Raphael asks.

"The wedding? We're working on it. We're thinking October."

"I meant the bachelorette party, Tracey. I'll help you plan it! I have a great idea for a risqué party game!"

I'll just bet he does.

He puts the phone down to relay the glad tidings to Donatello.

Back on the line, he says, "We're both so thrilled for you, Tracey. I just knew Jack had it in him."

"You did not know that, Raphael."

"All right, I did not know that. I thought he was going to break your little heart."

Privately, I might have thought the same thing at times…but those days are well behind us at last.

"Where's the groom?" Raphael asks. "Put him on. I want to say congratulations."

"He's not here. He went to the hardware store."

"Are you sure, Tracey?"

"Ye-es…why?"

"No reason," Raphael says quickly. Too quickly.

I wait.

"Carl—" a former boyfriend of Raphael's "—once said he was going to the hardware store, but he was really down at Oh Boy, picking up some drag queen."

"I really don't think Jack is at Oh Boy picking up some drag queen, Raphael."

"I'm just saying…"

"Thanks for the concern, but he's at the hardware store. Trust me. Listen—" I decide to change the subject to distract him "—I want you to be in the wedding."

"You do? Oh, Tracey! I would love to be your man of honor!"

"Actually, I was thinking bridesmaid."

"But Tracey, bridesmaids are female." Typical Raphael logic.

"You know I love you, Raphael, but my mother would kill me if I didn't have my sister as maid of honor."

"Oh." He seems to ponder this for a moment. Then he

exclaims, "Oh! Oh, I know! I'll throw you an engagement party."

"How sweet, but—"

"We can do a chocolate fountain, and mojitos, and—oh! I wonder if we can get crocodile sirloin or warthog in New York, because I got the most amazing recipe in Afri—"

"Raphael, Jack's mom is actually throwing us an engagement party in Bedford, in June."

And I would hazard a guess that warthog will not be served.

"Ooh, that's even better! Then we can just relax and mingle."

I murmur a halfhearted agreement, suddenly struck by a vision of Raphael and Donatello circulating among Wilma's tony Bedford friends wearing gold lamé G-strings.

You know, this wedding stuff really is more complicated than anyone ever lets on.

For a brief moment, I wonder whether Jack and I should just call off the whole extravaganza and go down to city hall. Or Vegas. Just the two of us.

Then Raphael says warmly, "You know, Trace, you're going to be a beautiful bride. I've got tears in my eyes just picturing you."

And suddenly, I've got tears in my eyes, as well.

Of course Jack and I don't want city hall or Vegas for two. At least, I don't.

I want to have full-blown wedding festivities to share with the people we love…and that's exactly what we're going to have.

7

I swear, every single time I fly home to Buffalo, there seems to be a problem of some sort. Weather, mechanical problems, delays or cancellations....

This blustery Saturday morning in March is no exception.

The flight seems to be oversold. Yes, *oversold*. Buffalo at 7:00 a.m. in March. Hot destination?

It must be, because the gate attendants are trying to find a pair of passengers willing to be bumped in return for a later flight and a free round-trip ticket anywhere the airline flies in the continental U.S.—and get this: *there are no takers*.

You would think people would be knocking each other over to storm the counter and trade their seat for, say, a noon arrival in Buffalo and a future weekend in sunny southern California or West Palm Beach.

Nope.

These grim-faced travelers—who appear to be part of

some tour group, probably bound for Niagara Falls—are hell-bent on getting to Buffalo this morning, dammit.

Then again, so are we.

"What do you think?" I ask Jack, who skipped breakfast to save room for the famous Connie Spadolini lasagna and is now hungrily eyeing a stranger's half-finished Egg McMuffin as it sails into a trash can. "Should we bump?"

He looks at the overcast sky behind the plate-glass window. "It's supposed to start snowing hard by noon."

"The next flight is at 11:43. That would give us a whole seventeen minutes to get off the ground before the blizzard blows in."

"It would not. Even if they board it on time, by the time they push back from—"

"I know. I'm just trying to keep our options open here. We could get a great honeymoon out of it," I add, thinking Palm Beach might not be all that exotic, but it beats the cabin in the Catskills.

Jack raises an eyebrow at me.

"I'm just saying…"

"No, I know. You've got a point. But what about getting up there today? You've been looking forward to telling your parents for weeks."

This is true.

But I'm strangely relaxed about it.

Strangely?

Okay, my relaxed state is directly related to the Xanax I took in the cab on the way to La Guardia in anticipation of the flight. The prescription is left over from my post-Will days of panic attacks, therapy and prescription drugs.

I've been off the daily medication—which I used to call my pink happy pills—for a while now. But I keep Xanax around just in case I have another panic attack—or have to fly, which invariably leads to a panic attack.

It takes the edge off, that's for sure.

At this point, I don't have a care in the world.

"It's no big deal if we have to wait a few more hours to tell my parents we're engaged," I tell Jack with a glib shrug. "Especially if we get two free round-trip tickets to anywhere in the United States."

"Yeah, but the airlines run sales on domestic flights all the time," Jack points out. "Is it really worth giving up our seats just to save a couple hundred bucks at the most? We might not get out today at all with the storm coming."

I shrug, the newly crowned queen of laid-back. "Whatever. You decide."

"Good. Let's keep our seats."

But when the gate attendant ups the ante—two free round-trip tickets to anywhere the airline flies, period—it's an obvious no-brainer.

"Let's do it," I tell Jack, picturing him lounging in a Tahitian water hut.

"You sure?"

"Yes! I've waited this long to tell my parents. What's another couple of hours?"

"Yeah?"

"Yeah. We can go get something to eat, hang out and catch the next flight."

"I don't want to eat anything. I'm saving room for lasagna, remember?"

We grin at each other, then jump up to claim our prize.

"Do you fly to the South Pacific?" I ask the attendant as she hands us vouchers.

"Yes, I believe we do."

Yes! She believes they do! Exotic honeymoon, here we come!

Eight hours, half a dozen false imminent preboarding announcements, and not a crumb of food later…

"To those of you in the gate area who have been waiting to board flight 398 with nonstop service to Buffalo, New York, I'm sorry to inform you that your flight has been canceled due to the inclement weather."

Inclement weather? It's a raging March blizzard out there.

What a waste of Xanax.

Jack, crankier by the minute from low blood sugar, meets my gaze from behind the *Us* magazine he's holding, with its cover photo gallery of reportedly anorexic starlets.

No, Jack usually isn't big on celebrity gossip—that would be my department. But he's read everything he brought—and subsequently bought—before moving on to my stack of carry-on magazines.

"I knew this was going to happen," he says. "We shouldn't have gotten bumped. We'd be at your parents' house in Brookside eating your mother's lasagna right now if we had stayed on that flight this morning."

"Yeah, and we'd be planning a honeymoon at my parents' house in Brookside, too," I point out, "because we wouldn't be able to afford anything else. With these airline vouchers we can go to Tahiti or—"

"Or your parents' house in Brookside, because we can't afford hotels in Tahiti anyway."

Hotel? Who wants to stay in a hotel when huts-on-stilts are an option?

I can see that I have my work cut out for me where the honeymoon is concerned, but the vouchers are a start. For now, there's nothing to do but rebook our flight for next weekend and go home.

One week, five hectic workdays, countless Client crises, a massive spring thaw and another dose of Xanax later, Jack and I find ourselves driving along the slushy streets of Brookside in a midsize airport rental car. No problems with the weather today, just a one-hour delay at the gate waiting for a connecting flight to come in.

I told you flights to Buffalo are never without some kind of problem. But at least we made it.

Huddled in the passenger's seat in my boots, jeans and too-bright-for-Manhattan Gore-Tex Mountain Guide Gold parka Jack gave me for Christmas, I'm swept by a familiar sense of nostalgia as we drive past familiar landmarks.

Lookee there, it's the gray stone library where I was a Saturday-morning regular! Ooh, and I see my old redbrick elementary school with its newly added one-story annex! Ah, it's Most Precious Mother church where Jack and I will exchange our vows, and the adjacent church hall where our reception will *not* be held.

As usual, everything looks smaller in reality than it does in my memories. It's kind of like when you go back to see your elementary school teachers after moving on to middle school, and think that everything—the desks, the lockers, even the teachers—appeared to have shrunk.

Or am I the only dork who went back to visit my elementary school?

Probably.

Maybe the rest of the world transitions from milestone to milestone without ever looking back. Or trying to go back.

But I've always been the nostalgic type, especially when I'm here. So naturally, my hometown is loaded with scenes from my dorky past.

Thank God I outgrew it. Being dorky, not the town itself.

Though I guess I outgrew Brookside, too.

It was once—long before I was born—a busy rail destination and a major port on Lake Erie. But urban renewal ravaged it in the seventies. These days—apparently unlike Schenectady: The City That Lights and Hauls the World—Brookside is a small, increasingly run-down, unambitious city. Like the better part of upstate New York, the dwindling population here is plagued by unemployment as once-thriving factories and mills continue to lay off or shut down altogether.

You know, it's depressing that so many people have abandoned this town, because it used to be a great place to grow up, raise a family...

Mental note: You have also abandoned the town, remember?

Well, moving to Manhattan was the right thing for me to do at the time—even if part of the reason I moved in the first place was to follow Will to New York.

But it doesn't matter now how or why I got there. What matters is that I know I belong there—with Jack.

I just can't help feeling a little guilty for so easily aban-
doning Brookside. And yes, I'm wistful, too, as we drive
along the familiar streets lined with majestic old trees and
affordable two-story frame houses.

The problem: who can make a decent living here these
days? My family is among the lucky few who are still gain-
fully employed...so far. My father and my oldest brother,
Danny, are hanging in there at a local specialty-steel plant
that's also hanging in there...so far. My middle brother, Joey,
who worked his way through college and has an account-
ing degree, just started commuting to a job at a Buffalo ac-
counting firm. My youngest brother, Frankie, is a licensed
electrician. And Mary Beth, who mostly relies on alimony
checks from her philandering ex-husband, Vinnie, is going
back to a full-time teaching job next fall.

What would Jack do here? What would I do, for that
matter? How would we make a living in Brookside? It's not
like we can open our own ad agency and start landing
million-dollar accounts.

Still, it's tempting to daydream about buying a Victorian
fixer-upper for roughly one-twentieth of what the same
house would cost in the New York suburbs....

Although now that I've got this ring on my finger and a
future as Jack's wife in New York, I need to accept that
there'll be no coming back here to live. Ever.

Of course I don't have any regrets about that. And I've
never really considered moving back here anyway. It's
just...that door is about to close for me now. And closed
doors make me a little sad.

Like the one that recently closed with Buckley. Every time

I hear from him—and it's mostly been e-mail—I'm reminded how much I care about him, and that we're destined to stay friends…and nothing more.

I know that's not really news to me, but it sure feels like it. He and Sonja are in the midst of moving to a bigger apartment on the West Side, and are having trouble trying to extract themselves from their current lease. Plus, they're going full speed ahead with their July wedding plans. Or should I say *her* July wedding plans? He doesn't seem that gung ho about it.

But enough about Buckley and the road not taken.

As the tires splash through yet another slushy puddle that sprays the windshield with muck, I assure myself that I have absolutely no desire to ever move back to this dreary wintry weather. Sure, the white stuff is great when you're bustling around Christmas shopping, hoping for a white Christmas—which is as guaranteed here as a hot Fourth of July is in Miami.

But by March, this weather is depressing. The snow may be long gone four hundred miles away in Manhattan, but here in the blizzard belt, it's still heaped in dirty, crystallized, gravel-studded banks along the curb or in crusty mud-flecked drifts on muddy lawns.

Gazing at the bleak landscape beneath a low-hanging iron-gray sky, I'm seized by renewed urgency to set an October wedding date. Any later than that, and this is what we get as a backdrop for our photos, pretty much until May.

The first thing we're going to do after we drop our bags and eat lasagna—for which Jack has been waiting a week—is head out to Shorewood and book the date. I didn't have time to call there during business hours this week to make sure it's still available. I figure if it's not, we'll just take whatever we can get—a Friday night, maybe, or even a Sunday.

Now that we've arrived in Brookside, I feel like we should definitely spend our wedding dollars here. After all, what better way to combat blight than by pumping revenue into a community? Noblesse oblige, and all that.

Okay, maybe it's a bit ridiculous to imagine that the Candell–Spadolini wedding can save Brookside...but it can't hurt. All those out-of-town guests will need a place to stay...

Then again, I can't quite picture my future in-laws or, say, Kate and Billy, feeling at home at the Super 8 out on the highway.

They'll just have to book rooms at the Greenway Inn, a charming bed-and-breakfast outside of town.

Mental note: as soon as date is set, reserve the entire Greenway Inn for that weekend.

Jack doesn't make a single wrong turn en route to my parents' house, and I congratulate him on his Brookside navigational skills as he pulls in to their driveway.

"I'm impressed. And surprised," I add, flipping down the visor mirror to see if my face looks as pasty as it did back at La Guardia.

Yup. Pasty as overcooked orzo, but there's not much I can do about it now.

"Are you kidding?" Jack says smugly. "I've been coming up here for a few years now. I know my way around."

All the more reason we should get married here! I tell him silently as he puts the car in Park.

We step out into frigid cold with a stiff wind blowing from

the west, off the lake a few blocks from here. The sky in that direction is heavy with black clouds that promise a fresh coat of snow before the afternoon is over. I gasp at the chill, which gives me a lungful of icy air.

Ooh, brain freeze.

Ooh, brain *storm*: what about a destination wedding in some far-flung tropical locale, say, Saint John in the United States Virgin Islands?

I open my mouth to blurt the idea to Jack, but am stopped by two things:

1) the sight of my mother, Connie Spadolini, flinging open the front door and gleefully calling out to us…

And 2) the thought of convincing the aforementioned Connie Spadolini to fly to the Virgin Islands for my destination wedding.

Don't get me wrong—my mother is all for *virgins*. As far as she's concerned, I should have stayed one till my wedding day. And said wedding day should most definitely take place at Most Precious Mother, the local shrine to her personal all-time favorite virgin, Mary, Mother of God.

But the Virgin *Islands?*

She's about as likely to trek down there for a wedding— even mine—as she is to dye her hair blond, lose forty pounds and get a tattoo.

"There you are! Finally!" she calls, standing there shivering in her stretch pants and a red fleece Kiss the Cook sweatshirt. She holds out her arms, so blatantly happy to see us that I feel guilty for not coming home more often.

(In case you haven't noticed, my Catholic guilt complex kicks into a higher gear whenever I'm in Brookside.)

"Finally?" I echo, covering the last few icy yards of sidewalk to the door, my ring safely hidden beneath my gloves. "Ma, our plane was only an hour late, and we called to tell you that!"

"No, I mean *finally*, because you were supposed to be here last week!" More guilt. Maybe we shouldn't have given up those seats. "Come here…let me look at you."

She hugs me hard, enveloping me in Jean Nate, then pushes me back a little so she can study my face. The wind is whipping my hair across it, and she lovingly pushes it back.

"Where's your hat?"

"I forgot it," I lie, because it's easier than admitting I never wear hats anymore. They squash my hair and itch and make me look like a twelve-year-old boy.

"You're pale," she decides. "You're not eating enough."

"Ma, I'm eating plenty." Not really. I lost two more pounds this week without trying, thanks to Abate.

The high-maintenance Client, not the product itself.

"Come on, we can eat right now. The lasagna is ready. Jack!" she exclaims, leaning past me to hug him warmly. "I hope you're hungry!"

"I've had a whole extra week to work up an appetite, Mrs. Spadolini," he tells her, and she smiles so hard I can see all her silver fillings.

We step into the warm house and I inhale the familiar smell: fragrant Italian cooking, my father's citrus-scented aftershave, Comet cleanser, a hint of bleach and that indescribable something else I can never put my finger on. It just smells like home.

It sounds like home, too. Connie Francis—my father's

"second favorite Connie," as he likes to say—is singing in the background, almost drowned out by the din of voices. Naturally, the entire Spadolini clan is in residence. Only my parents actually live here, of course—the others, in long-standing family tradition, have homes within walking distance.

There's Danny and his hugely pregnant wife, Michaela, plus their children, Kelsey and Danny Junior. Joey and his wife, Sara, and their little Joe Junior. Frankie and his cute redheaded, freckled wife, Katie. And of course, my sister, Mary Beth, with her two boys, Nino and Vince Junior.

I take in the sound and sight of them, for the moment so glad to be home again that I forget why we're here. When I remember, I feel as though my heart is absolutely bursting, pushing a lump of emotion into my throat.

I look for Jack over my brother Frankie's shoulder as he sweeps me into a bear hug. I find him, swinging my gleeful nephew Joey high into the air.

"Guess what? He's going to be your uncle Jack!" I want to tell Joey exultantly, but it's not time.

Not yet. Soon.

After a whirlwind round of hugs and chatter, we shed our coats—and my gloves—and make our way, en masse, toward the dining room. My left hand is securely tucked into the pocket of my jeans, waiting for the big moment.

Aside from the Christmas decorations being removed, the house looks exactly the same as it did last time we were here, in December. Which is pretty much exactly the same as it's looked my entire life.

The bric-a-brac never moves an inch. Nor do the gazillion picture frames, though new ones are slipped among them every time the grandkids go to the Wal-Mart—for some reason everyone here calls it *the* Wal-Mart—for a sitting.

Sure, an occasional piece of furniture might be swapped out, but the replacement is always similar, and it always goes precisely wherever the old piece sat. When the walls are painted it's in the same color they were before. On rare occasions that window treatments or carpets are replaced, the color scheme and style are identical to the original.

When Connie Spadolini likes something, she sticks with it. Forever. Not just when it comes to decor, either.

The Conster has been wearing her dark hair in the same style my entire life, trends be damned. It's short and kind of poufy, a little teased and sprayed but not drastically so. She goes to have it "done" every Wednesday morning without fail at Shear Magique.

We pass the wall that holds a trio of framed family wedding portraits, plus the empty hook and faint whiter-than-the-white-wall rectangle where the fourth, Mary Beth's, used to hang. I find myself wondering whether my mother left the hook in hope that my sister's marriage might somehow survive after all, or in hope that I'd eventually get married and she could hang mine there.

Probably a little of both. Like I said, Ma doesn't believe in divorce. To this day, she's more heartbroken over Mary Beth's failed marriage than anyone, including Mary Beth. My sister finally woke up and realized she's better off alone than married to a man who cheated on her constantly, even when she was in labor.

Ma doesn't necessarily agree.

And as critical as she is about my sisters-in-law, she

would be absolutely destroyed if any of my brothers' marriages disintegrated.

There she is at each of their weddings, looking exactly the same, give or take fifteen pounds and the shade of her dress. Teal, aqua, powder…it's always blue, always long and shiny with a cowl neck. The hair is identical right down to the little forward curlicues at the tops of her cheekbones.

Maybe I can get her to change it up a little for my wedding. The hair *and* the dress. Not that I care, personally. I just don't want her to feel funny next to Wilma, who is incredibly chic.

Then again, I've never in my life seen my mother looking insecure, so maybe it's just me that I'm worried about.

In the dining room, the long table is set with the extra leaves and layered with two of my mother's "good" fake-lace vinyl tablecloths. It's already loaded with cold food—crudités, chips and french onion dip, a relish tray, a cold-cut platter, a basket of rolls, an enormous antipasto. My mother, sister and sisters-in-law immediately start carrying in the hot dishes: baked ziti, eggplant Parmesan, veal Parmesan, sausage and peppers, and of course, the famous lasagna.

I elbow Jack and whisper, "Do you want to say it, or do you want me to?"

"I want to. After we eat," he adds, riveted by the sight of my mother cutting the first gooey, piping-hot wedge of lasagna and putting it on his plate.

"But I'm going to have to sit on my hand until then!" I hiss.

"Oh. Right. Okay, let's tell them first," he says—somewhat reluctantly, I might add.

I guess that's understandable. My mother's lasagna *is* pretty amazing. My own mouth is watering furiously.

But as hungry as I am, I'm anxious to share the big news with my family at last. I've been waiting weeks for this day.

Weeks? More like *years*.

Only I used to imagine, in my sadly misguided relative youth, coming home to announce my engagement to Will, God help me. Not that I'd have thought—if I ever stopped to *think* back then, which I don't seem to have done—that anyone here would rejoice at that news.

Will, with his dramatic flair and raging actor's ego, never did grow on my family the way I'd hoped. He fit in around here like a stray and slightly bitter arugula leaf in a good old-fashioned iceberg salad.

Not Jack. He might have come from a drastically different background than our family's, but he fits in like a sweet and very welcome extra tomato in that Spadolini salad.

And I can't wait to tell them all that he's here to stay.

When everyone seems to have filled their plate, I nudge Jack.

But before he can move or speak, my mother shouts for quiet. "Who's going to say grace today?"

"I will!" That, of course, is my nephew Nino, the biggest ham in the family.

We bow our heads.

"GodisgreatGodisgoodletusthankhimforourfoodamen."

"Amen," everyone echoes.

Brimming with anticipation, I look at Jack.

He opens his mouth, but before he can speak, Vince Junior announces, "I don't get it."

"What don't you get?" Mary Beth asks, cutting up

Nino's food into tiny pieces. Have I mentioned that she babies him?

Then again, she learned from the best. There seems to be this thing about Italian mothers and youngest sons. At least, there is in my family.

I glance over at my mother to make sure she isn't cutting Frankie's veal.

She's not, but she is spooning a little extra sauce on his lasagna without asking him and of course he's letting her, because that's how he likes it.

Katie, long accustomed to this quirky little scenario, pays no attention.

"Why," Vince Junior is asking, "do you start out by saying God is great, then you say he's only good?"

"Because that's how the prayer goes," Nino informs his brother stubbornly. "Sister Joseph Anthony taught it to me in CCD."

"Yeah, but it's stupid when you say it in that order."

"Mommy! Vince just called me stupid!"

"I did not. I said the prayer was stupid. Great, then good? That means God is going downhill. It should be good, then great."

"Then it wouldn't rhyme," Mary Beth protests. "And we don't call prayers stupid."

"It doesn't rhyme now," my brother Joey points out. "Good—food?"

"Maybe it's supposed to be *fud*." With a sly smile, his wife, Sara, pronounces *food* to rhyme with *good, hood* and *wood*.

"Or maybe it's supposed to be *gewd*," Katie puts in, pronouncing *good* to rhyme with *nude, lewd* and *dude*.

"You're all nuts," my father declares jovially, his eyes twinkling behind his glasses as he shakes his balding head. "Connie, pass the zau-zage."

That's how people say it here in Brookside. Or at least, my family does. Zau-zage. I never even noticed until Jack pointed it out once.

My mother passes it, but not before putting another choice morsel on Frankie's plate and asking, "Jack, did you get enough zau-zage?"

He did. He got enough everything. His plate, I see, is heaped higher than anyone else's. My mother beams.

"The sausage is even better than usual," Jack tells her. "Did you get it someplace different or something? It's amazing."

My mother looks at my father, who looks at Danny, who shakes his head just a little.

"What?" I ask.

"Nothing," all three of them say in unison—and exchange another furtive glance and headshake.

"Seriously, what?" I ask.

"Nothing," my mother says. "Danny just has a connection. That's all."

"Ma!" Danny protests.

"A sausage connection?" I ask.

"Forget it," my father says.

"Can you get some for me?" Frankie asks Danny.

"No! Ma, why'd you have to go and say something? Lou doesn't want it getting out."

"It's Lou?" Joey's eyes widen. "Lou's back in business? Whoa."

"No! It's not Lou," Danny lies—badly.

"Hey, listen, I won't say anything," Frankie tells him. "Just hook me up, will you?"

"He's your brother, Danny!" Michaela says. "Hook him up with the zau-zage."

"I'll see what I can do," Danny says grudgingly.

"For me, too," Joey says, and Danny glares.

I look at Jack, who clears his throat and starts to push his chair back again.

"For God's sake, Danny, get your finger out of your nose." We all glance over, I guess to make sure that Michaela is speaking to her son and not my brother.

Yup, but you never know.

I nudge Jack. He starts to push his chair farther back, then stops as my mother remembers she forgot the salad and hurries to get it from the trunk of her car.

That's as much a Brookside thing as bootleg sausage. Everyone uses their car trunk as a spare fridge when they're entertaining during the cold months of the year—pretty much from Labor Day till Memorial Day.

Of course, you have to time it all very carefully in the actual winter months, or you wind up with your food frozen solid. Worse yet, you might not be able to get at it at all, if an unexpected squall blows in.

But March is safe, and my mother returns with the nicely chilled iceberg salad, which she swiftly and expertly dresses in a homemade balsamic vinaigrette.

Then everyone has to pass the cheese, the salt, the pepper, the butter, the wine, the plastic liter bottles of Pepsi, Diet Squirt, loganberry.

Then people are starting to eat, and Jack is still waiting for God knows what.

Catching him sneaking a bite of ziti, I nudge him again and whisper, "Well?"

"I'm waiting till everyone's ready."

"That'll never happen!" I can't help but think he's got a lot to learn about being a part of this family. "You can't wait, you've just got to jump in and do it."

"Do what?" whispers my niece Kelsey, eavesdropping on Jack's other side. "Poop? Because Mommy says never wait. That's how accidents happen," she informs Jack solemnly.

"Thanks," he says just as solemnly. "I'll remember that."

After flashing me an amused smile, he pushes his chair all the way back and stands up. Yes!

No. Now my mother has dashed back to the kitchen for another forgotten item. He pauses, waiting for her.

"You better hurry. I hope you make it," Kelsey tells him. "Good luck."

"You hope he makes what, hon?" my brother Danny asks from the opposite side of the table.

"Jack has to go poop."

"Is that any of your business, Kelsey?" Michaela asks.

"He told me!"

"What? He said he has to go poop? That's terrific." My mother has come bustling back in on the tail end of the conversation. She sets a stack of extra napkins in the center of the table and proudly tells us, "Joey and Sara have been working on it."

"On what?" I am thoroughly confused now.

"On getting Joey to tell them when he has to go poop. He can't start preschool until he's trained."

Vince leans over and sniffs Joey Junior's butt in the high chair beside him. "Uh-oh...I don't think he made it. Smells like he went in his pants."

"Poop!" Joey Junior shouts. "Poop!"

"We weren't talking about Joey!" Kelsey protests, screaming with laughter. "We were talking about Jack!"

"Jack went in his pants?" her older brother asks in disbelief, and all the kids gape at Jack, horrified.

"No," Jack protests, looking shell-shocked. "I—"

"I don't do that anymore," Nino informs everyone proudly. "Right, Mommy? I have big-boy pants."

"So? Jack has big-boy pants, too," Vince Junior says. "And I bet he doesn't have accidents in them like you do."

"I do not. And Danny said Jack just went in his pants! That's an accident," his brother retorts.

"Poop!" Little Joey shouts gleefully again, and I wish my brother and sister-in-law would shut him up, but they don't believe in what they refer to as "tough love."

"Is this any kind of conversation to be having at the table?" my father asks, pounding his fist, a lot less jovial than before.

I look at Jack, who has shrunk back into his seat and refuses to meet my gaze. This would never happen at the Candell dining table. *Never*.

"Jack did not...poop," I tell them all.

"But he has to," Kelsey adds helpfully.

I sigh and manage to say evenly, "No, he does not have to. He just has something to tell everyone."

"Well, I hope it doesn't have anything to do with the bathroom," my father says.

"Why would you think that?" my mother swats his arm. "What's the matter with you?"

"What's the matter with *me?*" my father protests. "I'm not the one who—"

"Don't worry, it doesn't have anything to do with the bathroom," I cut in. "It's good news."

"The bathroom is good news when you're getting potty-trained," Kelsey informs me and turns to my sister-in-law, who's trying to tie a bib on her squirming toddler. "Right, Aunt Sara?"

"Right, honey, but we're not talking about Joey getting potty-trained right now."

"Poop!" little Joey shouts, and bangs his high-chair tray, laughing demonically.

"Honey!" Sara helplessly tosses the bib aside and shoots Jack an apologetic look. "Sorry. Go ahead."

Jack looks at me. I shake my head slightly.

I mean, who wants their engagement to be announced in the midst of this circus? "Everyone just eat," Jack says. "We'll tell you later. Go ahead."

I pat Jack's arm, wondering if he's having second thoughts about marrying into this madhouse. Who would blame him?

"Tracey!" Katie blurts, then clasps her hands over her mouth. "What?"

"Never mind," she says, averting her gaze abruptly.

But now Mary Beth is gasping and staring, too. At me. Below the neck.

"What? You guys, is there a bug on me?" I ask, brushing off my clothes fervently.

"Where? I love bugs!" Danny Junior announces.

"What bug? It's March," my mother protests, "and we're inside. No bugs. What's going on?"

Oh.

My ring. I forgot to sit on my hand and obviously Katie caught a glimpse when I patted Jack on the arm. Mary Beth saw it, too.

So much for the big surprise. It's now or never.

"It's not a bug," I say, standing and pulling Jack up with me. "Jack has something to say. Go ahead, Jack."

He nods, chewing a huge mouthful as the room falls silent.

Jack swallows audibly, puts his arm around me to pull me close and announces, without further ado, "Tracey and I are engaged."

And there it is.

A moment of silence...

Then the room erupts. Sheer bedlam. Laughter, tears, screams of joy, my mother wailing something in Italian that sounds suspiciously like a prayer of thanks. Through it all, Joey Junior bangs on his high-chair tray triumphantly shouting, "Poop!"

Of course everyone has to hug us, then see the ring.

Except my father, who doesn't care about the ring and only wants to hug me hard, too choked with emotion to say anything other than, "I'm happy for you, baby."

"That ring is absolutely gorgeous," Ma says tearfully, mostly to Jack.

"Huge stone, too!" Mary Beth puts in approvingly.

"You have excellent taste," Ma says, this time entirely to Jack.

"He does, doesn't he?" I jump in before Jack can mention that the diamond came from his mother's engagement ring.

I forgot to tell him that we need to keep that little tidbit to ourselves till death do us part, as far as my family is concerned, anyway. For all I know there's some old Sicilian superstition about engagement rings from failed marriages cursing anyone who wears them afterward.

Beside me, my father is pumping Jack's hand and saying heartily, "Well, it's about time, son, don't you think?"

"Dad!" I protest.

"What? It's been three months since he asked me for your hand. I've been wondering what's taking so long."

"You asked for my hand?" Stunned, I turn to Jack.

"Of course he did. That's how it's done," my father informs everyone. "Just like Vinnie asked me for Mary Beth's hand."

"Yeah, and you should'a said no," my brother Frankie mutters, and my sister glares at him even though she's probably wishing Pop had said no, too.

"When did you talk to Pop?" I ask Jack, amazed that my father didn't tell my mother and she didn't tell my sister and my sister didn't tell me.

Or maybe he did...

Nah. My mother and sister can't keep secrets from each other or anyone else. Everyone—especially my father— knows that.

"I asked him when we were here for Christmas," Jack says with a shrug.

"Really? Where was I?" Probably upstairs going through Jack's luggage, looking for the ring.

Just kidding. I didn't resort to that until we were in the Caribbean in January. Even then, I wasn't looking for the ring, technically. I was looking for a warm sweatshirt. I found one, and the ring, too.

I was so convinced we were going to get engaged on that trip. But it took him another month.

"You were asleep when I asked him," Jack informs me.

"Jack and I sealed the deal with some Black Velvet," my father puts in fondly. "Didn't we, Jack?"

"We sure did, Mr. Spadolini."

"Call him Dad," my mother instructs him. "And call me Mom. No more of this Mr. and Mrs. stuff."

Uh-oh. I'm not so sure Jack is going to go for that. I mean, he's so close to his own mother, he might not feel comfortable calling somebody else *Mom*.

In my family, that's as much a tradition as it is for the bride to exchange her maiden name for her husband's.

Tracey Candell.

That'll be me before the year is out.

Which reminds me…

"We've got to go make arrangements for the reception as soon as we're done eating," I tell Jack, who's looking a little dizzy amid the frenzy.

"Get the champagne glasses, Connie," my father directs. "I want to toast Jack and Tracey."

"With what?"

"Don't worry, I've got it covered. I've had a couple of bottles of Asti Spumante out in the trunk of the Buick since December. Don't worry, it doesn't freeze," he says, seeing the look on Jack's face. "But if you didn't get your butt in gear, I was going to have to move it into the fridge. Then Connie would have been all nosy."

"Me? Nosy?" Ma laughs as if she's never heard such a ridiculous thing in her life, and opens the hutch to start handing out mismatched champagne flutes she's accumulated through the years.

I get one that was a favor from my cousin's wedding; it's etched *Mario and Loretta, 5-16-99.*

Yes, they're still married. I take that as a good omen.

Pop fills everyone's flute with sparkling wine. I'm sure Jack's father toasts with Moët or Veuve Cliquot, but this is the sweetest wine—and toast—ever.

"To my beautiful daughter Tracey, and to her future husband, Jack." Pop's voice is a little hoarse. "May your lives be blessed with riches—and by that I don't mean diamonds and gold, I mean love, health and children. Because in the end, that's all that counts. *Cent' anni.* That means a hundred years," he adds for Jack's benefit.

"*Cent' anni,*" we all echo, clinking glasses all around and sipping contentedly.

For once, I think, smiling so hard my face hurts, something has lived up to my expectations.

8

"So when's the wedding?" Michaela wants to know as we set down our champagne flutes and pick up our forks at last.

"October," Jack says promptly, as if it's all settled.

"We *hope*," I speak up hastily. "We've got to make the arrangements while we're here today."

"I'll go call Father Stefan." My mother is already on her feet. "I'll see if he can meet us before four-thirty mass."

"Connie, sit down and eat," my father says, but my mother is already scurrying to the phone in the kitchen.

Sara looks at me. "I really hope you were planning on getting married at Most Precious Mother," she says dryly, "because if you're not…"

"Where else would they get married, babe?" Joey says, retrieving his son's tossed sippy cup from the floor.

"I don't know…the Beaver Club?"

I don't dare look at Jack. "I'll be right back," I say, setting down my fork and pushing back my chair.

"Where are you going?" Mary Beth asks.

"Bathroom."

"You are not."

She's right. I'm not.

In the kitchen, I find my mother already hanging up the phone. "It's all set," she tells me. "We're meeting with Father Stefan in forty-five minutes at the rectory because he has another appointment later."

"*We?*"

"You, me, and if Jack wants to come, he can."

"Don't you think he should?" I ask wryly. "Being the groom and all?"

"Do you think he wants to convert?"

"*What?*" Where did *that* come from?

"Jack. Is he going to convert?" she asks as if that's the most logical question ever.

"No," I say firmly. "And please don't start with that, Ma."

"I was just asking."

"Why were you asking?"

"Father Stefan wanted to know."

I sigh. This meeting is going to be one big happyfest. I can tell already.

"Did you ever check with Jack to see if he's willing to convert?" my mother persists, because that, and cooking, are what she does best.

"No."

"Then how do you know—"

"Can we please just talk about this later, Ma? Because I have to go to the bathroom."

She shrugs and returns to the dining room with a Saran-covered platter of something because she never walks out of the kitchen empty-handed when there are guests in the house.

I immediately pick up the phone and dial the number for Shorewood, which I long ago committed to memory. I ask to speak with the banquet manager, but wouldn't you know he won't be in for another hour?

"Can you do me a favor," I ask the girl on the phone, "and just check to see if the third Saturday in October is still available for a wedding?"

"Sure, hang on."

I do, holding my breath, praying *"pleaseGodpleaseGod-pleaseGodpleaseGod,"* until she comes back on the phone.

"I'm sorry," she says. "It's booked."

Exhale.

Thank her.

"Then is there anything available that Friday night?" I ask hopefully. "Or Sunday?"

"Everything's booked here right through New Year's," she informs me. "That's our busy season. We might have a Saturday in mid-January…"

I weigh my opposition to crepe-paper-festooned basketball hoops against the odds of a January Buffalo blizzard stranding the bride and groom, most of the wedding party and half the guest list in New York.

"No, thanks," I tell Shorewood Country Club, and feel like I'm enduring the second most heart-wrenching breakup of my life.

I slink back to dining room, mission unaccomplished.

Now what?

Crepe-paper-festooned basketball hoops, here I come.

By the time we're finished eating that enormous meal followed by coffee and dessert—homemade canoli—wouldn't you know there's just no time to do the dishes.

"Leave them for me." That's resident dish-doer Connie Spadolini, already slipping into her good brown tweed dress coat and grabbing her tan vinyl purse.

"Ma, don't be silly. We're not going to leave them for you," Mary Beth protests. "We'll do them."

By "we" she means herself and our three sisters-in-law, because my father and brothers are immune to kitchen work. Imagine my mother's surprise—and dismay—when Jack started clearing the table the first time he visited.

"Jack, put that down right now!" she'd commanded, as if he were a toddler and the Corning Ware casserole dish were priceless crystal. "You go sit down. Tracey and I will get the dishes."

He'd tried to argue with her, but soon figured out that it's useless. She absolutely refuses to let him—or any man—touch a thing in the kitchen, unless it's food itself.

Crazy, I know. But somehow, the residents of Brookside—or at least, the Spadolini segment of the population—seem to have missed the entire women's lib movement. Back in the seventies, while the rest of her gender were burning their bras and demanding equal pay for equal work, my mother was bustling around in her apron frying onions and garlic, serving up elaborate meals, scrubbing pots with Brillo and I'm sure secretly longing for a dishwasher.

Pop got her one as an anniversary present—their twentieth, it must have been, because I was just a kid. I've never seen her so exhilarated. Watching her hug and kiss my father, I thought it was the most romantic thing he could have done.

Then I grew up and realized the most romantic thing he could have done was learn how to load, run and unload it once in a while.

But some things just don't change, and I honestly don't think my parents want them to. They're comfortable with things the way they are.

As for my brothers, they might get away with sitting on their butts after meals in our mother's house, but I know for a fact that my sisters-in-law don't let them do it at home.

The drive over to the church rectory literally takes two minutes. Ma sits in the front with Jack and I sit in back trying to figure out whether I'd rather A) postpone the wedding for a year or B) have the reception at Most Precious Mother church hall or—God help me—the Beaver Club, after all.

None of the above, I think glumly as we pull into the empty parking lot.

I really had my heart set on that Saturday at Shorewood. I was so sure it was meant to be, especially when they had that last-minute cancellation and the date opened up again after all. I took that as a positive sign.

What if it's a bad omen that the date is booked again?

I don't know, maybe it's for the best. After all, how were we going to pay for it even if it wasn't booked?

I mean, it's not like I expected my parents to hand over a check for thousands to put toward a deposit.

I guess I just figured the problem would somehow work itself out if I ignored it. We'd head over to Shorewood to book the date and *poof!* A bundle of cash would materialize.

Very realistic, I know.

But a girl can believe in miracles, can't she?

A girl can dream.

A girl can completely delude herself into thinking that she won't be forced to begin married life on the same basket-ball-court-slash-dance-floor where she once threw up after too much zau-zage and birch beer at a CYO mixer.

Jack parks behind the rectory and comes around to open the passenger's-side door for Ma, then the rear door for me.

"Whatever happens in there," I whisper to him as we hurry through the chill toward the door, "don't let them talk you into converting."

"Are they going to lash me to a pew and brainwash me?" he asks dryly.

That's one of the things I love about Jack. It takes a lot to throw him.

Unlike me. I get thrown by the slightest bump in the road.

Not that Shorewood being booked is a slight bump. More like a major pothole. But for now, I need to sidestep it and move on, because Father Stefan is opening the door.

He's pretty young for a priest—early forties—but he's been here at our parish since before I left Brookside. Natu-rally, we're on hugging terms; he's spent many a Sunday af-ternoon at the Spadolini dining-room table eating spaghetti and playing Michigan rummy.

He's got less hair and more face than he did the last time I saw him, and he smells kind of sacred yet musty: incense. Now that we're out of my mother's house, I can smell the garlic-and-meatball smell wafting strongly from the three of us.

Mental note: do not let Ma cook anything on wedding day, lest people smell fried onions when they kiss the bride.

"Tracey! I hear we've got cause to celebrate," Father Stefan says warmly. "And this must be Jack."

"Nice to meet you, Father." Jack politely shakes his hand.

Father Stefan invites us into his study to chat. The three of us sit on the nubby maroon couch facing him. On the wall behind him is the biggest, most grisly crucifix I've ever seen; I can't seem to drag my gaze away from the plaster blood and gore.

"When did you want to get married?" The priest is flipping through the pages of a big leather-bound desk calendar.

"Around the third weekend in October." Finally, I turn away from the bloody pulp that is Christ's left hand and watch Father Stefan flip to the right page.

"Let's see, I've got a twelve o'clock wedding that Saturday. You can have the two-thirty slot. Oh, and I'll put you in touch with the noon bride so you can make arrangements to share flowers."

"Share flowers?" I echo.

"You would split the cost," he says. "It's more economical that way."

Economical? He says it in his pious way, insinuating—at least to me—that being economical is my Christian duty.

"But…" What does one say to such a bizarre suggestion? "Wouldn't that be kind of…bizarre?"

"Not at all. That's how it's usually done these days."

Maybe in Brookside. But I'd be willing to bet that

nowhere else on the planet do brides form floral teams with complete strangers.

My mother is nodding vigorously as she echoes the priest very reverently, "It's so economical."

Call me a selfish spendthrift infidel, but… "What if the noon bride doesn't want the same flowers or color scheme that I want?"

Father Stefan assures me, "I'm sure you can come to an agreement together."

He is? Because I'm really not feeling it.

"The savings are significant," he adds.

I look at Jack, who shrugs. I look at my mother, who is smiling happily.

Well, of course. Who doesn't love economical savings and God?

She's probably wondering if Noon Bride and I are the same size, and how long Noon Bride plans on wearing her gown after the ceremony, in case we can share that, too.

"She's away on a eucharistic ministers' retreat this weekend and won't be back until Monday morning," Father Stefan is saying cryptically.

"Who's away?" I ask, wondering what I missed and afraid of the answer.

"Mary. The bride who will be sharing the flowers with you."

Noon Bride again. Don't you hate her? Especially now that we know her name is Mary and she's a eucharistic minister spending her entire weekend at a religious retreat. She's making me look bad.

"I don't know," I say with a slightly defiant lift of my chin. "I think I'll just do my own flowers."

"Tracey!" my mother exclaims, as though I've just announced I don't believe in the Immaculate Conception.

"It's all right, Connie." Father Stefan writes something on the page.

Probably *Bride is Uncooperative and Extravagant*.

As he closes the calendar and swivels his chair to open a file cabinet, I sneak another peek at Jack, who probably wouldn't care if we festooned the altar in wilted dandelions.

He smiles encouragingly, though, and I feel a little better.

Father Stefan attaches a form to a clipboard and picks up a pen. "All right, I need to take down some information. Bride's name…we know that." He writes it down. "Bride's phone number?"

I give him my cell, since I'm rarely home these days. Not that I expect to be in regular hands-on communication with my home parish over the next seven months....

Or should I?

"Bride's address?"

I tell him, wondering if he's planning to visit, too. Who knows, maybe he's envisioning Sunday spaghetti and Michigan Rummy at my apartment. In which case I would definitely have to keep Raphael and Donatello and their gold lamé G-strings far, far away.

Father Stefan asks, re: my address, "Now is that in downtown Manhattan?" *May-an-hay-ayat-an*. That's how everyone in Brookside pronounces it. All those flat *A*'s.

"It's actually uptown," Jack puts in.

Father Stefan looks a little blank.

"I think he meant, is it in the city," I translate. When people around here say downtown, they don't mean lower

Manhattan. They aren't at all familiar with New York City geography. To them, "downtown" just means right in the heart of the action.

"Oh, right," Jack says, nodding. "Yeah, we live in the—"

I kick Jack. Hard enough to shut him up.

He looks at me in shock, wincing as if to ask, *Why'd you do that?*

I raise my eyebrows to say, *You can't tell him we live together! He's a priest!*

Jack frowns cluelessly to indicate, *As usual, I have absolutely no idea what you're trying to tell me and you might as well be speaking Swahili.*

"Groom's name?" Father Stefan has moved on.

Uh-oh. Is he going to ask for all the same information about Jack?

"Jack R. Candell," my unwitting fiancé says.

Father Stefan pauses with his pen poised on the page. "Is that your given name?"

"No, my given name is John R. Candell."

"Middle name?"

"Rufus."

"How…interesting," my mother murmurs. "Are you named after someone? Your middle name, I mean."

"No. My mom just liked it."

"Rufus?" Ma asks in disbelief.

"Right."

"Oh," says Concetta Josephina Sarafina Abondanza Spadolini, who was named after many people, all of them long dead. She knows her parents were helpless; they were just following Italian tradition.

Jack's family is a different story, though. I can see that Ma is wondering what kind of woman would willingly name her son Rufus. Yes, she's deciding, right before my very eyes, that there's something seriously wrong with Jack's mother.

Terrific.

"Groom's phone number?" Father Stefan asks, and Jack provides our home number.

I try to catch his eye but as usual, he either pretends not to notice, or he really doesn't see me.

Father Stefan asks, "Groom's address?"

I kick Jack.

He jerks his head toward me. *What?* his eyebrows demand. *Don't—*

Too late.

There he goes, rattling off our home address.

Cue theme from *Psycho*.

Well, what did I expect, you may ask?

I expected Jack to know enough to lie to the nice priest, dammit.

That's what I expected.

What in God's name is wrong with him?

Him? you may ask. *What's wrong with you?*

To which I would say…

Help me, Jesus.

Father Stefan's pen seems to have stalled on the paper. He looks up slowly at Jack, then at me.

"You live together."

"It's very economical," I say, very Christian-like. "The savings are significant."

He can't very well argue with his own words, now, can he?

He sets the pen down ominously, and I'm thinking he very well can.

My mother mutters "Madonna" under her breath.

Jack, who was just moments ago spouting his home address like there was no tomorrow, says nothing at all.

"Tracey, do you go to mass?"

Huh? Has Father Stefan merely gone back to the questioning process? Is he going to let me off without an admonishment for my sinful lifestyle?

"Yes, I go to mass." I nod vigorously, relieved. "Absolutely."

Which is true. I do go to mass…every chance I get.

Not every week…but that's not what he asked.

I wait for him to write down my answer.

He doesn't. He just moves on to the next question, and he doesn't seem to be reading off the form. "When you go to mass, do you take communion?"

"Definitely. I always take communion. Every single time I go to mass." *See, Father? I'm a stellar Catholic even if I am living in sin.*

I'm starting to relax a little more, though I am wondering why he's not filling in my answers.

Then he starts shaking his head.

I say *starts* because he doesn't stop.

"You can't take communion, Tracey."

I know I'm going to regret asking, but… "Why not?"

"Because you're breaking God's law and disrespecting the sacrament of marriage and your own human dignity by having sexual relations out of wedlock."

Wow.

"I…" *don't know what to say.*

Maybe I should point out that almost everyone I know has sexual relations out of wedlock. We just got caught because we're living together.

Or maybe I should claim that we don't have sexual relations at all, because really, how is anyone going to prove it?

Sexual relations.

The icky phrase alone makes me feel shameful, especially with my mother sitting right here. I feel my face flaming.

"This is very serious indeed, Tracey."

I nod at Father Stefan; I can tell by the look on his face that it's very serious indeed.

He seems angry, but more than that, he's disappointed and...I guess *sorrowful* is the right word. It's like he's really sad for us, going around having sexual relations, heedless of our human dignity.

Maybe a speedy Act of Contrition will help.

Oh my God, I am heartily sorry for having offended thee....

And Father Stefan, I insert for good measure.

And my mother, Connie Spadolini....

"Tracey?" he interrupts my prayer. "Do you have anything to say about this?"

"I'm sorry," I pretty much whisper.

"So am I," he says heavily. "So am I."

I should point out that Father Stefan is still shaking his head continuously and Jack is still silent and my mother is now weeping into a handkerchief.

I should also point out that Father Stefan is directing all of this solely at me. He hasn't looked at Jack since he asked him his address. My lucky Protestant fiancé is obviously off the hook.

"Most couples who live together before marriage don't stay married," Father Stefan announces dispiritedly.

He's right. It's true. I read that somewhere. Oh, God.

Are we doomed, Father?

Why did I let Jack lead me into temptation? Why?

I sneak a peek at Jack, who offers an encouraging smile and reaches out to squeeze my hand.

I love him so much.

"Does this mean we can't get married in the church?" I ask Father Stefan in a small voice...because of course we're still getting married, even if our chances for survival are grim.

"No, it doesn't mean that," he says to my relief.

"Oh, good." I was starting to think we'd have to turn to Reverend Devern and Bedford Presbyterian after all.

"However—"

Don't you hate *howevers*? They never herald anything good. You rarely hear people saying things like, "However, you have won five million dollars," or, "However, I'm giving you this miracle pill that will allow you to eat all the deep fried Oreos you want and lose a pound a day."

"—it's my responsibility to share the church's views with you," Father Stefan goes on, "and to set you on the right path to salvation."

Salvation? My ears prick up at that. Salvation sounds good to me.

"You'll need to make your confession, of course—"

"Of course," I insert almost giddily.

"And then you'll need to separate for some Christian reflection."

"Separate?"

"Move out," he clarifies, "until the wedding."

My jaw drops. Move out? As in move out of my apartment? Separate from Jack?

"You'll spend that time engaged in virtuous activity."

I nod as though I know exactly what Father Stefan means, but I'm thinking *virtuous activity?* What is that? Is it just not having sexual relations? Because it's not like Jack and I are rabbits, humping every chance we get. In the grand scheme of your average twenty-four-hour day, I'm basically virtuous, so why go to all the trouble and expense of moving out?

Father Stefan feels the need to clarify: "By this I mean you'll be praying for guidance and reading scripture to prepare for marriage."

I nod as if I knew that all along. Of course. Totally logical. Yup.

I try to envision myself moving to some run-down apartment and spending every virtuous celibate day between now reading Scripture instead of *Modern Bride*.

"Frankly, Father, the chances of my doing that are about the same as your moonlighting as a Chippendale dancer."

No, I didn't really say that. But man, I want to.

What I say is…

Are you ready for this?

I say, "Okay."

Yes, friends, I have just agreed to move out of the apartment I share with Jack and live a virtuous, prayerful, scripture-reading life for the next seven months.

I don't dare look at Jack, whom I know well enough to know that he knows I don't mean it.

Nor do I dare look at my mother, whom I know well enough to know she thinks that I do mean it.

I keep my focus on Father Stefan, who seems satisfied with my bold-faced lie because he's finally stopped shaking his head. He's not exactly beaming at me, but he definitely has hope for my salvation. I can tell.

He asks a few more random questions on the form and writes down the answers, all of which apply to both of us but are answered by me because Jack obviously took a sacred vow of silence when I wasn't looking.

"Finally," Father Stefan says, steepling his hands, "you'll need to enroll in Pre Cana. That's a required course on marriage taught by the Catholic church," he adds, presumably for Jack's benefit, or maybe for mine, assuming I'm a fallen Catholic.

"Can we do Pre Cana in New York?" I ask, and Father Stefan nods agreeably, back in our corner now that we're no longer roommates.

I'm starting to feel sick, and not from too much zau-zage. Am I going to burn in Hades for lying to Father Stefan?

Maybe I really should move out and start reading scripture.

At the very least, I probably should have crossed my fingers when I said okay to Father Stefan's holy commands.

But Satan doesn't care about crossed fingers. Crossed fingers don't save souls from the fires of hell.

My gaze settles once again on Christ, hanging gruesomely on that crucifix behind Father Stefan.

Please, please, Jesus…please don't let me burn in hell. Please send me some kind of sign that you understand why I did what I did. That you forgive me like you forgave Simon Peter and Judas Iscariot.

But Simon Peter and Judas Iscariot didn't falsely promise a priest that they'd abstain from sex for seven months. Did apostles even have sex? I mean, sexual relations? They were probably chaste in the first place.

"I think we're all set for today." Father Stefan sets the form aside, incognizant of my inner tug-of-war.

"One more thing." That's my mother, speaking up at last.

Jesus, Mary and Joseph, what could she possibly want?

"We need to book the church hall for the reception."

But of course.

"I'm so sorry, Connie," Father Stefan says seamlessly, "but it's not available."

Blink.

Did he just say it's not available? Or did I imagine that in all my psychotic delusion?

"It's not available?" My mother sounds as if she's echoing Father Stefan, so I guess he did say it. Maybe there's some rule about the church hall being off-limits to sinners.

Father Stefan elaborates. "The noon bride already has it booked that day."

Hallelujah!

That's my sign!

Thank you, Jesus, Mary, Joseph and also Mary the economical eucharistic minister!

"Oh, no! What are we going to do?" My mother turns to me, distressed. "We'll have to change the wedding date."

"No, we'll just have the reception someplace else," I say illogically.

"The Beaver Club," she says.

"No!" I shout. Then, tempering my voice the best I can,

I say, "Ma, I cannot start my married life at a place called the Beaver Club. No way."

"Well, where else is there?"

"Shorewood Country Club." That, at last, is Jack, breaking his vow of silence.

Talk about illogical.

I wave a dismissive hand at him. "Shorewood isn't available that day."

"Sure it is."

"No, it isn't."

"I think it is."

Is he annoying or what?

"Well, it's not," I say succinctly, "because I checked a little while ago. Somebody already booked it."

"Did you ask who it was?"

"Do I care?" I mean, what kind of question is that? It makes no difference to me who's having their reception at Shorewood that—

Wait a minute.

I'm noticing that Jack is looking mighty smug.

"Jack..." I say slowly, not daring to hope.

"Yee-es?" Still smug.

Can it be?

I say, without breathing, "Don't tell me...you didn't..."

He nods. "I booked it. It's ours."

"Oh, my—" *God* is what I was going to say, but I've got enough trouble here without taking the name of the Lord in vain, so I leave it at that, and say it again. "Oh, my!"

Jack grins, obviously pleased with himself.

I'm more than pleased with him. I am absolutely head over heels with this man.

I want to launch myself at him and smother him with kisses, but I hug him instead. A decidedly chaste hug, of course.

I sneak a glance at Father Stefan to see if he's noticed how virtuous we are.

He seems to have lost interest in the conversation and is checking his watch.

"But Jack," I say breathlessly, wondering if anyone in the history of the world has ever loved anyone as much as I love this man, "what about the money?"

"We can't afford Shorewood," my mother puts in, sounding worried.

"No, it's okay." Jack shrugs. "I sold my stock."

"The stock your grandmother gave you for your birthday?"

"His grandmother gives him stock for his birthday?" my mother echoes incredulously. I can see the wheels turning beneath her Shear Magique hairdo. She's thinking, *No wonder his mother named him Rufus. Obviously, his whole family's weird.*

"I didn't want you to have to do that," I tell Jack, trying to sound mollified, but I'm having a hard time pulling anything other than pure exhilaration into my voice.

"Why not? I can't think of a better investment than starting our marriage with the wedding you've been dreaming of."

I boldly give him a kiss, not caring that Father Stefan and my mother are sitting right here.

"Thank you, Jack. You're…amazing."

He grins. "You're welcome." I'm surprised to see that his eyes look a little shiny.

And it's all fallen into place, just like that.

My parents sit us down that night and tell us they're going to give us the amount they would have spent on the church hall wedding. We'll still have to come up with a whole lot of cash by October, but I know we can do it. I just have a gut feeling.

A girl really *can* dream.

From here on in, I tell myself, the wedding-plan nightmare is behind us.

9

The next time I have a gut feeling about anything, do me a favor and slap me.

Back in Brookside in March, I think I actually said something about wedding plans being smooth sailing from there on in.

As I recall, that was the same day I promised my parish priest that I would separate from Jack for intensive prewedding spiritual preparation.

Yeah, that didn't happen. None of it.

Here it is many weeks later, and the wedding machine has kicked into high gear. My mental checklist is getting longer by the second—and mostly unfulfilled.

A few days after we got back from Buffalo, we took the train up to Westchester and told Jack's father the big news. He didn't cry and wish us *"Cent' anni,"* but he was very—for lack of a better word—cordial.

Then again, I guess *cordial* is the perfect word to describe Thomas Candell's reaction. He shook Jack's hand, gave me a kiss on the cheek and told us he'd look forward to the wedding.

"That was it?" Wilma asked, mildly outraged when we stopped by afterward to recap the conversation.

"What did you expect him to do, Mom? Break out in song?"

"No, Jack, but I'd expect him to break out the checkbook. He didn't say he's going to help you with the wedding?"

"No, but we don't need his money," Jack assured her.

The thing is…we so do. We've been scrimping in every possible way, but I'm worried that we're not going to have enough to pay for the big day when it finally rolls around.

"We'll get money for our wedding," Jack tells us.

I want to remind him that we're in credit card debt, and we want to have a down payment on a house.

But I can't say that in front of his Mom, and anyway, I have enough to worry about for now.

Priority number one: I really need to order the navy velvet dresses for my bridesmaids, and I plan to, tomorrow.

I thought I had the whole thing nailed months ago, long before I had a ring on my finger. There were going to be eight bridesmaids. Just eight. Plus Raphael.

As of last month, there were still going to be eight girls, plus Raphael, and I had asked all of them already, gotten their deposits and dress sizes.

Then I decided I seriously want to have Jack's sister Jeannie, too. She's been really supportive in all this. She even offered to make me a headpiece if I can't find one I like. She's pretty crafty and made her own for her wedding.

So far I haven't found anything that works with my boring

straight brown shoulder–length hair unless I put it up. Jack did mention that he doesn't like it that way, but what does he know?

I definitely don't want a tiara or a headband or silk flowers or, God forbid, one of those little hat-type things. And I don't want a big puffy cloud of white illusion floating around my head, either. So I may take Jeannie up on the offer to make the headpiece. I definitely want her in the wedding party either way.

I figure Emily and Kathleen can't feel left out because there are two of them—if there were just one sister who wasn't getting to be a bridesmaid, it would be a different story. Jack agrees. Or maybe he just said he agrees because he wanted me to get out of his face when he was watching the Yankees' home opener a few weeks ago, which was probably not the best time for me to bring up anything that needs a thoughtful opinion.

Anyway, Jeannie was thrilled when I called the other day and asked her to be in the wedding.

So that brings the bridesmaids' head count up to nine, plus Raphael. Ten.

I know that's a lot, but there's nobody I'd want to leave out.…

Well, okay, if you want the truth, Brenda, Yvonne and Latisha have been a little distant these last few months. Not that I want to cut them, but…

An invisible wall seems to have gone up between me and the three of them. I feel like we're all going through the motions, having lunch and going to the occasional happy hour same as usual—when my schedule will allow, anyway— but there's something a little…off.

I'm starting to wonder if they resent my promotion after

all. I mean, I know they were the ones who encouraged me to go after it in the first place, and they were really supportive when it first happened...

Lately, though, I'm just not feeling the love. Good thing I don't have much time to dwell on it. I've been working seven days most weeks, and I've had to travel a few times to Cleveland on Client business.

But it's Friday night, and I want to forget about everything work related.

Jack and I are getting ready to go out to dinner with Buckley and Sonja. We've been trying to schedule it for months, but everyone's life has been too crazy, especially with their move and their wedding only two months away.

Now we're running late, Jack is still in the shower, I'm missing an earring—and of course, the phone is ringing.

I grab the cordless and see my parents' number in the caller ID window.

Oh, crap, crap, CRAP.

I probably don't have to tell you that the Conster isn't exactly thrilled that I haven't moved out of our den of carnal sin. Every time she calls, she wants to know if I've found a new place to live yet. The first few times she asked, I actually told her I was looking.

Then I decided it wasn't fair to lead her on, so I finally confessed that right now a move just isn't practical—or financially feasible. Of course, I assured her that I'm being virtuous and prayerfully preparing for marriage right where I am. Which is somewhat true, because I've been so stressed and exhausted between work and wedding plans that I'm asleep most nights before anything the least bit carnal can unfold.

Anyway, my mother made the sound she makes with her tongue whenever people go astray and she realizes she can't lead them back to righteousness. She dropped the subject—but only for the duration of that particular conversation.

When I see that it's her calling now, I almost don't pick up.

Then I think, what if someone's dead?

I learned that from my mother herself. It's what she would always say whenever the phone interrupted dinner and my father would tell her to just let it ring. (They didn't get an answering machine until long after they got the dishwasher.)

"What if someone's dead?" she would ask.

"They'll still be dead in ten minutes, but my food won't still be hot." Good old Frank Spadolini logic.

So I pick up the phone. I swear, if it turns out everyone is alive and well, I'm going to regret this. "Hello? Ma?"

"Tracey! There you are."

"Here I am. What's up?"

"Your cousin Joanie said you promised her she could be a junior bridesmaid."

Oh, Lord.

Why couldn't this have been something easier, like a death in the family?

Preferably, Cousin Joanie's.

Okay, I'm kidding. I love the kid. But she's been a gargantuan pain in my butt from the day she was born. Literally. She threw up some kind of curdled soy formula all over me in front of Bruce Cardolino, my first crush, and Bruce called me Tracey Puke-alini for years afterward.

Okay, I know that doesn't sound all that earth-shattering now, but believe me, at the time, it was tragic.

And now Joanie's claiming I promised she could be my junior bridesmaid? Why on earth would she think—

Wait a minute. Now I remember. Last Christmas back in Brookside, she did ask if she could be my junior bridesmaid if I ever got married. Doubting that myself at the time, I probably said something like, "We'll see."

Or maybe "Maybe."

And that has evolved into a promise that now involves my mother because, well, Joanie is a Spadolini and that's how things work in our family. Give an inch and they'll puke all over you, then take a mile.

"I never *promised* Joanie she could be a bridesmaid, Ma," I say as I go back to rooting through my jewelry box, looking for my other silver hoop earring.

"*Junior* bridesmaid. And," my mother goes on, sounding as if she's ticking items off a list, "you'll have Toni and Donna as bridesmaids, too, because Uncle Cosmo has always been good to you."

Again: pretty much how things work in our family. Not that I have anything against my cousins…but do I really owe them bridal-party status because their father used to give me a piece of Bazooka and a half dollar every time he saw me?

Yes, I do, in accordance with longstanding-family tradition.

Don't get me wrong, I love Uncle Cosmo, even if he is graphically vocal about his irritable bowel syndrome. And I love my cousins, too—but there are plenty of people I love just as much, or even more, and I am already leaving them out of the wedding-party lineup.

"Ma," I say reasonably—and hastily, hearing the shower

turn off in the bathroom. "How can I ask Donna and Toni to be bridesmaids without asking Michaela and Katie?"

"You didn't ask Michaela and Katie?"

"How can I? I've already got too many bridesmaids—I can't add two more. Five more, if I put the cousins in. Jack doesn't have enough ushers to match up with the girls as it is."

Okay, to be entirely truthful, he doesn't have *any* ushers—yet.

It's becoming a sore subject around our house. So far, Jack has said only that he wants his friend Mitch as best man, but he has yet to officially ask him, and whenever I try to discuss the ushers he'll probably want to have, he changes the subject.

"We've got plenty of family he can use," is my mother's solution. "Your brothers, your uncles, Fat Naso, and I'm sure Aldo and Bud would love to—"

"Ma, no." I shudder at the thought of marching down the aisle behind my teenage cousins, who, *word,* think they're gangsta rappers these days. Or, God forbid, behind my father's *compare,* Fat Naso, or my uncle Cosmo and his spastic colon.

"Tracey—"

"Ma, please. Jack has his own friends. I'm sure he'll figure it out soon."

Not really, but I need to get off the phone.

"Well, make sure you call Joanie as soon as you can. She really has her heart set on being in your wedding party."

"I will call her," I say agreeably as Jack comes into the bedroom wearing only a towel, "and I'll let her down easily, I promise."

"Let her down? No, that's not what I—"

"The dresses are already ordered," I cut in, crossing my

fingers and telling myself it's only a white lie. And less than twenty-four hours from now, it will be the full-blown truth.

"Tracey, Joanie's going to be very—"

"Listen, we're really late for this dinner we're going to, so I'll talk to you soon. I love you. Bye."

I hang up the phone and toss it onto the bed with a frustrated scream.

"Your mother?" Jack asks, dropping the towel in front of his dresser and opening a drawer.

"How'd you guess? Because I said *I love you?* How do you know I wasn't arranging a rendezvous with my *othah lovah?*"

"Because lately you're too stressed out to rendezvous with one *lovah,* let alone two." Ha, point taken.

Mental note: later, no matter how tired you are, be sure to Put Out.

"Speaking of stress, what's up with the Conster this time?"

"She wanted to add three more bridesmaids to the herd," I tell Jack.

"What did you tell her?"

"I said what the hell, the more the merrier."

"You did not."

"I did not. Hey, speaking of the wedding party…"

"Please don't." He pulls out a pair of boxer shorts.

"Don't what?"

"Don't ask me if I've asked Mitch to be my best man yet, because I haven't had a chance."

"That's not what I was going to ask—but Jack, I mean…how can you not have had a chance? You see him all the time."

"All the time? I do not."

"You just went to the Yankees game with him last night."

"That's not all the time. That's one occasion."

"You could have asked him then, though."

"In the middle of the game?" he asks, poised with one leg in his boxers.

"Why not? You both love baseball, the Yankees were winning big from the first inning on… I think that would be a perfect place to ask him."

"I'm not *proposing* to Mitch, Tracey."

"Right, if you were *proposing* to him, I'd expect you to take at least another six months." I stick out my tongue at him.

He laughs good-naturedly. Then he gives me a closer look and asks, "Are you wearing *that* to dinner?"

I look down at my black crepe dress. "No, just threw it on to clean the toilet in. I'm going to change."

"Good, because I was going to wear jeans."

"Jack, hello, I was being sarcastic. Yes, I'm wearing this."

He groans. "What kind of restaurant is this? Is it fancy?"

"I doubt it. It's just some tapas place in Chelsea." Having found my other earring at last, I put it on and check myself in the mirror. I look great, if I do say so myself. I've lost about seven pounds since Valentine's Day without even trying. No time to eat.

"So if it's not fancy," Jack asks, holding a folded pair of jeans hesitantly, "why are you all dressed up?"

"I'm not." I feel my face growing hot. "I mean, it's not like I'm wearing a gown or something."

"Well, how can I wear jeans if you're wearing that?"

"You can wear whatever you want." *Just don't accuse me of getting all dressed up for Buckley's benefit.*

Not that he would ever suspect that's what I'm up to.

"Up to"? Interesting choice of words, don't you think? Inner Tracey pops up to ask. *Why would you be up to anything? You're practically someone's wife.*

Of course I wouldn't be up to anything, don't be ridiculous, I tell her.

The fact that I decided to look especially nice tonight has nothing to do with the fact that I haven't seen much of Buckley in ages and I miss him.

Nope, not buying it, says Inner Tracey, who really needs to get a life—other than mine, I mean.

All right, so maybe I *do* want to hear Buckley tell me I look good, the way he always does when I take extra care with my appearance. He's a good friend. He notices things like that.

So does Jack, of course. He's supposed to; he's my fiancé.

It's just kind of nice to be appreciated by a man who isn't Jack, even if I am almost a married woman and my secret crush on Buckley is ancient history.

I feel pretty. So sue me, Inner Tracey.

"Listen," I tell Jack, "I don't care what you wear, just put something on quick because we have to get moving."

He decides to switch to every male's when-in-doubt uniform: khakis, a blue chambray button-down, loafers.

"All set?" I ask, checking my teeth for lipstick one last time. I must say, I haven't looked this good in ages. My complexion has cleared up thanks to this great ointment Kate gave me, my cheekbones haven't been this pronounced in—well, ever. I'm at my lowest weight since middle school, and I feel great.

Hopefully I can keep the pounds off long enough for all the pictures we're going to want to take on our honeymoon. You can hardly go around in a hip-camouflaging blazer in Tahiti.

We head down to the street, where Jimmy the doorman whistles at me as we scurry past him. "Looking hot tonight, Mrs. C."

He's been calling me that ever since we got engaged. Being referred to as *Mrs.* gave me butterflies the first few times he did it, but now it makes me feel kind of...like someone else.

Nobody specific.

Just—not me.

On the avenue, Jack scans the oncoming, downtown-bound traffic stopped at the light. "Let's get a cab."

"Subway's cheaper." We're trying to save every possible penny for our wedding.

"Cab's faster." Jack checks his watch. "We're supposed to be there in seven minutes. We'd have to change trains three times to get there."

"You're right." What's an extra ten bucks in the grand scheme of wedding things?

Well, I'll tell you what it is. It's three and a third French onion soup appetizers.

We've been going over the catering menu for our reception, and found that we've had to make a few compromises.

Instead of offering filet as the red meat choice, we're doing a lesser cut.

And we're serving the wedding cake as, rather than in addition to, dessert.

But Jack still has his heart set on a French onion soup appetizer, and I think we can make it happen if we cut some corners.

Just as I still have my heart set on an exotic South Seas honeymoon, and I think we can make that happen, too.

The airfare is taken care of, thanks to our vouchers, though we haven't booked anything yet. We can't until we find a way to swing that hut-on-stilts, which is considerably more pricey than three hundred French onion soups.

But I'm hoping Jack will come around to my way of thinking.

After all, he owes me one: I agreed to the soup.

Of course, it helped when Jack pointed out that cooked-onion breath isn't nearly as pronounced as raw-onion breath. And I'm brilliantly combating potential reek with our wedding favors: each guest will get a little tin that's imprinted Thanks a Mint, Jack and Tracey, and filled with killer-strong wintergreen drops.

Clever, I know.

Kate helped me come up with that idea.

Well, actually, what she said was that she makes Billy pop a Wint-O-Green Lifesaver every day because his morning breath still makes her nauseous, and I ran with it from there.

Now, as we careen along the streets in the cab, zigging south and zagging west, I try to figure out how to bring up the possibility of having Buckley in the wedding party.

But every time I'm about to mention it to Jack, either I chicken out, or the cabbie swerves around the corner and I get violently slammed against the door, which tends to break my concentration.

I guess it can wait.

We can't get across Fifth Avenue in the Twenties or Teens because there's some kind of protest march going on, so we have to go farther south, skirt Washington Square Park and come back up through the maze of pedestrian-and-traffic-clogged streets of the West Village. What a pain.

You know, I really am starting to get sick of living in Manhattan. But I promised Jack I won't bring that up anymore—not until November, at least. He said we have enough to think about just trying to pull off this wedding, and he's right.

The thing is, of the two of us, I get the impression I'm the only one who's giving that much thought anyway.

The cabbie makes Eighth Avenue his own personal speedway and we get to the restaurant a mere twenty minutes after our reservation.

As we climb out of the cab, I can see Buckley and Sonja waiting out front. Their arms are folded and they look extremely pissed off, which I assume is because we're late. But then they see us and immediately brighten, and I realize maybe they must have been pissed at something else.

Like each other.

I find myself wondering how things are going with them. Buckley hasn't said…but then, I haven't spent much time with him in the past few months.

He gives me a quick hug and an appreciative once-over. "Hey, you look great tonight."

What'd I tell you?

"Thanks." I try hard not to beam, conscious of Jack's and Sonja's presence. Not that either of them is paying the slightest bit of attention. Sonja is hugging Jack and telling him how happy she is that we're engaged.

When she lets go, Buckley shakes Jack's hand and offers a hearty, "Congratulations, bro!"

Bro? Since when does Buckley call anyone *bro?*

He's trying really hard to be dudelike and jovial, I decide. And it's not working.

Sonja excitedly grabs my hand. "Let me see your ring, Tracey! Ooh! I love it! Buckley, did you see her ring?"

"I saw it." Yup, his smile seems a little tight. "Good job, Jack."

At least he didn't attempt bro again, because that's so not him.

Inside, the hostess informs us they gave our table away— no surprise there, it's a Friday night and the place is hopping. But at least she's apologetic about it, so we decide to stay even though we have to wait in the bar until they can seat us.

Jack and Buckley decide to order Spanish beers, and I'm pretty much set on a glass of white wine cut with seltzer until Sonja tries to talk me into a mojito.

"You'll love it, Tracey. It's so refreshing."

"Wine spritzers are also so refreshing."

"Come on, just have a mojito with me. You like rum, right?"

But it probably isn't a good idea to have it on an empty stomach, and I haven't eaten since the half a bagel I scarfed down at a breakfast meeting.

Sonja, however, can be very persuasive.

Exhibit A: the rock on her own fourth finger. Exhibit B: her bumped-up July wedding, which is bearing down on us like a black funnel cloud.

Okay, I should probably pick a more upbeat analogy.

I just can't think of one. "Bearing down" just happens to have an ominous connotation, and Buckley's the one who phrases it that way, not me.

Jack says, as we wait for our drinks, "So you guys have

moved up the date to this summer, huh? That's exciting. It's right around the corner."

And Buckley says, "Yup, it's bearing down pretty fast."

I can't help but picture him running frantically for his life, tossing wild-eyed glances over his shoulder as a wedding gown–clad Sonja chases after him, cackling.

We sip our drinks, and she's full of excited chatter about their wedding, which will be held in some quaint old inn outside Boston. In fact, they're mailing out the invitations Monday morning.

"We had to pull the wedding together so quickly that it's going to be a lot smaller than we originally thought. I felt so awful when Raphael said something the other day to Buckley about it because unfortunately, he and Donatello aren't on the guest list."

For a moment I think maybe that's a big hint that Jack and I aren't invited, either.

But then she says, "You guys will love this inn. It's so romantic. You should think about going back up there for your honeymoon. The foliage will be gorgeous around then."

"We're actually going to Tahiti for our honeymoon," I can't resist saying as I sip my mojito, which is truly so very refreshing. And piercingly strong.

"Tahiti? You are?" Sonja is sounding a little envious.

"We *are?*" Jack is sounding a lot sarcastic.

Buckley has nothing to say about our honeymoon plans, just sucks down the rest of his beer and announces, "I'll get another round."

He's gone before any of us can point out that we've barely made a dent in our own beverages.

We talk about Tahiti—rather, I talk about it, and Jack sits there mostly shaking his head. Then when I halt my travelogue to pick a mint sprig out of my teeth, he asks Sonja if Buckley is okay because he doesn't seem like himself tonight.

"He's a little stressed," she says somewhat apologetically.

"Cold feet?" I ask.

"Why? Did he say something to you about that?"

"No. I'm just… I mean, a lot of guys get cold feet. I just assumed…"

I trail off as Buckley reappears. He sets another refreshing mojito in front of me and there's nothing to do but suck down the remainder of the one in my hand.

Well, technically, there might be other things to do, but this is definitely my best option at the moment. Sonja's, too, I notice, watching her guzzle her first drink and slam down her empty glass like a brauhaus regular.

"Hey, go easy. Those are strong," Buckley warns her.

"You're the one who got me another one," she snarls.

Yup, I'd say there's definitely some tension brewing between bridal couple #1.

As the conversation meanders along, I notice that whenever Sonja brings up the subject of their looming nuptials, Buckley changes it.

After a while, I can't help but feel kind of sorry for her. I mean, she's trying so hard to be excited about their wedding, and he seems anything but.

Then again, she did manipulate him into it. He'd have been content to wait a little longer, unlike Jack, who really wants to get married this year…and who went to all that trouble and expense to book Shorewood for me.

I'm so very lucky, I think as we sit down at last in a cozy booth for four. And so very wasted.

I'm not as familiar with tapas as the others are, but I say yes to everything they suggest ordering. A pitcher of white sangria? Hell, yes. Alongside another pitcher of mojitos? You bet. Chorizo-and-goat-cheese-stuffed figs? Why not? Beef snout with tripe? No problem. Ximxim? Bring it on—whatever it is.

I'm telling you, all that rum on an empty stomach has me loving everything and everyone, even snout. Even Sonja.

We're in one of those booths where the curved bench goes around three sides of the table and the fourth side is open. Buckley and Jack are seated on the outside edges facing each other across the table; Sonja and I are on the inside facing out, doing all the talking, mostly to each other.

As we work our way through the many platters and, I think, many pitchers, we compare notes on wedding dresses, flowers, menus, cakes, honeymoons.

"Are you really going to Tahiti?" she asks wistfully.

"Definitely." I ignore Jack's eye-roll. "What about you guys?"

"I want to go to Beirut—"

"Wow," I say. "Beirut." And I don't mean that in a good way.

"—but Buckley just wants to do a few days in Kenne-bunkport."

"Kennebunkport, huh?" I glance in Buckley's direction for the first time in a while.

"It's pretty scenic up there." He sips his Dos Equis.

"I'm sure it is."

"And the Maine coast has gorgeous beaches."

"Well, Lebanon has gorgeous beaches, too," Sonja says defensively. She knows this because, "My boss's aunt Gwelda went last year."

"Your boss's aunt Gwelda went to Afghanistan and said that was beautiful, too. I'm thinking your boss's aunt Gwelda has a death wish."

"Buckley!" Sonja looks pissed, and I hide my snicker behind my sixth or seventh refreshing cocktail.

I must say, I enjoy these mojitos.

I must also say, Buckley looks pretty miserable, and not just because it looks like he'll be spending the better part of July in Beirut.

"Come on, Sonja, who goes to Afghanistan on vacation?"

"It was a while ago," Sonja snaps. "And I'm sure it was beautiful, back before it was so…"

"Desolate? Unpaved? Dangerous? War torn?" Jack supplies helpfully. "Take your pick."

"All of those!" She flashes him a big loopy smile. "Anyway…what was I saying?"

Beats the hell out of me. I'm just sitting here munching on an inebriated apple slice I plucked from the dregs of the sangria pitcher.

"You were talking about Beirut," Jack prompts. "Afghanistan. Kennebunkport. Aunt Gwelda."

"Oh! Right! I just want a honeymoon we'll remember for the rest of our lives. A real adventure. But Buckley never wants to go anywhere exciting," Sonja complains as I swig my sangria.

"Don't worry," I say, suddenly feeling like I've discovered my long-lost soul sister. "Jack doesn't, either."

"Sure I do," my fiancé says amiably.

"Where? Name one exciting place you want to go."

"Home to bed," he says, stretching and yawning.

"That's not exciting."

"Not lately." He raises a suggestive eyebrow at me. "But you have the power to change all that."

As I grin flirtatiously at him, I notice he's a tad blurry.

"You guys can't go home yet," Sonja informs us, and darned if she isn't slurring. Or maybe that's just me.

Wait! I'm not talking!

It's her: "Le'ss have dessert and after-dinner drinkssss."

"If I drink any more I'm going to be trashed, like you," I protest.

"Who caresss? Tomorrow's Saturday."

"You're right! Who caresss?"

We newfound soul sistahs order dessert wine and flan, then traipse off to the ladies' room, where we both pee and I ask Sonja to be one of my bridesmaids.

Yes, that's right.

Don't ask me why or how it happens.

Just know that it does, right around the time that we both come out of separate stalls to wash our hands.

For a second, I'm sure I imagined I said it in the first place. I mean, I wasn't even thinking about it. I was mainly wondering whether the flan will come in caramel sauce.

Maybe, I think hopefully, that's the question I posed aloud.

"Yes!" Sonja squeals, hugging me, hard. "Definitely!"

Okay, are you thinking she loves caramel sauce as much as I do? Because that's what I'm thinking.

"Oh, Tracey, that's so sweet!"

Yes, yes, caramel is very sweet indeed.

She hugs me again, then cries out, "I can't believe you want me to be in your wedding party!"

I can't believe it, either!

"I wish I could have you in mine," she goes on, accepting a paper towel from the smiling bathroom attendant, "but we're only having Buckley's brother and my sister. He just wants a best man and maid of honor. How many attendants are you and Jack having?"

Let's see, so far, I'm having about twenty and he's having none.

"We're having quite a few," is what I tell her as she leans into the mirror to apply more lipstick, "including you and Buckley."

"Buckley's in it, too?" She looks positively giddy with joy all over again. "I didn't know that!"

Coincidentally, Jack doesn't, either!

"Don't say anything to him—Jack hasn't asked him yet," I tell her. "But he's definitely going to."

"Maybe he's asking him right now!"

"Maybe he is!"

And maybe I'm a drunken lunatic who should go home to bed before I ask the smiling bathroom attendant to be my flower girl.

Saturday afternoon, I manage to pull myself together to keep my date with Kate.

I use the term *pull myself together* very loosely, because I've looked and felt like dog-doo ever since I rolled out of bed at eleven forty-five, even after scarfing down a huge brunch at the diner with Jack.

Wearing a huge hoodie sweatshirt of Jack's, sneakers and

jeans that are falling off my newly shrunken hips, I meet Kate at her brick town house on a leafy block of Thirty-eighth off Park, not far from the bridal boutique.

"Good gracious, sweetheart, what happened to you?" she drawls, giving me a once-over as she answers the door.

Under ordinary circumstances, I feel vaguely dowdy and unkempt in Kate's company. Today, I'm definitely the ugly stepsister to her Cinderella-with-child; she's fully made up and wearing one of her darling maternity ensembles: silk blouse, cardigan and pants, all in sherbet colors that complement each other and her fair coloring.

"Mojitos and sangria—that's what happened to me. Do you have any ginger ale?"

"Hay-ell, yes. Come on in, as long as you think we have time."

"If I don't sit down and sip some ginger ale right now, I'm going to vomit."

"Join the club."

She leads the way through her elegant grown-up house, which is filled with real furniture. Whenever I return to our apartment after visiting Kate and Billy, I realize that Ikea and pressed wood lack a certain *je ne sais quoi*, and feel like Jack and I are merely playing house.

Kate is going with me for another dress fitting, and we're going to order the navy velvet bridesmaids' gowns.

I'm armed with nine checks from the girls for a hundred dollars each and a spreadsheet I compiled containing wedding-party info, including the bridesmaids' sizes. I apparently got Sonja's last night in my drunken stupor because this morning in my purse I found a cocktail napkin that's scribbled: *Sonja size 2*. I also found a wad of five twenties Jack said she handed me as her deposit for the dress.

"You asked Sonja to be a bridesmaid?" Kate shouts incredulously as I plop down on her leather couch in utter misery.

"Oh my God, Kate. Shhh!"

"Oh, don't worry. Billy's at Chelsea Piers golfing."

"No, I mean *shhh,* you're screaming and my head is killing me," I tell her, rubbing my throbbing temples. "Not *shhh,* I don't want Billy to know I've asked everyone and their mother to be in our wedding party. He'll think I'm certifiable."

That's what Jack thought when he found out I'd asked Sonja to be in our wedding.

Well, he didn't say it when he first found out…which was pretty much the second we returned to the table after the bathroom, holding hands.

"Tracey asked me to be in the wedding!" Sonja announced.

"*Our* wedding?" Jack asked, gaping. At least he didn't say, "Why?"

Not then, anyway.

But as I recall—mind you, my memory is a bit spotty— he asked it a few times during the cab ride home. He also told me that I was out of my mind. He also told me, a little later, I think, to roll down the window and stick my head out. Later still, back at home, he advised me to put one foot on the floor so the bed would stop spinning.

It didn't.

God, I feel lousy.

And I must say, Jack could have been more sympathetic today.

Okay, he did bring me a really strong cup of coffee in bed.

He also said he'd consider having Buckley in the wedding party—which he claims I begged him to do in my last burst of coherence before the spinning bed got the better of me.

So at least something good came out of the evening.

"You're talking about Buckley's Sonja, right?" Kate clarifies, lowering herself into a Stickley chair as if she's nine months pregnant and huge instead of five and barely showing. "Big-boobed Sonja with the hair?"

"What other Sonja is there?"

"I know a few."

"Well, I don't, so what other Sonja would I possibly be asking to be in my wedding party?"

"Hay-ell, Tracey, I can't imagine that you'd ask *this* one."

"That makes two of us." I sip the ginger ale Kate poured for me—she's got an entire fridge full—and say, "It's just…I mean, I was drunk."

"Being drunk is no excuse to go around asking random people to stand in your wedding."

"I didn't go around asking random people, Kate."

"Sonja is random, wouldn't you say?"

"She's just one person, though—I wouldn't say *people*. I didn't go around asking everyone in sight." Thank God. It could have been so much worse.

Still, you have to admit, this is pretty bad. "What am I going to do?"

"Uninvite her," Kate says with a shrug. "What else *can* you do?"

"I can have her as a bridesmaid. I've got her size and her dress deposit."

"Tracey, you *cannot* do that. You don't even like her!"

"I like her." Last night I did, anyway. Last night we were soul sistahs.

And we're going to be moving to the suburbs together, buying houses next door to each other, babysitting each other's kids and playing bridge—or something like that. I have a vague recollection of that conversation happening over flan.

Flan.

Creamy. Rich.

Sweet, sticky caramel sauce.

Oh, ick.

"Come on, you only hang out with her because she and Buckley are a package deal," Kate says.

I open my mouth to protest but it's swept by a wave of bile before I can say a word.

Sangria hangovers are the worst.

"Seriously," Kate goes on as I try really really hard not to vomit on her heirloom rug, "if they broke up tomorrow, would you care if you never saw Sonja again?"

It's purely a rhetorical question, I know.

Which is why it's so damn ironic that the very next afternoon, I get a call from Buckley who says, "Tracey? Listen, I thought you should know…Sonja and I just broke up."

"What?" I immediately aim the TiVo remote and freeze the television screen, where a young-looking Billy Crystal is in the midst of explaining to a younger-looking Meg Ryan that men and women cannot be friends unless they're both involved with other people.

"We broke up," Buckley repeats somewhat glumly—but not as glumly as one might expect.

"But…how can you break up? You're getting married."

"Not anymore."

"You called off the wedding?" I am now off the couch, pacing around the living room in my bare feet. "Why?"

"I had to. It would've been a mistake to go through with it."

"But…I mean, Buckley, you guys have broken up and gotten back together before. I'm sure you can—"

"Sonja burned the invitations."

"Oh."

"And every picture of us she could find. It's over, Tracey."

It can't be! Sonja's in my wedding, dammit! I just ordered her a nonreturnable size two navy velvet sheath!

I'm dying to say it, but that would come across as selfish. Wouldn't it?

Yeah, it pretty much would.

And here I am, fresh from Sunday mass, where this week's sermon was about how we should all strive to be more like Jesus; how we should stop ourselves whenever we're in doubt and ask, *What would the Lord do?*

(Yes, I've been going to mass weekly ever since that confrontation—I mean, conversation—with Father Stefan. What, did you think I wasn't following through on at least part of my promise to him?)

Anyway, Jesus wouldn't be worrying about dealing with a random buxom bridesmaid, would he? He'd be concerned with his dear friend's well being.

I am anxious to prove that I'm a Christlike friend to Buckley; a friend who isn't the least bit worried about herself.

So rather than condemn his sucky timing, I nobly and calmly ask Buckley if he's okay.

"Yeah, I'm hanging in there. I just had to get out of the apartment—she's upstairs packing her stuff right now. She's going to go stay out in Jersey with Mae and Jay—remember them?"

Of course. Mae is Sonja's old roommate, an investment banker, and Jay is her psychiatrist husband. Mae and I were both there when Buckley met Sonja; she and I were both involved in long-distance relationships at the time. Obviously, hers ended happily ever after; mine was already over and everyone knew it but me.

"How's Sonja holding up?" I ask Buckley, remembering my own heartache when Will dumped me.

"She's pretty upset."

Yeah, well, who isn't?

My mind is spinning faster than the bed did last night. You know, a mere forty-eight hours earlier, I'd have heralded this news. We all know I wasn't wholeheartedly rooting for Buckley and Sonja's man-and-wifedom.

"So what happened, exactly?" I ask. "Did you guys have a fight?"

"It started over the guest list and escalated from there."

"The guest list for the wedding?"

"Yeah. I told her she was being a bitch about it. She didn't want to invite Raphael and Donatello and they just had us at their wedding. But she said that was different."

Different. Yeah, that certainly describes Raphael and Donatello's wedding, all right.

"She actually said it wasn't a legal marriage so it doesn't count—can you believe that?"

Yes, but it's pretty wenchy, even for her.

"She said Raphael is known for inviting hundreds of

people to every party he throws, so of course we'd be invited. I told her Raphael is my friend and I want him at my wedding, and she wouldn't budge."

"So you called off the wedding over Raphael?" I ask incredulously, thinking our good friend's ego is going to love this.

"No, it wasn't just because of Raphael. It was—" Buckley hesitates. "That was just the tip of the iceberg. There were a lot of other…issues."

"Like…?"

"I don't want to talk about it right now. But trust me, this has been a long time coming, Tracey."

Yeah? Then why, why, why couldn't you have broken up with Sonja before Friday night?

Better yet, why couldn't I have waited to ask her to be a bridesmaid?

Waited? Ha!

Here's a thought: how about if I hadn't asked her at all?

Damn those mojitos, and damn my big fat bridesmaid-inviting mouth.

"Where are you right now?" I ask Buckley, trying to focus unselfishly on my dear friend in need.

"In the Starbucks across the street from my building."

"Do you want me to come down there?" I offer. Jack is over at Mitch's apartment watching the game with a bunch of guys, and I'm on my own for the rest of the afternoon. I figured some serious Couch Time—sweatpants, chick flicks and Choc-Chewy-O's eaten straight from the box—would be the order of the day, but if Buckley needs me…

"No," he says. "I'm good, actually."

He does sound good, actually.

Much better than I do as I ask a bit desperately, "By any chance are you guys still going to be…you know, a couple? Even though you're not getting married or living together?"

"Nope, we're definitely through." Buckley sounds—dare I suggest it?—almost cheerful. "We were all wrong for each other. I guess deep down I always knew it."

"So did I," I admit without thinking first. Oops.

"You did?" Buckley sounds dismayed. "Then why didn't you ever say anything about it?"

Caught off guard, I offer a lame "I guess I didn't think it was my place."

"So you were going to let me marry the wrong woman." Okay, now he just sounds pissed.

"You didn't need my permission, Buckley. I mean, that was your decision."

"But…Tracey, we're friends. I count on you. I'm the one who coached you through your breakup with Will, remember? I'm the one who told you to be strong when he came crawling back. Remember?"

"Yes…"

"I wouldn't have let you marry Will."

"He didn't want to marry me, Buckley. It was never an issue."

"But if it had been an issue, I wouldn't have let it happen."

"No? What would you have done?" I have a sudden vision of Buckley galloping up to Most Precious Mother, shouting, "Halt!" and spiriting me away on horseback. The church has been transported to a bucolic countryside. I'm wearing my white gown and my hair is flowing, and Buckley's wearing all white, too. Very picturesque.

"I would have sat you down and talked some sense into you."

Oh. Well, as fantasies go, that's not nearly as dramatic as the white-knight rescue scene in my head, but reality seldom is.

"If I wanted to marry Will," I tell him, "nothing you said would have changed my mind. I would've had to figure out on my own that it was wrong, just like you did."

He's silent for a moment.

Then he says, "Tracey, if you had ever said I shouldn't marry Sonja, I would have listened."

"Oh, come on—you can't pin this on me!"

"I'm not. I'm just saying…you could have told me what you thought long before it came to this."

"And if I had, and you had married her anyway, you would have resented me for it. Same thing with Kate. I mean, I could have told her I didn't think Billy was right for her, and where would we be now? Probably not even friends."

I think of how I resented her back when Will was my boyfriend and she was convinced he was gay. We're lucky our friendship withstood the tension.

"So if I didn't think you should marry Jack," Buckley says, "you honestly wouldn't want to know?"

That gives me pause.

Would I want to know?

Is that really how Buckley feels?

"You don't think I should marry Jack?" Yeah, I guess I do want to know.

He hesitates. "I didn't say that. I asked if you'd want me to tell you if I thought he was wrong for you."

"No," I say simply, "I wouldn't."

I'm in love with Jack. I'm going to marry Jack. He's right

for me, and nothing anyone says would change my mind about that.

Buckley lets out a heavy sigh. "I guess we're just really different, then."

"I guess we really are."

"I should go," Buckley says then, and I don't argue.

We hang up.

I aim the TiVo remote and press Play again.

"—the person you're involved with," Billy Crystal resumes saying, "accuses you of being secretly attracted to the person you're just friends with, which you probably are—"

I scowl and aim the remote again, zapping Harry and Sally and their ridiculous theories into oblivion.

10

Flash forward to a gorgeous Saturday morning in June, the better part of which I have now spent drinking bad coffee at JFK airport in Queens.

You're assuming I'm waiting for a delayed flight to Buffalo again, aren't you?

Wrong!

I'm waiting for a delayed flight *from* Buffalo.

On the flight are seven Spadolinis: my parents, my grandmother, my sister, Mary Beth, my brother Joey, my sister-in-law Sara, and my nephew Joey Junior, newly potty trained.

Or maybe he isn't, because he reeks. I can smell him coming from a few feet away when my family finally appears in the baggage-claim area.

Yes, my family. I know, I can hardly believe it either but here they are in New York City for the first time.

They came, of course, for the engagement party Wilma is throwing for us tonight in Bedford.

I couldn't believe it when they decided to fly in for it. My parents haven't been on a plane since my great-aunt Phyllis's funeral in Fort Meyers years ago, and my grandmother never has, even though Great-Aunt Phyllis was her favorite sister.

But she finally decided it was time she got over her fear of flying.

When I asked her why, I thought she might say, "Because you're my granddaughter and I want to be there to celebrate your engagement."

Nah. Her explanation: "I'm at the end of the road anyway. If I go down in flames now, I'll get a head start."

A head start on eternal salvation. Now there's something to strive for.

But here she is, in one piece. Here they all are. Here I am, enveloped in hometown hugs right in New York, with a sudden, unexpected lump in my throat.

"Oh, no, what's happened to you? You're too skinny!" my mother shouts at me in dismay, and everyone within earshot turns around expecting to see Nicole Richie. "Aren't you eating?"

"Yes, Ma, I'm eating."

"Dolce mia!" cries Grandma as she pushes past Connie the Cobra's fervent maternal embrace to hug me herself.

"Hi, Grandma! I'm so glad you could come. And you look beautiful," I add, because as usual, she's waiting to hear it, and because as usual, it's true. She's wearing full makeup, heels and what she likes to call "a slacks suit." She's also wearing lots of perfume, which I bet went over about as well with her fellow passengers as little Joey's loaded diaper.

Sara gives me a quick hug, then rushes away to find a changing table, carrying my stinky nephew and a diaper bag.

"I still can't believe we made it!" my mother announces loudly and dramatically enough for everyone else in the terminal to turn around and wonder if their plane lost a wing over Syracuse.

"I told you we would, Ma," my sister says, but she looks a little shaken. She's never flown before either, and this is her first time away from Vince Junior and Nino, who are spending the night with their father. They've never done that before even though Vinnie's supposed to have them every other weekend per the divorce agreement. He always claims he doesn't have room for them to stay over. That's fine with my sister, who lives for the boys and doesn't want to spend every other Saturday night in an empty house anyway.

"Ma was convinced we were going down over Elmira," my brother informs me with an eye-roll.

"I can't help it. I'm a nervous flier," my mother says, like she does it all the time.

"So was it a rough flight, then?" I ask.

"No, it wasn't bad at all, once we got off the ground," Joey tells me. "They just held us on the runway forever because there was some problem with air traffic on this end. The seat-belt signs were on the whole time, so we couldn't take poor Joey to the bathroom."

"The plane stunk to high heaven by the time we took off, thanks to that kid," my grandmother says, then cracks up maniacally, because puns slay her. "Get it?" She elbows everyone in proximity—me, my father, my brother—painfully in the ribs. "Plane! High heaven! Bwa-ha-ha-ha-ha!!!"

Joey asks me under his breath, "There're going to be drinks at this party, right?"

"Plenty."

Drinks, food, music, waiters passing hors d'oeuvres on silver platters. Wilma is going all out: she's having this soiree at Toute l'Année, "a lovely restaurant with sweeping views of the countryside."

That's how she described it to me, like she was reading from a brochure.

"And Toute l'Année means all year round, Tracey," Wilma had added helpfully, "so I'm sure the view is lovely all year round."

"And sweeping," I couldn't resist saying, and she smiled.

She's been such a sweetheart about the party, the wedding, everything. And she said she's going to be giving us money toward the wedding. I told her the engagement party could be her gift to us, but she told me not to be silly.

"Jack is my only son," she pointed out. "This is the only time I get to be mother of the groom. I want to be a part of things."

It made me feel guilty for thinking she was trying to commandeer our wedding way back in February at Gallagher's.

Even my own mother hasn't done that, for the most part. I'm sure it's because the reception is off her home turf. She wouldn't dare tangle with Charlie the banquet manager of Shorewood, who has a formidable reputation around town.

"Where's Jack?" she asks as we walk arm in arm toward the baggage-claim area.

"He went up to Bedford last night so he can help his mother set up."

"His father doesn't help?" my father asks disapprovingly.

"Frank, they're dee-vorced." That's my mother, masking her own disapproval with a big happy mother-of-the-bride smile.

I can tell she's decided to embrace the Candell family, dee-vorce and all, this weekend. She promised me she would. Good for her. Good for me. Good for everyone involved.

It takes almost as long to get their luggage as it did for the actual flight from Buffalo. When it finally comes rolling out, I swear every other bag on the conveyer is marked with a bright red, white and green striped ribbon. Yes, like the Italian flag. These, apparently, are the colors for Team Spadolini, cleverly selected by my mother so that their bags would be readily identifiable.

Never mind that no other living soul would possibly mistake most of the Spadolini luggage for their own. My parents have matching suitcases they got years ago at a garage sale—the kind with the hard sides. I'm sure the last owners were a flapper and a bootlegger, and God knows they didn't fill them with rocks as my parents must have, because it takes three of us to hoist them off the belt. They're covered in something my mother insists is "Gen-u-ine walrus leather," though I have never seen a walrus in quite that shade of green. Or any shade of green, come to think of it.

Oh, and did you know that walrus skin, according to the Conster, is reportedly the heaviest, thickest leather in the world? Which is why these days it's probably used to cover, say, armored trucks, black boxes and nuclear-bomb shelters. As opposed to a matched set of luggage.

My sister, on the other hand, is traveling ultra-lightly. She's packed her stuff in the boys' bright blue-and-red Thomas the Tank Engine duffel, which reads Choo Choo! in a big white dialogue bubble emblazoned on the side. Wouldn't you know, Vinnie the cheating louse got all the grown-up luggage in the divorce because, as Mary Beth put it at the time, "Where do I ever go?"

In addition to blessedly ordinary-looking rolling bags—four, mind you, and they're large—Joe and Sara have checked a car seat and a shiny red tricycle with a rubber horn and handlebar streamers.

Yeah. You read that right.

They said Joey Junior screamed bloody murder when they tried to leave it behind, so they gave in and brought it along. Yes, that'll show him who's in charge: the tyrannical toddler himself. Brilliant move.

And then there's Grandma.

Grandma seems to think she's spending the summer abroad, because it looks like she's brought a steamer trunk.

Oh. My. God.

I gape at the towering heap of…stuff. "How are we going to get all of this to the hotel?"

"Is there a nice big limousine?" my grandmother asks, looking around as if expecting to see one parked right here in the baggage-claim area. "They always take a big limousine on my stories."

I'm trying to be patient here, really I am, but I hear myself barking, "Who? Who are 'they'?"

"Well, Desiree and Destiny—they're twin sisters—"

"They're characters on one of her soaps," my mother cuts in.

"Yes, and Desiree's husband, Vlad, is—"

"I'm sorry to interrupt, Grandma," I say, "but we've got to get moving. There's a bus that goes right to your hotel—" they're staying at the Grand Hyatt, which I chose because it's right near both the airport bus and Grand Central Station, where we'll be catching the train up to Bedford later "—but we can't get on a bus with all this luggage. We're going to have to take a cab."

"I've always want to take a real New York City taxi," Sara says excitedly, then screams, "Joey, noooo!" as he runs down an elderly couple on his tricycle.

"Do they make a taxi big enough for all of us and all the luggage?" my sister asks dubiously.

"That would be a bus," I say crisply. "Listen, we're going to have to split up into groups. Let's go."

I attempt to hustle them through the crowd out to the taxi stand: Grandma in her heels, my mother clinging to me in sheer intimidation, little Joey veering left and right on his trike, everyone else pushing rented carts piled high with luggage—at a mere three dollars per cart, "highway robbery" according to my father.

As we stand on the world's longest line, I give them a crash course in overall taxi etiquette, tipping and the hotel's location.

When we reach the top of the line, I dispatch Joey, Sara and little Joey in the first cab, with my nephew shrieking at the driver, who insists on stowing the trike in the trunk with the rest of their stuff. Unfazed by the tantrum, the driver shrieks right back at him in Pakistani, then gives him an affectionate belly tickle and Joey laughs hysterically in response.

As they drive off, it occurs to me that if my overly indulgent brother and sister-in-law sent him to live with Abdul-Hakim for a week at Camp Tough Love, Joey's terrible twos would be tamed in a hurry.

"Next!" the taxi dispatcher bellows, and I shove my parents toward the open doors of the waiting cab, shouting after them, "Don't forget to tip twenty percent!"

"Twenty!" my father echoes. "I thought you said fifteen to twenty. Now it's twenty?"

Glancing at the sweating elderly driver as he struggles to lug those prehistoric walrus bags into the trunk, I resolutely tell my father, "Twenty. Maybe twenty-five."

Away they go, with my father grumbling and my mother, God love her, swatting his arm and saying something about "when in Rome."

And then there were three.

It takes me, Mary Beth, the driver, the dispatcher and a Good Samaritan traveling businessman to wrestle Grandma's chest into the trunk. And for once, when I say "Grandma's chest," I'm not talking about the famous bullet boobs, which are resting sedately in the backseat along with Grandma.

I tip the dispatcher and thank the businessman profusely before settling into the seat with Grandma, Mary Beth and Mary Beth's choo-choo duffel, which didn't fit into the trunk.

As we careen toward the Belt Parkway, reggae music blasting from the radio in the front seat, my grandmother holds on to me for dear life and insists that we all say a rousing rosary.

"She did this on the plane, too," my sister hisses into my ear.

★ ★ ★

She does it on the Metro-North train, too, six hours later. Well, she starts, anyway—the moment the lights and ventilation system turn off in the tunnel as the train picks up speed.

"It's okay, Grandma," I cut in. "This happens all the time."

And then there was light.

And ventilation.

And a clear view of my nephew standing on his seat in madras shorts and a preppy Baby Gap polo, staring down a pair of rough-looking tweens in the seat behind him.

"Sit down, little Joey," I coo, reaching across the aisle and past my sister-in-law to touch his shoulder.

"No!" he shouts, bouncing wildly on the seat.

"I don't want him to get hurt," I tell Sara.

"Hmm? Oh, he's okay. He's holding on to the seat."

Yes, I think, turning away from potential bloodshed, *but the tweens might be armed.*

And it's a good thing I don't carry a firearm around in my purse because by late afternoon, after showing my family around Manhattan, I'd have been tempted to turn it on myself.

It was hard enough to keep from diving off the observation deck of the Empire State Building when my father asked where the twin towers used to stand, then loudly announced that it was too bad our country hadn't learned its lesson yet, and kicked out all the "foreigners."

Keep in mind that his own parents were Italian immigrants, that he spouted this gem within earshot of a virtual melting pot of tourists, and that he had complained just five minutes earlier that we wouldn't have time to see the Statue of Liberty until tomorrow.

Why is he so anxious to see it? Does he have a can of spray paint and a diabolical plan to change the inscription to "*Keep your tired, your poor, your huddled masses...*"?

Then again, at least he didn't request a stop for coffee and danish every five minutes despite a hearty lunch at the hotel restaurant. No, that was my mother, the bottomless pit.

My father was the one who complained nonstop about the cost of coffee and Danish and everything else in Manhattan.

For her part, my sister spent most of the afternoon on her cell phone, fielding frequent calls from Nino and Vince Junior, who have been bickering and needier in her absence than they are when she's around, which I didn't think was possible. Keep in mind that she dropped them off at their father's apartment just *this morning* and she'll be picking them up again tomorrow afternoon.

Her end of the conversation always tends to go something like this: "Hi, sweetheart...I know, I miss you so much too... He did what?... Did you tell him to stop?... Put him on... Hi, sweetheart, what did you do to your brother?... You didn't?... He did what?... Where's Daddy?... Well, go wake him up...(*or knock on the bathroom door,* or *tell him to get off the phone with his girlfriend*)..."

You get the picture. Poor Mary Beth, who has never spent a night away from her children, gets a little weepy whenever she hangs up after talking to them. But her phone invariably rings again five minutes later and she's right back in it.

And then—once again—there's Grandma.

Wouldn't you know, her steamer trunk contains twenty pairs of shoes—all of them skinny high heels? She was limping five minutes into our sightseeing jaunt, and by the time I dropped everyone back at the hotel to get ready for the party, her feet were bloody stumps.

But she turned down my offer to pick up a pair of sneakers for her—she's got a pair of "gorgeous gams," as Grandpa used to call them, and dammit, she's going to show them off. So now she's wearing tall, strappy hot-pink sandals that perfectly match her hot-pink well, hot pants is the best way to describe what she's wearing, though she prefers to call it a "skort."

Mary Beth, who is sharing a room with Grandma and a train seat with me, assures me in a whisper that this outfit is preferable to the "Batgirl getup" Grandma was planning to wear.

Um, Batgirl getup? Dare I ask?

"It was shiny, and long, and…skintight," my sister informs me with a shudder. "She made it herself out of some bargain fabric she got at Joanne's."

"She still sews her own clothes?"

"Yup."

I should probably be thinking, "God bless her."

Instead, looking at her sitting there across the aisle in those hot pants, I'm thinking, "Holy varicose vein, Grandma. You're an octogenarian!"

I don't dare say it, though. She prides herself on looking great for her age—and great for anyone a few decades younger, too. I just wish she wouldn't flaunt so much skin in front of my future in-laws. Or people in general.

Grandma is lugging along a mysteriously bulging Hens and Kelly shopping bag, filled with God knows what. She won't tell me, just keeps insisting it's "for the party."

I'm sure it's safe to assume she didn't buy whatever it is at Hens and Kelly, a blue-collar Buffalo department-store chain that vanished before my allowance days. Then again, you never know, because when I ask her if she made her hot pants, she says, "No, I bought them down at the Montgomery Ward."

Which pulled out of Brookside at least a decade before I was born.

My mother, who goes nowhere empty-handed, actually asked if we could stop at a supermarket this afternoon; turned out she wanted to throw together a "dish to pass." She was thinking a nice salad. She even had the foresight to pack a paring knife, a Tupperware container and "good" olive oil because we must not have "good" olive oil here in the most vast and diverse metropolitan area in the country.

"Station stop...One Hundred and Twenty-fifty Street, Harlem," intones the mechanical voice.

"Did they say Harlem?" Grandma asks loudly. "Is it safe here?"

Dear God.

I pointedly ignore her. So does my sister, whose cell phone is ringing again.

"Off!" Little Joey bolts from the seat and makes a mad dash for the doors as they open.

My brother the superhero leaps forward in a single bound and snatches his son just inches from the platform.

"Off!" protests little Joey in a piercing voice.

What a far cry from "On!", which is what he was screaming back in Grand Central when we were waiting for the doors to open. "On!" It echoed through the cavernous tunnel and everyone else on the platform gave us a wide berth.

"Joey, you love trains," my sister-in-law claims as my

brother marches little Joey back to their seat. "Choo choo! Remember?"

"No! I hate choo choos! I want my bike!"

Terrific. I had to force them to leave it back in the hotel room. Yes, they were planning on bringing it to the party. They thought it would keep him entertained, and who doesn't know that a toddler zipping around on a shiny red trike would be a welcome addition to any engagement party?

Honestly, it's scary the way parenthood has challenged Joey and Sara's common sense. Between that and Kate's miserable pregnancy, I'm seriously thinking Jack and I need to wait a good two or three years before we even consider having children.

"Biiii-iiike!" Joey howls.

Maybe four or five years.

"Here, have a treat, honey." That's my mother saving the day as only an Italian grandmother can: by shoving something sweet—this time, a chocolate doughnut—into Joey's mouth. It immediately shuts him up, of course.

No, Ma doesn't carry doughnuts in her purse in case of emergencies.

I assured her earlier that the party food was taken care of, but she showed up in the hotel lobby toting two boxes of Krispy Kremes she had sent my father out to pick up for the party.

When I protested, "Ma, you don't have to do that," she shrugged and said, "Oh, I wanted to."

I mean…what do you say to that?

I'll tell you.

You say: "Really, Ma, it's not necessary. Go put them back in your room and eat them later."

But then she looks wounded and asks, "Why? You don't think Jack's family likes Krispy Kremes? Are they some kind of health nuts?"

Some kind of health nuts. In my family, that is the ultimate insult, right up there with *some kind of liberal.*

"Everyone likes Krispy Kremes, Connie," is my father's response. "And they were selling them four for a buck."

Ah, his first New York bargain: day-old doughnuts.

Luckily, I'd had the foresight to visit the Grand Central ticket kiosk earlier this week and pick up a bunch of off-peak round-trip tickets to Bedford. I can just imagine what my father would say to spending almost twenty bucks a head just to get to the party. Needless to say, he's still freaked out about the forty-five-dollar cab ride—not including tip and toll—from the airport this morning.

So here we have it: Mom and her twenty-three remaining donuts; Dad and his perpetual sticker shock; Grandma and her inscrutable shopping bag; Mary Beth and her long-distance bickering boys; indulgent Joey and Sara and their unruly toddler, whose face is now smeared with chocolate icing....

A far cry from the Candells and people of that ilk.

Still, regardless of everything...

They're my family and I love them. I'm glad they're here to celebrate my engagement. All of them.

Even Grandma.

11

Yes, I'm thrilled Grandma came all this way to celebrate my engagement...until the moment she pulls me aside to ask me in a loud whisper why Jack's family is protesting the wedding.

Which occurs pretty much the moment we walk through the door into the private party room at Toute l'Année.

Protesting? What can she possibly be talking about? I look around, half expecting to see Jack's siblings sporting Down With Tracey sandwich boards.

Nope.

In fact, no one has even glanced in our direction yet, including Jack, who is helping himself to a tasty morsel from a passing tray, and Wilma, whom I spot conferring with a tuxedoed waiter.

The party is under way and the guests are elegantly mingling, munching and sipping Candelltinis, the signature drink Wilma and the bartender created just for tonight. A pianist is playing a jaunty version of "Just The Way You Are" on a baby grand in the far corner beside a tall window. Beyond that is a view—yes, sweeping—of the blooming garden against a backdrop of stone walls, rolling hills and a tangerine sunset.

I turn back to my grandmother, flummoxed. "What makes you think anyone is protesting the wedding, Grandma?"

"Look at them! They're all in black from head to toe! They look like they should be at a wake!"

Yes, and you're in hot-pink hot pants and spike heels. You look like you should be hooking by the Lincoln Tunnel.

Aloud, I say only, "Grandma, this is New York. Everyone wears black. It doesn't mean they're protesting anything. I promise you."

"It's just so…somber," my mother comments in a stage whisper. Balancing her Krispy Kreme boxes in one hand, she reaches up to nervously pat her hair, and I glimpse an unfamiliar vulnerability in her black-lined eyes.

"Ma—" I put an arm around her "—come on. Let's go meet Jack's mother."

"Which one is she?"

I point out Wilma and feel my mother stiffen beneath my grasp.

"Do I look all right?" she asks anxiously, and I see her seeing Wilma's flattering black sleeveless dress, her youthful haircut, her real jewelry.

I look at my mother. She's a head shorter than me, her roly-poly figure draped in a silky red dress with a cowl neck. She's wearing a new cubic zirconia pendant and matching earrings she ordered from QVC especially to wear to the party.

My heart overflows and I hug her. "You look beautiful, Mom. Come on, let's go get Jack so you can meet everyone."

"We look like we just got into town with the circus," Sara mutters as we head over.

"What do you mean?"

She gestures at the other guests. "They're all in black."

Et tu, Sara? Et tu?

"It's a New York thing," I tell her soothingly. "And you look great."

"I look gaudy." She gestures at her lemon-yellow sundress. "And so does poor Joe. I made him wear that. I got one for him and one for your dad for Father's Day last week."

It's a Hawaiian shirt covered in turquoise hibiscus blossoms. My father's is similar but his blossoms are orange.

They are a pretty colorful crew, especially with little Joey's loud shorts, Grandma in hot pink and Mary Beth in a pale lavender pantsuit.

Being the bride, I'm all dressed in white—corny, I know. But I went shopping with Rachel a few weeks ago and found this crisp Ralph Lauren skirt and top that set off my new fake tan, which was Raphael's engagement gift to me.

"You're giving me a *tan?*" I asked when he told me about it awhile back.

He nodded vigorously. "You want that Palm Beach glow, Tracey."

He's right. I do. Now that I have it, anyway.

At first, though, I wasn't crazy about the idea of stripping down to my underwear under bright lights in a little booth and being sprayed head to toe by a stranger with some kind of bronzing mist. But then Tiffany—she, of course, is the tanning technician—started explaining how she was contouring my thighs and stomach with strategic spraying, to make me look more toned—and you know what? She was right. It really does. I even got a touch-up last night after work.

Now Jack's eyes widen appreciatively when he sees me, and he greets me with a kiss and a fervent, "You look gorgeous."

"Thanks. So do you." He's in a dark suit and tie with a white dress shirt and polished wingtips. I love it when he's all dressed up like this. It makes up for all the stinky socks and holey sweatpants.

He warmly hugs all of my family and takes the doughnuts from my mom, saying, "Krispy Kremes! That's the best thing anybody could bring to a party. I'm having one now."

Good old Jack.

"We're missing three," my mother says apologetically. "Little Joey got hungry on the train."

Hungry?

Little Joey was out of control on the train. Especially after my mother had pumped him full of sugar. By the time we reached our stop, he was literally hanging from the overhead luggage rack.

Wilma comes bustling our way calling, "At last! Welcome!"

"Are we late?" my father asks. "I thought we were early."

"Oh, no, no. I mean, it's about time we're finally getting to meet. I feel like you're family already!" Wilma throws her arms around my mother: Chanel No. 5 meets Jean Nate.

Mom looks instantly relieved. "It's so nice to meet you."

"You, too. I've heard so much about you."

"You, too."

"We brought doughnuts," my grandmother speaks up, wanting to be noticed.

"Krispy Kremes." Jack holds them up.

"Oh, we love those!" exclaims Wilma, promptly debunking the "health nut" accusation, though nary a cruller has crossed those frosted-pink lips in all the time I've known her.

I introduce her to everyone, especially Grandma, who beams when Wilma tells her she and my mother could be sisters.

"People say that all the time," she claims.

"Tracey!" I turn around to find Yvonne, Latisha and Brenda, all dressed becomingly—yes, in black.

"Hi, guys!" I hug each of them, touched that they made the trek up here.

There's still a subtle level of unspoken tension between me and them at the office, and I really wasn't sure they'd come, but here they are.

I introduce them to my family and Wilma as "bridesmaids and dear friends."

"Now, whose mother are you, again?" I hear Grandma asking Yvonne.

Uh-oh.

"Nobody's. Whose daughter are you, again?" Yvonne asks good-naturedly in return, and my grandmother titters girlishly.

I watch the two of them—both aging, unnatural redheads in clingy clothes—head off to the bar together. How about that.

Wilma has taken my parents under her wing, escorting them around the room making introductions.

Jack is off greeting some of his cousins, who just got here.

Joey and Sara have taken little Joey outside to "blow off some steam," thank God.

"So how long have you two worked with Tracey?" Mary Beth asks Brenda and Latisha as the four of us sip our Candelltinis.

"We were there right from the start," Brenda tells her, "back before she became a big shot with her own office."

She means to say it lightly—and maybe she even does— but for some reason, it stings.

"I'm definitely not a big shot," I protest.

"You're a bigger shot than the rest of us," Latisha points out.

"And," Brenda adds, "we really miss you out in the cubes."

"The cubes?" my sister asks.

"Tracey used to sit with us in the cubicles. Now she's way off down the hall."

"Not that far," I tell Latisha. "And anyway, we still eat lunch together—"

"When you have time."

"When I have time," I agree with Brenda. "And I know I haven't had much time lately. They've been piling on the work since I got promoted."

"Tracey was so excited about that promotion," my sister contributes. "And we were all so proud of her back home. My parents tell everyone about her."

I look at Mary Beth in surprise. "Ma and Pop tell people about me? What do they say?"

"That you're an executive in Manhattan." May-an-hay-at-an. Mary Beth's flat *A*'s are coming through loud and clear.

"An executive?" I echo. "They actually say that?"

She nods. "You've done better than anyone else in the family. They're really proud of you. Dad is always telling people you made it in New York and 'if you can make it there you'll make it anywhere.' You know how he loves Frank Sinatra."

"But…I thought New York was a problem for him and Ma. You know, that they were upset that I moved away."

"Only because they miss you like crazy. But trust me, they brag about you every chance they get."

"Wow." I stare across the room at my parents, who are holding glasses of red wine and politely listening to Jack's brother-in-law Bob, Kathleen's husband, talking about something really boring.

No, I can't hear what he's saying. I don't have to. Everything Bob says is really boring.

As he talks, the twins are busy with the nearby chocolate fountain. No, they're not dipping the strawberries or butter cookies that are artfully arranged beside it. Ashley is, however, dipping her fingers, and Beatrice has cupped her hands beneath the trickling chocolate. Nice.

Even from here, I can see that my parents are making note of this scene and deciding that the Candell grandchildren are spoiled brats.

I can't say I disagree.

But then, I feel the same way about the Spadolini grand-child, who can currently be seen running amok through the lovely sweeping view beyond the window.

"You know, I can't believe they say good things about me living in New York and working in advertising," I muse, turning away from my parents, back to my sister.

"Why not?" Mary Beth asks.

"Because they've never said it to me directly."

"They're not like that."

"No, I know…I just…" I'm suddenly feeling really emotional. I'd love to go over there and give my parents a huge hug right now—and not just to spare them some painfully involved tale about people they've never met. Bob and Kathleen like to keep everyone apprised of their friends' and neighbors' lives in addition to their own.

"You know, Tracey," Brenda says, "I'm really happy for you—that you got promoted and everything."

I look up in surprise. I had forgotten all about her and Latisha being here. I notice now that their expressions have softened considerably.

"Are you sure?" I can't resist asking.

"Is she sure about what?" Yvonne has rejoined us, having left my grandmother to flirt with the twentysomething studmuffin tending bar.

Mental note: rescue studmuffin ASAP.

"I just told her I'm happy about her promotion."

"We all are," Yvonne agrees, "and we're jealous as hell of your door, view and raise, but don't mind us. We'll get over it."

"The view isn't that great," I tell her, "and the raise doesn't make much difference at all, after taxes."

"Whatever, we just feel like we've lost you, girlfriend," Latisha says.

"Why? I'm still around."

"Yeah, but now you know stuff that we don't," Brenda says.

"Like who's getting fired."

"Nobody's getting fired," I tell Latisha. "Not that I know of, anyway."

"You knew about Julie."

"I did not. You guys knew before I did."

"Yeah, right." That's Yvonne.

"You said Adrian told you in advance that there were going to be layoffs on Choc-Chewy-O's," Latisha points out.

"Hello?" That's Mary Beth, answering her cell phone again. She listens for a minute, then excuses herself to go take the call.

"Julie just thought you should have warned her she might lose her job," Brenda tells me. "She felt really bad."

"But…" What I want to say is that I had no clue what Adrian was even talking about.

Then I realize that if I did know, it still wouldn't be my place to warn Julie. I mean, there's going to be certain information I'm privy to on my level now, and it's not a good idea to go spreading it around the office.

And if my friends think I should be engaging in corporate espionage…well, they're wrong.

"Listen," I say, "you guys have to understand that my job depends on my being professional and responsible, just like your jobs do. I'm trying really hard to do this right, and I'm completely overwhelmed with work and crazy Clients, and I feel like you guys haven't been supportive at all lately. You're pissed at me for something I didn't even know anything about. And anyway, you would do the same thing in my shoes."

For a moment, there's silence. I guess they're not used to me sticking up for myself. Maybe they were expecting an apology and a promise to keep them apprised of future clandestine Blaire Barnett developments.

"Tracey's right," Yvonne speaks up. "We've been a bunch of jealous assholes."

"I didn't say *that*," I protest.

"You probably should have." Brenda leans over to give me a squeeze. "I feel really bad."

"So do I." Latisha shakes her head. "Girl, just you need to slap some sense into us sometimes."

"Tracey? Come here for a second and meet my cousin Anne." That's Jack, touching my arm.

I excuse myself from my friends, feeling a whole lot better about everything.

I meet Jack's cousin Anne, then his old neighbors Clyde and JoEllen, his godfather, Ted, and, at long last, Reverend Devern—who is young, laid-back and cute, with a ponytail and an off-color sense of humor.

"If you need anything at all, Tracey, remember, I'm not all that far away from Manhattan," he says.

"Thank you, Reverend Devern."

"Oh, call me Rev Dev." He heads off to get another glass of wine.

"I love him," I tell Jack wistfully. "He's so awesome and hip."

"Father Stefan is awesome and hip, too."

"Not really."

"Not really," Jack agrees. "But he cares about us and he'll do a great job on our wedding ceremony."

"I know. That reminds me...my parents want to go to early mass at Saint Patrick's Cathedral tomorrow morning. I don't suppose you want to come?"

"Sure."

"Really? I thought you'd want to stay home in bed."

Jack pulls me close. "Only if you were there, too. I missed you last night. I'm really glad you didn't move out."

. "Me, too." I grin, feeling head over heels, just as a bride should at her engagement party.

Jack kisses me.

"Hello, young lovers, wherever you are," a voice trills, and we look up to see Raphael.

"What the heck are you wearing?" I ask him.

He looks down. "Green and yellow madras pants and a green argyle sweater vest over a pink Lacoste shirt, Tracey. Oh, and loafers, no socks."

"I know *what* you're wearing," I say patiently, "but *why?*"

"To blend in with the country-estate crowd." Raphael pulls both of us into a warm embrace. "I'm so happy for you two! Are you having fun tonight?"

"Absolutely," Jack tells him. "Where's Donatello?"

"He's over there with Billy, getting us drinks." Raphael gestures at the bar, where I see the bartender filling Billy's glass with top-shelf single malt.

Wilma wanted nothing but the best for this party, so I'm sure the Scotch will meet with Billy's snobbish approval. I'm also sure it will be a different story when he gets to Brookside, but you know what? At this point, I really don't care.

"Where's Kate?" I ask Raphael as Jack excuses himself to go greet someone.

"She's in the bathroom throwing up."

"Morning sickness again? I thought she was past that. Bummer."

"No, she's just carsick. Billy drove a hundred miles an hour on the Saw Mill Parkway coming up here, and you know how curvy that is."

"Poor Kate. Do you think I should go see if she's okay?"

"No, stay away from her. She's in a really bad mood. She just told me I look like someone's halfwit caddy."

I look him over again. "I hate to say it, Raphael, but—"

"Egad, who is that?" he screams, clapping his palms over his cheeks and gaping.

I follow his gaze.

"That," I inform him, "is my grandmother."

"She's too much, Tracey! I love her!"

"So do I, actually," I say. "Even if she is a little out there."

"I love her outfit! I always knew the culotte would come back."

"I honestly don't think Grandma realizes the culotte ever left," I tell him. "And anyway, she calls it a skort."

"Skort! Tracey, I *have* to meet her! Ooh, look…there's a child!" he exclaims, clapping his palms over his cheeks and gaping all over again. "And we have matching pants! Oh my God, Tracey, is he precious or what?"

I turn to see little Joey on the opposite end of the room, reaching up toward a burning votive candle.

"That imp!" Raphael exclaims as Joey sprints away from Sara, a miniature torch runner with the flaming candle clutched high in his outthrust hand.

He passes dangerously close to someone's diaphanous skirt. Instant visions of Superbride to the rescue: I can just see myself tackling the woman to the ground and smothering her with a tablecloth.

Raphael turns all the way around to watch the small Olympian dash outside with his parents in mad pursuit.

"Who is he, I wonder?" he asks, mesmerized.

"He's my nephew."

"Tracey! Are you serious? I love your family. Especially that precious little guy!"

All right, old ladies in hot-pink culottes have a certain charm. That, I can understand.

But torch-bearing children are downright scary, no?

"Since when are you so into kids, Raphael?"

"Since I realized I want to be a daddy, Tracey."

"Are you serious?"

"Yes! But Donatello and I are having marital woes."

"Oh, no."

"Oh, yes."

"What's going on?"

"It's the oldest story in the book—I want to start a family and my husband doesn't think we should bring another child into the world," Raphael laments. "I'm thinking I might just have to go ahead and do it anyway, and pretend it was an accident."

"Ooh, aren't you the crafty little wife."

"I'm serious, Tracey."

All right, then, I have to ask: "You do know you can't get pregnant, Raphael?"

"Tracey! Of course I know that! I mean, I'll mail in the preliminary adoption application we filled out a few weeks ago, before Donatello completely puts his foot down. I'll pretend it got mixed in with the bills."

"I don't think that's such a good idea."

"But Tracey, I really want a baby, especially after going to Africa and finding out about all the thousands of children who need homes. I just ache to go back there and bring them all home with me."

"Okay, Angelina, keep me posted."

He sighs deeply.

"Listen," I say, "have you talked to Buckley today?"

"No. Why?"

"I told him to check with you or Kate about getting a ride up here for the party. I guess he must have decided to take the train after all."

He didn't seem very keen on that idea, though, when I last talked to him. In fact, he was sounding very un-Buckley, now that I think about it. Kind of unenthusiastic about the party.

I figured maybe he felt funny coming alone, which is why I suggested his hitching a ride with the others. He and Sonja are still broken up.

I'm assuming she's still in the wedding, though.

I say assuming because she never called to say that she was dropping out of the bridesmaid lineup. She hasn't called me, period. I haven't heard a peep from her since the night she and Buckley broke up. It's like she fell off the face of the earth.

So, yeah, it's a little awkward.

Wilma sent her an invitation for the engagement party. I had her mail it care of Mae's address, which Buckley gave me. But he has no idea whether Sonja is even living there; he hasn't heard from her, either. For all either of us knows, she's run off to Lebanon with her boss's aunt Gwelda.

When Buckley found out Sonja was invited tonight, he sounded even less enthusiastic about coming.

Which is why I probably shouldn't be so surprised that he hasn't shown.

Then again, he's one of my closest friends, and I thought he'd be here for me.

I find myself keeping an expectant eye on the door as I introduce Raphael to my grandmother, who hits it off with him immediately. The two of them chat like old friends about vintage fashion, show tunes and their mutual fondness for Judy Garland—the pianist is currently playing "Over The Rainbow"—and, naturally, Liza Minnelli.

Then Raphael excuses himself to get a drink, and Grandma whispers, "Poor thing. I can tell he's not over you, Tracey."

I look around, confused.

"What? Who?"

"Your handsome friend Ralphie. He's in love with you. I can tell."

"I don't think so, Grandma," I say with a straight face.

She taps her temple, wearing a sage expression. "You listen to your old grandma. I'm more intuitive than you think. I wasn't born yesterday, you know."

"I know."

"And back in the day, I had my share of Ralphies, Tracey, even after I met your grandfather. All the most handsome, talented boys in the drama club were crazy about your grandma."

"No kidding," I murmur.

"Sure. I broke a lot of hearts the day I walked down that aisle with Grandpa. And I'm sure you'll be breaking a few the day you get married, too."

I chat a few more minutes with my grandmother, the unwitting former fag hag, then tell her I've got to get back to mingling.

I join Jack's father and his sisters Jeannie, Rachel and Emily.

My future father-in-law greets me with a perfunctory peck on the cheek.

"I hope you're having a nice time," I tell him.

He almost didn't come, saying he was supposed to be in a golf tournament in Palm Springs this weekend. But somebody—Rachel, I assume—talked him into skipping it.

"Jack is so glad to have you here," I add—bold-faced lie.

"I'm glad I came," his father says, but he doesn't particularly seem to mean it.

"You look gorgeous tonight, Tracey," Rachel tells me. "I love your dress."

"So do I," Jeannie chimes in. "Emily, it's kind of like the one you had on last weekend, isn't it?"

"Not really," Emily says briefly. "Oh, look, Dad, isn't that George Barnes over there by the bar?"

"No," he says. "I don't think so."

Moment of awkward silence. I can't think of a single thing to say.

"Bacon-wrapped scallop?" a waiter asks, sidling up with a trayful, and, relieved, I seize one—along with the opportunity to move on.

"Is it my imagination," I ask Jack when I manage to work my way back to his side, "or is your sister Emily cold-shouldering me?"

"Probably not your imagination," he says promptly. "She's really upset that you didn't ask her to be a bridesmaid."

"*What?* How do you know?"

"Rachel told me."

"Why didn't you tell me? Oh, God, I feel so bad. What did she say?"

He shrugs. "Just that Emily's hurt because she's the only one you left out."

Terrific. I should have known.

I accept my fifth Candelltini from a conveniently passing waiter. No, I'm not wasted at my own engagement party. I keep getting drinks, taking one sip, setting them down, then getting dragged away to meet someone or pose for another picture.

"Well, what about Kathleen?" I ask Jack. "I left her out, too."

"Yeah, but you're having the girls, so she figures that covers her. She's fine with it."

Is it my imagination, or is Jack suddenly speaking gibberish?

"What are you saying?" I ask him impatiently, thinking it's been one long day.

"The girls," Jack repeats cryptically. "I guess Kathleen feels like they're stand-ins for her, or something."

Okay, he's making no sense whatsover. I'm about to ask him how many Candelltinis he's had when he adds, "And anyway, Kathleen said it's better that she's not a bridesmaid. She gets low blood sugar and passes out if she's on her feet too much."

"I know that," I say impatiently, because who doesn't? By now my parents probably know Kathleen's medical history, real and imagined. "But what are you saying about the girls? What girls?"

"Beatrice and Ashley…you know, that they're the flower girls, so Kathleen—Hey!"

In the midst of sipping, I just spewed Candelltini all over my fiancé.

"Geez, what are you doing?" He wipes himself off with a blue *Jack and Tracey* cocktail napkin.

Too shell-shocked to apologize, I manage to ask only, "Did you just say Kathleen thinks Beatrice and Ashley are our *flower girls?*"

"Yeah…why?"

"Because they're not. That's why! Didn't you tell her they're not?"

"Obviously I didn't, or we wouldn't be having this conversation."

"Why didn't you? How could you not tell her?"

"Because I didn't know they weren't our flower girls. How would I know that?"

"How would you *not?*" I snap before remembering that this is the man who just this week finally decided who his groomsmen would be, and would probably be hard-pressed to rattle them off now without prompting.

Oh, and in case you were wondering, yes, he did ask Buckley. Which is why it makes it all the more frustrating that Buckley isn't here. Jack also asked Mitch, Jeff, his two brothers-in-law, my three brothers, his old roommate/my former boss, Mike Middleford.

Which leads me to wonder…

"Jack, did you get mixed up somehow and accidentally ask your nieces to be our flower girls?"

"You're not serious, are you?"

"Then why does your sister think this?" I wail, setting my drink down. "Listen, you need to go tell Kathleen right now that the girls are *not* in our wedding party."

"Why not just have them in it?"

Why not? Because we have too many people already, that's why not.

But if I bring that up, he'll throw it back in my face and tell me he's the one who just wanted a maid of honor and best man.

So I say, as calmly as I can, through clenched teeth, "Because if I had your nieces I'd have to have my niece, too."

"So have her."

That does it. He's off his rocker, truly.

"What about Cousin Joanie?" I ask shrilly. "Huh, Jack? What about her? Did you even give Cousin Joanie a second thought?"

"Have her, too," he says with maddening calm. Then he has the gall to grin. "Seriously, who's going to notice one more face in the crowd that's coming down the aisle as it is?"

"Hardy freaking har, Jack." I can't believe he's taking this so lightly. "How about if you have Aldo and Bud as your ushers? Hey, maybe Fat Naso can be your best man. How would you like that?"

He just shakes his head. "Calm down, Tracey."

"I'm sorry…" I rake a hand through my hair. "You have got to talk to your sister."

"Relax, Tracey." He gives me a little hug. "We'll straighten it out, okay? I promise."

That's better.

"I just don't get why on earth Kathleen would get such a crazy idea into her head," I say queasily. "I mean…we should go tell your mother about this, so she can help us—"

"Oh, she knows."

"She does?" That stops me short. "Are you sure?"

"She was saying something about taking the girls shopping for their flower-girl dresses, I think."

"What?"

Oh my God.

I cannot believe I was just rhapsodizing about Wilma not commandeering our wedding, because obviously there's a complex Candell conspiracy afoot here. There really is.

"Where's your mother?" I ask Jack, seething.

"Right there." Jack points her out, a stone's throw away, talking to a white-haired man, Uncle-somebody, who's been wielding a camera all night.

"Wilma?" I call.

She turns around and the man she's with says something to her.

"Smile!" Wilma descends upon us, putting an arm around each of us. "Uncle Jim wants to take another picture of me with the two of you!"

We smile.

Well, mine is more like bared teeth and it's all I can do not to snarl, after the flash, "Wilma, can we talk to you about something for a second?"

"Sure. What is it? Is everything all right? Are you having a good time?"

Wilma, I notice with a pang of remorse, is positively glowing tonight. She's having such fun, being the hostess at this wonderful party.

I soften a little.

I mean, I'm sure it isn't her fault her crazy daughter thinks I want demonic flower girls.

I take a deep, cleansing breath, then say, "There seems to be a misunderstanding, and Jack and I are hoping you can help us straighten it out."

I look at Jack and realize the only thing he's hoping is that someone will come rescue him from this hell.

Obviously, it's going to be up to me to straighten things out here. Big surprise there.

"Kathleen seems to be under the impression," I say cautiously, "that the twins are going to be flower girls in the wedding."

"Oh, I know. The girls were so excited I couldn't tell them no."

"Listen, Wilma, I need—"

Wait, *she* couldn't tell them no?

Where was I when Wilma was voted stand-in bride?

I stare at her, slack-jawed.

"They kept begging Kathleen," she explains, "because a little friend of theirs had just been in a wedding—"

Beelzebub the ring bearer, no doubt.

"—and Kathleen said she'd ask you about it, but she was too shy to do it."

Kathleen? Shy?

Okay, I'm really starting to feel like I just rode up the Saw Mill in the backseat of Billy's Beemer.

"So she asked me to find out if you'd mind, and I said I would," Wilma goes on, "but I kept forgetting—I've just been so caught up in planning this party, I guess."

Is there such a thing as Presbyterian guilt? Because I could swear she's laying it on right now, thicker than fresh mozzarella on my mother's lasagna.

"Then the other night the girls asked me about it, and they were so earnest and adorable I said yes. I was sure you wouldn't mind, Aunt Tracey," Wilma says cheerfully, and gives me a big hard squeeze. "After all, the more the merrier—that's what Jack said your philosophy is about your bridal party, and I think that's very refreshing."

No, mojitos are very refreshing.

And man, could I use one right now.

"Wilma," I begin....

But before my future mother-in-law discovers that Aunt Tracey is actually a bitch on wheels, my grandmother appears out of nowhere, looking distressed. She's toting that shopping bag again and it's starting to tear from the weight of whatever is in it.

"Tracey, there you are! I need to talk to you."

"What's wrong, Grandma?"

"In private." She drags me—and the shopping bag—off to a distant corner near the corridor outside the restrooms. "I wanted this to be a surprise for you, so I hate to do this, but—"

She pulls something out of the bag and hands it to me.

I find myself holding a roll of toilet paper, and my flower-girl woes are instantly forgotten.

Oh, God, no wonder she hates to do this, poor thing.

And I certainly am surprised. Nobody said anything about Grandma having trouble with bowel control.

My first thought: she probably shouldn't be going around wearing hot pants, all things considered.

My next thought: it's probably time she went into a nursing home, where people are trained to handle this sort of thing and let her maintain her dignity.

My next: of all the people in this room, she chose *me*—the guest of honor—to wipe her?

But she's my grandmother and I love her, and I'm sure she did the same for me when I was a baby.

"Grandma," I say gently, and have to pause, a little choked up at how life comes full circle, "we should probably go into the ladies' room so that I can—"

"And here's the rest." She pulls something else out of the bag.

It seems to be a plastic doll—a stiff, generic version of a Barbie, the kind you buy at the dollar store. She's wearing a hand-crocheted frilly white veil and matching dress with a huge, droopy ruffled skirt.

Grandma lifts the skirt, plunks her unbending plastic-doll legs down into the core of the toilet-paper roll I'm holding, and smooths the skirt over the roll.

"I made it myself. What do you think?" Grandma asks.

I stare down at the bizarre object in my hand.

What do I think? I think I'm looking at some kind of twisted toilet-paper-cozy-meets-antebellum bride gone wrong.

"Well?" Grandma prods.

"It's...so..."

"Tacky?"

"Tacky? My God, no," I sputter. "Why would you think that?"

"Because your mother just said it was."

She *did?*

I look around and spot my mother heading in our direction. She's looking vaguely alarmed.

"Why," I ask Grandma, "would anyone say such a thing about this—this—creative homemade, um, creation?"

Which begs the additional question, why in the name of all that is good and holy would anyone *make* such a thing?

"Is this a present for me, Grandma?" I ask, eyeing the still-bulging bag a tad uneasily. "Because I love it!"

"I knew you would!" she says triumphantly—and snatches it back just as my mother arrives. "Connie, Tracey said everyone will love them."

"Pardon?" Uh-oh. An ominous thought has just appeared on the horizon.

"She made two dozen of those as party favors for tonight, to surprise you," my mother explains.

Two dozen? There are two dozen of these things?

"But once we got here and I saw how—fancy—the party is, I didn't think it would be right to hand them out."

"She doesn't think they're fancy enough," Grandma sneers.

"Well, they're very fancy," I say, fingering the doll's very *very* fancy ruffled skirt. "It's just—"

"I know what you're going to say. I didn't bring twenty-four rolls of toilet paper. Just this one, for an example, so they can see how it's supposed to work. They'll have to use their own T.P."

"I'm sure they won't mind, Grandma, but—"

"I know what you're going to say," she cuts in again. "There aren't enough of these to go around. Well, that's not my fault. I thought you said Jack had a small family," she adds accusingly.

"He does. Compared to ours." And if I had to guess, I'd say the vast majority of Jack's family—and our friends—probably aren't toilet-paper-cozy kind of folk.

"Well, I was thinking we could pull numbers to see who gets them, or give them away as door prizes," Grandma suggests, "or—"

"What are we talking about, girls?" That's Raphael, popping out of the men's room and sidling right into the conversation in his Raphael way. "Oh my God, what *is* that?"

"It's..." I falter helplessly.

"Oh, I love it!" Raphael grabs the toilet-paper bride out of my hand. "It's so kitschy! Tracey! Where did you get it?"

"I made it," Grandma says proudly.

Raphael screams with joy. "Of course you did, Grandma! I should have known!" Raphael hugs her. "You're the modern-day Martha Stewart!"

Okay, Martha Stewart is the modern-day Martha Stewart, and I wouldn't necessarily call my grandmother a modern-day anything. Nor can I imagine Martha crocheting two dozen bridal latrine dolls. But Raphael is gushing and Grandma is glowing, so who am I to rain on their little parade?

"Someday when you have time, Grandma," Raphael tells her, "I'd love it if you'd make one for me!"

"You can have one right now, Ralphie!"

"Are you serious, Grandma?"

Hugs abound; there is much rejoicing.

Never in the history of the world have two people been more delighted with each other.

I look at my mother, who turns her hands up a little, as if to say, "What do you want from me?"

"Tracey? The Carsons have to leave now." Wilma has penetrated our little huddle outside the ladies' room door, and she has a middle-aged couple in tow. "They wanted to ask you something about the wedding."

"Sure!" I aim a big, bright bridal smile at the Carsons,

Jack's childhood neighbors, who seem like nice people. "What is it?"

"We were just wondering how long a drive it is to get to your hometown—Buffalo, is it?"

"Brookside. It's about eight hours, give or take."

"Eight hours!" The Carsons exchange a glance.

"But it's an easy plane ride," my mother, the jet-setter, pipes up. "Just a hop, skip and a jump. We hope you can make it."

"We'll certainly try."

The Carsons and I do a couple of those double handshakes, each of us using both our hands to clasp both of the other person's hands—warmer and more intimate than a one-handed, businesslike handshake, but we're not on hugging terms yet.

Or maybe we won't ever be. I've noticed people don't hug as much in Jack's world as they do where I come from. Things are predictably more stiff and formal amid the country-estate crowd than among the country-bumpkin crowd.

Mr. Carson reaches into his pocket and takes out an envelope. "Congratulations."

"Oh, thank you!" These nice country-estate people just gave me a card....

And, good God, Grandma just gave these nice country-estate people a toilet-paper cozy.

"How...sweet." Mrs. Carson turns it over in her hands, not quite sure what to make of it, or of the batty old lady in the hot pants.

"I hope you like it," Grandma tells her a little huffily. "Too bad there aren't enough to go around."

Holy crap, Grandma! I silently scream. *Cut it out, would you!*

Mrs. Carson looks questioningly at Wilma, who smiles warmly at Grandma and asks, "Did you make it yourself, Theresa?"

"Yes." She lowers her head shyly, suddenly all fake-modest.

"Isn't she the *best?*" That, of course, comes from the president of Grandma's fan club.

Wilma and the Carsons agree with Raphael that Grandma is, indeed, the best.

Then the Carsons beat a hasty retreat, and my mother tells Wilma in a low voice, "I'm so sorry. She made them as party favors. I tried to tell her they were silly, but—"

"Not at all," Wilma returns with an easy smile. "I think it's really sweet. I wish my own mother had been that giving."

I want to point out that her own mother made my dream wedding possible, but I don't know if Jack told her that he sold his Disney stock, and I don't know if she'd mind that he did.

Turning to Grandma, Wilma says, "It was so nice of you to make those for the guests, Theresa. They're adorable!"

"But I don't have enough for everyone." Grandma can't resist sending a glare my way.

"Oh, that's all right. We'll just do first come, first serve," Wilma tells her.

"You mean first *leave,* first serve?" Grandma laughs hysterically at her—well, *joke* isn't really the word for it.

But Wilma, ever the good sport, chuckles. "Why don't you sit right in that comfy chair over there, Theresa, and hand them to people as they go."

Grandma is thrilled to death with that plan.

And you know what? I am right back to being thrilled to death with my future mother-in-law, Wilma.

So thrilled that I've instantly forgiven her for the flower-girl debacle and decide to consider—*maybe*—giving the twins from hell some kind of wedding duty—say, handing out programs.

I'm even more thrilled when, in the privacy of a ladies'-room stall, I peek at the engagement card the Carsons gave me and find an enclosed check for a hundred dollars.

Not only that, but as Jack's family and friends gradually make their way toward the door, I find myself holding more cards—presumably with more checks inside.

"I can't believe this," I whisper to Jack as yet another set of his relatives make their way out into the night, good-naturedly clutching their toilet-paper cozies. "Why are they all giving us money?"

"It's an engagement party. That's what people do."

"Not people in Brookside. It must be a local custom."

"Must be."

"We have our own local customs in Brookside," I say, watching Grandma explaining how the toilet-paper cozy works to an elegant-looking friend of Wilma's, who leaves wearing an affectionate smile.

At last, Grandma's shopping bag is empty, my purse is bulging with white envelopes and most of the guests are gone.

The party was a success, I'd say.

Wilma is my hero.

In fact—don't faint—Inner Tracey has almost convinced me to let the twins be flower girls after all. Along with Kelsey, of course. I mean, that's what Jesus would do, right, if he were a bride?

Brimming with bridal joy, I walk into the ladies' room.

It appears to be empty at first. Then I spot Jack's sister Emily, reapplying lipstick in the mirror in the far corner.

Uh-oh.

"There you are!" I say impulsively, as if I've been looking all over for her.

"Here I am." She doesn't smile or meet my gaze in the mirror.

I have to pee really badly, but instead of heading for the stall I step up beside Emily and manage to find my own lipstick in my purse without dumping any of the engagement-card booty onto the floor.

I normally don't put on fresh lipstick for a train ride home at this time of night, but I have to make things better with Emily somehow, because…

Well, again, what would Jesus do?

"Listen, Emily, I found out you've been really hurt because you thought—" *Wait…you thought?* "—that I didn't ask you to stand in the wedding…"

"You *didn't* ask me to stand in the wedding."

Right you are, Emily.

"God, I'm so sorry…I really thought I had!" I hear myself say. Huh? "Things have just been so crazy."

She's looking at me as if *I'm* crazy.

That makes two of us.

I quickly wipe the what-the-heck-am-I-doing? expression off my reflection's face. Then, to shut myself up, I get busy covering my mouth with a slick of frosted pink lipstick.

"You mean…you want me to be in the wedding?" Emily asks incredulously.

"You'd better be...I ordered you a dress!" There goes Inner Tracey, obviously having staged a coup. I scowl at the mirror and silently scold *Cut that out!*

"You ordered me a dress?" Emily asks.

I see Inner/Outer Tracey nodding vigorously, darn her. "Size two, right?"

Goodbye, Sonja.

Hello, Emily.

"Size two. Right. But..." She frowns. "I mean, wouldn't you have needed a deposit?"

"Oh, I've got your deposit covered." Beatific smile. I'm a bystander watching this tanned, white-draped all-but-unrecognizable Jesus-like creature take control of the bridesmaid situation and make it all better.

"I know you've been broke lately, so I didn't want to ask you for it."

A big, relieved grin spreads across Emily's face.

"Anyway, I'm really sorry for the misunderstanding," somebody—I swear it's not me—is telling Emily. "Of course I want you in the wedding. I would never leave you out."

"I didn't think so, but..." She shrugs and shakes her head. "Thanks, Tracey. I can't wait! It's going to be such a blast!"

"Yes!" I say. "A blast!"

Watching her leave the bathroom, I exhale shakily and look warily into the mirror.

She's gone.

Yup, that's me all right. Big, worried eyes, furrowed brow, clenched fists, emotionally drained.

Whoever would have imagined getting married could be so complicated?

Then again…at least the wedding-party issue is all straightened out now.

I'm adding three flower girls, but merely exchanging one bridesmaid for another. I'll send Sonja her hundred bucks back, care of Mae, and hope she gets it.

If she wants to get upset with me for kicking her out of the lineup, that's fine. Better her than Emily. I'm not going to be related to Sonja for the rest of my life.

Which reminds me…

Buckley never showed.

I wonder why.

12

"So you really want to know?"

That's Buckley, in response to my asking him—for the hundredth time this summer—why he didn't come to our engagement party back in June.

"Yes," I say, sipping from the cold Corona bottle in my hand. "I really want to know. But—" I hold up a finger and wag it in his direction, shaking my head "—I don't think you're going to tell me."

"Why not?"

"Because you always blow me off when I ask you about it. Why should today be any different?"

It's a sweltering August Sunday, late in the day. We're hanging on the beach in the Hamptons, where Jack's sister Rachel has a share in a house with a bunch of her friends. Everyone else—Jack, his friend Mitch, Rachel and her new boyfriend, Nick, and a bunch of their housemates—is still in the water.

Which is really choppy today. Not to mention freezing.

Even in the dog days of August, the sea here doesn't get much above seventy degrees. Apparently, Buckley and I are the lightweights of the group; we went in as far as our knees and returned promptly to the sand chairs and beer-stocked cooler. Here we sit comfortably beneath a bright blue umbrella watching the surf, with our bare legs sprawled before us in the hot sand, portable radio cranking U2.

"Today is definitely different," Buckley informs me mysteriously, and sips his own beer.

I find myself glancing down at an icy drop of condensation that's fallen from the bottle onto his bare, tanned chest.

Big mistake.

There I go again, being slightly attracted to my good friend Buckley.

I can't help it. Blame it on the inherent sexiness of the moment: Bono's wailing love song, all this bare sun-kissed skin, the pervasive scent of Coppertone. Our little patch of umbrella shade feels oddly intimate amid the glaring stretch of sand, with no one in earshot but a scavenging gull.

"Why?" I ask Buckley, glad I'm wearing sunglasses and he can't see my eyes drifting back to his chest.

"Why, what?" He's also wearing sunglasses, which makes me wonder where his eyes might be drifting.

Not to be vain, but…

Well, I'm looking pretty good lately. Better than I ever have—which is how it's supposed to be when you're getting married, right?

Buckley seemed kind of surprised when he first saw me this morning. It's been awhile; I've been busy with work and the wedding and he was busy finding a new place to live. There was no real reason to move, other than that he said he wanted a fresh start. Can't blame him for that.

Just before the Fourth of July, Jack and I helped him move into a great studio in Tribeca. Then he skipped town around the date he and Sonja would have been getting married. He went out to Long Island and visited his mother, then spent a few weeks with his sister in California. We've e-mailed, of course, but only sporadically.

Meanwhile, I've lost a few more pounds, mostly because of stress. But Brenda, Latisha and I have been doing this yoga class the agency is offering after work a few nights a week, so I feel more toned than I ever have before. And my fake tan, courtesy of Raphael, has developed into the real thing, thanks to a couple of beach weekends like this.

Look, I'm no beach bunny and I'm not wearing a bikini, by any means. But I have to say it's good to put on a bathing suit and not be tempted, for a change, to pull one of Jack's old T-shirts on over it.

"So…why is today different?" I ask Buckley.

"Because…there's no one else around right now. That's why."

"You can't discuss this with anyone else around?"

"Nope."

Hmm.

I probably should treat this topic like a sun-baked leather seat under a bare butt, and get off of it, pronto!

But you may have noticed I'm not the most prudent gal in town.

"Okay," I tell Buckley, after another swallow of icy

lime-tangy Corona, "Why didn't you come to our engagement party?"

"You really want to know."

"Yes, Buckley, I really want to know."

"I don't think you do."

I let out an exasperated sputter. "Yes! I do! Tell me!"

"Okay. Here goes..."

Suddenly, a banner-toting plane buzzes overhead, and we
both glance up at it, shielding our eyes.

I see that the sky is darker blue now, tinted with telltale
pinkish-orange. It's getting late.

I also see that the plane's banner reads: BRING ABATE
TO YOUR NEXT BAR-B-Q!!!

The copywriters at Blaire Barnett came up with countless
clever slogans for the Abate/Barbecue campaign, but that's the
one the Client chose. What a waste of creative talent.

I've been rethinking my plan to become an ad agency
copywriter lately. I don't know if I want to deal with arrogant
Clients and their ridiculous demands for the rest of my career.

I have no idea what I want to do instead—but I'm pretty
sure agency account management isn't it. It's great for now,
but after the wedding, when things settle down again and
it's time to think about moving out of our apartment, I
really have to give my career path some serious thought, too.

I turn to tell this to Buckley, then remember that we're
on the verge of a big breakthrough revelation here. My professional soul-searching can wait.

"Go on," I prod, wiggling my bare toes in the sand, "I'm
listening."

"Tracey, I swear to God...I love you."

"I love you, too," I say in return. "Even if you didn't show up for me on one of the most important nights of my life. So just tell me why—"

"No, that *is* why," he cuts in. "I just told you."

"What?"

Why am I not comprehending him? Is it heatstroke? The beer? Bride brain?

I wish I could see his eyes and get a clue.

"I love you," he says again. "That's why I didn't come to the party. Because I didn't want to watch you celebrating with Jack. I was out-of-my-mind jealous. Because I love you. I've loved you for a few years now. I could never do anything about it because we were both with other people. Okay?"

Whoa.

Now I'm glad I can't see his eyes, and I'm sure as hell glad he can't see mine.

Speechless, I just gape at him.

"I told you you didn't want to know," he says with a shrug, and sips his beer, turning to look out over the water.

I follow his gaze, wishing Jack and the others would come splashing back in to disrupt this insane conversation, but they're way out there, tiny dots in the waves.

"I don't know what to say," I tell Buckley at last.

"Yeah, I knew you wouldn't. I probably shouldn't have told you, but...my sister said I should be honest with you. Just in case...you feel the same way."

"What?" I'm floundering, so far over my head that I might as well be out there in the surf.

Buckley takes a deep breath and looks at me again. This time, for real: he props his sunglasses over his forehead.

What I see in his green eyes takes my breath away.

"Tracey, I've never known anyone like you. You're clever and big-hearted and gentle and crazy and magnetic. Sometimes when we're together, just hanging out talking and joking around, you have no idea that I'm thinking about grabbing you and kissing you. And that I wish I could just grab your hand and run away with you."

The first wave—that heartfelt *I love you*—knocked me off my feet and now they just keep on washing over me, pulling me in way over my head.

"Buckley," I say hoarsely, "no. You can't..."

"I know." He nods. "I can't. But I do."

I turn to look at Jack. He's a speck on the horizon at the moment.

He has no idea that my friend—that our friend—Buckley is in love with me.

But I knew.

That's what I realize.

Maybe I wouldn't have used the word *love*. But deep down, I did know all along that Buckley had unresolved feelings for me.

Just as deep down, I have unresolved feelings for him.

Which we both need to resolve, right here. Right now. Because...

"I'm getting married," I say firmly, "in less than two months, and—"

"No, I know. Enough said." His sunglasses are back on. He resolutely lifts his beer bottle to his lips.

"No, *not* enough said. I mean, you haven't said anything at all, except that..."

"I love you. Yeah—" his laugh is as bitter as the hunk of lime in my Corona "—I think that's way more than enough."

"But...what did you expect me to say to that?"

"Nothing." He reaches for the cooler on the sand between us. "I didn't expect you to say anything. I just needed to say it." His empty bottle lands in the cooler with a clanking sound, and he retrieves another bottle.

I watch him looking around for the opener.

"Here," I say, handing him Jack's shoe, discarded earlier in the sand by my chair.

"Huh?"

"It has a bottle opener built into the sole."

Buckley just looks at it.

"Go ahead."

"I don't know. Is it bad form to open your beer with a guy's shoe when you've just told his girlfriend you're in love with her?" he asks then, and his mouth quirks with a wry smile.

Instantly, the mood is lightened. Thank God.

I laugh a little.

So does he.

"No," I say. "I don't think it's bad form. Open your beer, Buckley. And open one for me while you're at it."

He does.

"Fiancée," I say, trading my nearly empty bottle for the icy one he hands me.

"What?"

"I'm Jack's fiancée. You said girlfriend."

Silence.

"You know I'm going to marry Jack, Buckley, don't you?"

He nods. "That's what I told my sister."

"You talked to your sister about me?"

"Yeah. You came up a lot, actually, while I was out in L.A."

"Because…"

"Because she wanted to know why I wasn't getting married, and I told her."

"What?"

"You're not the only reason I broke up with Sonja, Trace," he says quickly. "Just part of it."

"Does she know?" I ask, trying to take this all in. "Sonja?"

He hesitates.

"Yeah," he says reluctantly. "She knows. I probably shouldn't have told her, but I did."

"That would explain why she never acknowledged the engagement party invitation. And she cashed the check I sent back to her for the bridesmaid dress last month, so I know she's still alive."

"I'm really sorry you went through all that with her," Buckley says apologetically.

We sip our beer in silence, listening to the waves and the gulls and the Edge's wailing guitar riff.

I think about how, just a few months ago, he was planning to marry Sonja and she and I were making plans to be a suburban foursome someday.

Maybe Buckley was thinking the same thing…only we'd be a suburban swinging foursome?

Nah.

He's as much a one-woman man as I am a one-man woman….

Which I am, aren't I?

Of course I am.

Otherwise, I wouldn't have sent Buckley packing way back when I realized I cared so much about Jack.

Jack is The One.

Buckley is…well, The One Too Many.

"So what do you want me to do with this?" I finally ask Buckley. "Just file it away and forget about it…?"

"That would be good."

"…because I don't think I can. We should resolve this."

"Resolve what? I've got feelings for you, you're about to marry someone else. I'd say that's pretty much resolved."

"No, I mean…it's not just you." I can't believe I just said that. In a mere whisper, but I said it, and he must have heard, because I can feel him gaping at me from behind his shades.

"Before I make the wrong assumption here…can you elaborate?"

"You're not the only one who—"

Nope. I can't say it.

"You mean you feel…?" Buckley can't, either.

"Something. Yeah."

I know what you're thinking, but look, I'm just being honest here.

Because that's what Jesus would do.

Oh, who am I kidding?

"Oh my God." The words rush out of Buckley on a gust of hope and I realize I've made a gargantuan mistake.

"But Buckley," I say quickly, "that doesn't change anything."

"It does. For me, it does. Just knowing—"

"It can't," I say firmly. "It can't change anything. I mean…yes, I'm attracted to you. But I'm not in love with you."

He winces.

"Maybe there was a time when I could have been, if I had let myself." I've softened my tone, fighting the urge to reach out and touch his arm. "But that wasn't supposed to happen."

"How do you know?"

"Because it didn't. And because I'm in love with Jack."

He winces again.

"Yeah. Okay." He plunks his beer bottle into the sand, sticks his feet into his flip-flops, and abruptly stands up.

"Where are you going?"

"For a walk on the beach."

"Should I come?" I start to look around for my own flip-flops.

Then Buckley says, "No."

And walks away.

"Do you ever think about what either of us would be doing if we had never met?" I ask Jack late one night a week later, when we're sitting at the table addressing three hundred envelopes.

Yes, three hundred.

That's how many people we're inviting. It really was a compromise, I swear.

I read in *Modern Bride* that you should count on two thirds of your guests showing up, so by inviting three hundred, we're actually throwing a wedding for two-hundred.

Forget that Jack's ideal number was fifty guests, tops.

I didn't say the compromise was an even split.

Fifty is just completely unrealistic. I mean, the wedding party alone eats up almost half of that number.

Anyway, we're not as worried about the guest list now that we've banked several thousand dollars courtesy of that engagement party Wilma threw for us.

We even booked a Tahitian honeymoon—another compromise.

Really, it is. I agreed to trade the hut-on-stilts for the less exotic but more affordable Sheraton.

So lately, life is overall pretty good, if a little more hectic than I'd like. All right, a lot more hectic.

I fully expect Jack to ask me why he would even be thinking about what we'd be doing if we'd never met—which is, of course, the safest answer.

But he doesn't say that.

He seems instead to be giving my question serious thought.

In fact, I address an entire envelope to Mr. and Mrs. Benjamin Sellers of Armonk, New York, whoever they are—Wilma's friends, I presume—in the time it takes Jack to come up with a suitable answer to my question.

Well, an answer, anyway: "I guess we'd both be with other people."

"Really?" I'm stunned, I must say. "Why do you think that?"

"I don't know…what did you want me to tell you?"

"I didn't want you to tell me anything specific. I'm just surprised you can see yourself with somebody else."

"You said if we had never met. Not now." He sounds a little defensive.

"No, I know!"

"What, you *can't* see yourself with somebody else?"

An image of Buckley pops into my head.

"No way," I say firmly, shoving Buckley out.

"So you think there's just one right person for you in the world? And I'm it?" Jack grins and reaches for another envelope.

"Don't you think that?"

He tilts his head.

"You don't," I accuse.

"Not really. I think it all comes down to timing."

Yeah, I guess I pretty much think that, too.

But I'm afraid to agree aloud.

"So you're saying that if you and I weren't together, we'd both still be out there looking for each other?" Jack asks.

"I'm just glad I found you. That's all I know."

Jack reaches across the stacks of envelopes and pulls me close. "Me, too."

I find myself wishing he were more the romantic type; that he'd told me I'm the only woman in the world for him. That it isn't about timing; it's about true love.

Maybe it's not realistic, and maybe neither of us believes it, but it would be nice to hear anyway.

In all this disruptive wedding planning, I can't help but feel like something—some part of who we were, or are, or wanted to be—has been…well, not lost, exactly. At least I hope not. More like temporarily misplaced.

And I really hope we can get it back.

"Oh my Gawd, Tracey. You look—"

I'm sure big-eyed, big-haired Brenda, who is perched on a cushiony red bench nearby, said *go-aw-jus*, but I blanked out for a second there.

Staring at myself in the mirror of the bridal salon, I'm pretty much stunned.

Suddenly, I really look—and feel—like a bride.

That's because, for the first time, I've brought my head-piece to the fitting. Jeannie made it and it's beautiful. Instead of illusion, she used a piece of exquisite French lace. It falls from a silk-covered comb: simple, old-fashioned and very unique. I even put my hair up in a bun to simulate how I'll have it done on our wedding day.

In this gown, with a veil on my head, I've gone all Natalie Wood in *West Side Story,* dreamy and swoony and I-feel-pretty.

"We'll have to take it in some more here," says Milagros around a couple of pins clenched in her mouth. She bunches some fabric at the waist. "See? You lost weight again."

So I did. A couple of pounds, by the looks of it.

"You really are getting so skinny, Tracey," Brenda says, shaking her head. "Be careful. You don't want to get anorexic."

"I'm not anorexic," I tell her. "Just...too busy to eat, mostly. And...you know...it's wedding stress."

Brenda nods. "I remember what that was like. It feels like there's so much to think about, and worry about, right? But don't wish it away, okay? Because someday you'll just have mortgage stress and baby stress and trust me, that's not as much fun."

"I'll be right back, ladies." Milagros bustles away to the back room, leaving the two of us alone.

"This stress isn't much fun, either," I tell Brenda. "I quit smoking months ago and lately, I've been craving a cigarette. Not that I'm going to start up again."

"Don't you dare. Your wedding is going to be great. You shouldn't worry so much."

I stare at myself in the mirror, toying with the edge of my veil. I look worried. Probably because I *am* worried.

"What?"

I look over at Brenda. "What?"

"Something's wrong. Oh my Gawd, Tracey, you're not having second thoughts, are you?"

"No!" I frown at her. "I'm fine."

"Are you sure? Because you don't look fine."

"That's because I'm not." I want to sag onto the nearest bench, but I'm under strict orders from Milagros not to sit and crush the gown.

"Oh my Gawd, you poor thing. What's wrong?" Brenda is up and at my side, touching my arm. "It's not too late, you know."

Too late for what?

Labor Day has come and gone; it's been several weeks since Buckley made his seaside confession. Neither of us ever said another word about it; by the time he got back from his walk, the others were out of the water, the sun was sinking fast and we were packing up to go. He was quiet the whole drive back to the city, but I don't think anyone else noticed.

I haven't seen him since. We've spoken on the phone a couple of times, but we both carefully avoided mentioning what happened that day.

Still, it's been gnawing at me.

Not nonstop.

For the most part, I really am too busy with work and the wedding machine to do much of anything—eat, think, sleep.

But it does hit me every so often:

Buckley is in love with me.

Buckley is hurting.

And, frankly, so am I.

But mostly for him, because he's the one who's alone.

I'm as sure of my love for Jack as I've always been... although it does bother me that our relationship has been so matter-of-fact ever since our future together was sealed with a ring. I guess taking each other for granted is just naturally what happens after a few years, especially when you've both pledged that you're going to be there for each other forever. I mean, it's only natural, right?

Still, I can't help but crave a little less predictability; a little more good old-fashioned romance. Candlelight dinners once in a while, maybe. Champagne. Roses. Poetic words.

"Do you want to back out of the wedding?" Brenda asks me. "Is that it? Because there's still time if you aren't sure—"

"No!" I shake my head vehemently. "I'm sure. I love Jack, and I want to marry Jack. Period."

No.

Not period.

"It's just...okay, Bren, if I ask you something, do you swear you'll tell me the truth, and do you swear you won't tell another soul that I asked this question?"

"I sway-uh," she says solemnly.

"You love Paulie, right?"

Her plucked-thin pencil-darkened brows furrow. "That's the question?"

"No, I mean...you do, right? You love him?"

"Of course. He's my husband."

"So do you ever… I mean, have you ever… Okay, were you ever attracted to another guy?"

"Yeah." She nods. "Tony, my old neighbor. We grew up together. But we were mostly just friends. Why?"

"Mostly?"

She gives me a sly smile. "We might've fooled around a little once or twice on the Fourth of July. There was always a block party, and you know…"

"Fireworks?" I grin.

"Yup."

"But this was before you met Paulie, right? That's not what I mean."

She hedges. "Nope. It was during Paulie." *Po-awww-lie,* she says it. Her accent gets more prounounced when she's nervous.

"Brenda!"

"What? He's gorgeous, Tracey, I swear." It takes me a second to decipher. *He's go-aw-jus, Tracey, I sway-ah* is how it comes out in her thick accent.

"I'll bet he is, but…you cheated on Paulie?"

"Not when we were married! I've known Paulie forever, remember? We've been going out since we were in junior high."

"Oh…so this Tony thing was when you were in junior high, then?"

"Mostly," she says cryptically. "And high school."

I raise an eyebrow.

"And then there was one last time after that," she admits. "When we were in college. One last hurrah. But when Paulie and I got engaged, that was it."

"You never hooked up with Tony again?"

"Tracey! What do you think I am? I'm married!" She tilts her head at me.

"But...? I smell a but."

"No buts. I don't commit adultery."

"I didn't think you did."

"And it doesn't count if you fantasize once in a while."

Aha!

"I mean...Tony's a fireman. He looks like he should be in one of those hot-firemen calendars, you know?"

"So you mean you're still attracted to him even now that you have a husband?"

"Hell, yeah. I'm married. Not dead."

Hallelujah.

Brenda and Paulie have one of the healthiest marriages I've ever seen. If she's not immune to the charms of a smokin'-hot fireman despite a ring on her finger, there's hope for me.

"Does Paulie know about this?"

"About what?"

"That you think Tony is...you know, hot."

"Are you sick? No, Paulie doesn't know. And I swear to God, Tracey, if you ever say anything in front of him—"

"I won't! I promise!"

"Why are you asking me all this, anyway?"

"No reason," I say airily.

Which normally wouldn't let me off the hook with her, but Milagros comes scurrying back in just then, and the subject is effectively dropped.

"Tracey? It's me."

Me, who? Oh...

"Will?"

"You didn't recognize my voice?"

"Uh, no." Aware that obscurity is the ultimate insult to Will McCraw, I probably should apologize.

Maybe the old Tracey, his ex-girlfriend, would have done that.

But you know what? I haven't felt like Will's ex-girlfriend in ages. That time in my life is so long ago and far away that I can barely remember what it felt like to be hung up on someone who didn't give a damn about me.

What a pleasant surprise. I've grown up and moved on. Yay, me.

Shuffling papers on my desk in search of a report I need for a meeting in about five minutes, I nearly knock over the half-full cup of cold coffee that's still on my desk from this morning. Crazy day, as usual.

"I guess it's been awhile," Will says.

"I guess it has. So how are you?"

"I'm good. Back from Transylvania."

Oh! Right! Transylvania!

How long has it been since I've even thought about that? Or him?

Well, it's about time I got to that point, wouldn't you say? We've been broken up for over three years now.

But I never have been very good at putting things behind me and not looking back. I guess I just don't like endings. Even those that are long overdue.

"How was your show?" I ask, finding the report and tucking it into a folder.

"It was great. I'm sure you were wondering why I wasn't back before now—"

Um, no.

"—but they extended our run a few times. I may be going back after the holidays, which would be terrific."

Terrific. Transylvania in the dead of winter.

"Listen, Will, I'm glad you're back, but I've got this meeting and—"

"The guy who was subletting my apartment didn't do a great job forwarding my mail while I was away," he cuts in. "Some of it got lost in the shuffle. So I was just wondering about the invitation to your wedding."

He was? Uh-oh.

"You're still getting married in October, right, Tracey?"

"Right." *But you're not invited.*

Just tell him, urges Inner Tracey, clearly over Will at last.

But I hedge. "The third weekend in October. In Brookside."

"So the invitations must have gone out then…"

"Right."

Tell him!

I should…but that would be quite a blow to him.

So? How many times did he hurt your feelings?

"I knew it. I didn't get my invitation," he says, sounding a little put out. "It must be on its way to Transylvania. I swear, I told—"

"No, you didn't get an invitation because you're not on the list, Will."

Silence.

"You're kidding…right?"

"No," I say firmly. "I'm not."

"But—I mean, you and I have been friends for years, Tracey."

Not really. We were much more than friends for the first few years, and far less than that for the last few.

"You're not inviting me to your wedding?"

"I'm sorry, Will."

"Oh, I get it," he says. "Is your fiancé jealous?"

"Of you?"

"I guess that makes sense," says Will, who is undoubtedly imagining Jack, green with envy over my past with an international stage sensation such as himself.

"No, it's not that. We really just had to limit the guest list," I say, and suddenly, I feel like a little girl who's been dragging around a flaccid balloon on a string, a sorry relic from some long-ago birthday party.

"So you cut me off the list?" he asks incredulously.

"Actually—you were never on it."

Silence.

"I've got to get to that meeting," I say, knowing that if I leave it like this—if we hang up now—I'll never hear from him again in my life. It would be the end of an era.

"Okay, then…" he says a little awkwardly.

"Goodbye, Will," I say.

And I hang up, letting go of Will McCraw at last…for good.

"What do you think of my fixing up Billy's sister with Buckley?" Kate asks casually a few days later.

I look up, startled, from the pile of white onesies we're folding. She got them—and a truckload of other layette loot—for her baby shower earlier that afternoon.

"I think that's a really bad idea," I tell her.

"What? Why? He seems so lonely lately, don't you think?"

"I don't know…I haven't seen much of him. Have you?"

"Billy and I ran into him at the movies the other night. He was there alone. We asked him to sit with us, but he said no. I think he's depressed."

And I think he, like the rest of us, isn't overly fond of Billy. But of course I can't say that to Kate.

"Amanda's boyfriend just dumped her," she says, referring to Billy's sister, a snobby, elegant ash blonde who was here for the shower. "I think she and Buckley would be perfect for each other."

"Why?" I ask sharply.

Kate shrugs and reaches past her cute basketball-like bump to add another onesie to the towering pile in the wicker laundry basket. "She's pretty, he's cute, he's romantic and good at wining and dining women. They're both single, and neither of them is really into settling down…"

"Buckley would be, if the right person came along."

"No, he wouldn't. Not now, anyway. Buckley can't commit to anyone—or anything, for that matter. Not a job, not even a lease. He bounces around the city freelancing, moving from apartment to apartment. Tracey, he has a lot of growing up to do."

I never thought of it that way.

She's right.

"I think I'll ask him to come to dinner and have Amanda here, too," Kate muses.

"No, she's really not his type." I shake my head. In response to her questioning look, I elaborate, "He's so down to earth. She's not. She's on the rebound—"

"So is he. And she's very down to earth, when you get to know her."

"Kate, she got you a thousand-dollar baby carriage imported from France. And she thinks you should name your baby Amadeus if it's a boy. She is not down-to-earth."

"Well, Sonja wasn't all that down-to-earth, either."

"Exactly."

"What do you mean?"

"Sonja wasn't right for him. Buckley likes down-to-earth girls. He likes…"

No. Don't say it.

"Me. He likes *me*, Kate."

Why did I say that?

"Actually…he *loves* me, Kate."

Why did I say *that?*

I wait for her to freak out.

"Um, yeah. No kidding," is all she says.

"What?" I gape at her, an unfolded onesie dangling from my fingertips.

"Hello? Don't tell me you never knew that."

"No, I didn't know that! Kate! How did you know? Did he say something?"

"No! It's just obvious. And I'm sure I'm not the only one who ever noticed it."

"I hope Jack didn't."

"Nah. Men are clueless about stuff like that. Jack wouldn't have Buckley standing in your wedding if he thought he had a thing for you, would he?"

"God, no. No way."

We fold in silence for a few seconds.

Then Kate asks, "So if you never realized Buckley was into you, how do you suddenly know now?"

"He told me."

Her jaw drops. "Really."

"Really."

"What did he say, exactly?"

"He said 'I love you.' And some other really sweet things."

"To which you said…?"

"I'm marrying Jack. I love Jack."

She nods. "Good. You did the right thing. Buckley's not husband material. Jack is."

"But…"

"But…?"

"Sometimes I see Buckley and I feel kind of…wistful."

"Yeah. That's how I feel sometimes, too—not lately, though," she says with a laugh, patting her rounded stomach.

"You're attracted to Buckley?" I must say, I am shocked.

"Lord-a-mercy, no! I'm attracted to Gabriel. My personal trainer."

Okay, not so shocked. I've seen Gabriel. Lord-a-mercy is right.

"God, I miss him," Kate says. "I swear, the second this baby is out, I'm so *there*."

"You mean…?"

She nods. "Back at the gym."

"Oh! I thought you meant—you know."

"Tracey! I would never cheat on Billy."

"So you're just attracted to Gabe, but you wouldn't do anything about it?"

"No way. Plus, he's a huge flirt."

"So are you."

"Exactly." She flashes a salacious grin. "Look, it's human nature to want what we can't have. But when you come right down to it, it's all harmless, as long as you don't act on it."

That's pretty much what Brenda said.

And it's what I believe, deep down.

Being attracted to Buckley even though I'm on the verge of marrying Jack isn't a bad omen. It doesn't mean I'm destined to become the Vinnie of our marriage a few years down the road.

I guess I just always expected that if you were married—or about to be married—you were supposed to be oblivious to all other members of the opposite sex.

Which really makes no sense whatsoever, because physical attraction stems, at least in part, from chemistry and biology, right?

Right.

And a ring appearing on your finger doesn't have an overnight impact on your chemical or biological self, right?

Of course right.

Why did it take me so long to figure this out? No wonder I stunk at science back in school.

Anyway, I can now accept that I'm destined to live monogamously ever after with Jack—and the occasional pesky but meaningless flicker of unacted-upon attraction for other guys.

The only question now is, can Buckley and I salvage our friendship?

I honestly have no idea. I've made my peace with it; the rest is going to be up to him.

13

"What if my plane crashes?"

That's me, talking to Jack in the wee-hour post-lovemaking darkness of a late-September Saturday, my head against his bare chest.

"Don't be ridiculous," he murmurs, but his arms seem to protectively tighten around me. "Who would even say something like that?"

"I would."

"Well, why?"

I don't know. I should be ecstatic. I'm getting married, I'm looking good, I've got a great job...

Why am I feeling so anxious lately?

"Maybe because for once in my life everything is about to fall into place," I muse aloud. "I'm so afraid something's going to come along and rip it apart."

Jack laughs softly. "That's my girl. The eternal optimist." The laugh evolves into a deep yawn.

"I'm serious, Jack. Maybe I shouldn't go up to Buffalo tomorrow."

"You mean today."

"Right—today." The digital clock by our bed reads 1:30 a.m. I have to be up and en route to the airport in four hours. I should be sleeping, not stressing.

"All right," Jack says drowsily, "so don't go."

"I *have* to go. They're throwing me a shower. I'm the guest of honor."

It's going to be held at the Beaver Club, of course. Most Precious Mother was booked for the day.

A shower at the Beaver Club is fine with me, particularly since only the women on my side of the wedding were invited. Jack's sisters are throwing me a shower here next weekend. At Tavern on the Green.

"So go," Jack advises me. "You'll be fine."

"You don't know that for sure. What if I crash and die? You won't even be a widower. They'll probably list you in my obituary as 'special friend' or something."

"Were you always this morbid?"

"Yes. You were just too crazy in love to notice."

He snorts but holds me closer still.

I think about how safe I feel with him; how lucky we are to have found each other; how much I love him.

When was the last time I even told him any of that?

It's been awhile.

And it's not like he goes around rhapsodizing about me, either.

Things have been so crazy lately, sometimes it feels like we just run past each other a few times a day and never even have a chance to talk, let alone sit still and absorb this tremendous step we're about to take.

Presuming everything goes as planned, that is.

It all seems so precarious all of a sudden. Like anything can happen between now and our wedding day. It can all evaporate, just like that.

I'm not morbid, really. Just…incredibly vulnerable for some reason.

Suddenly, I feel this tremendous need to reach out to Jack emotionally, to have a romantic moment, the way we used to. One that isn't just about the wedding. Or sex.

"Jack," I say softly into the darkness, "if anything happens to me, I want you to know that I'm happier with you than I ever thought was possible. And that I think our life together is going to be really great. I mean, obviously if I'm dead that can't happen, but it's what I want to happen. I love you more than anything else in the world. Without you in my life, I'd be… You just… I don't know how to say it—you make me feel complete. You complete me. Wait, I think I just stole that line from some movie. Which movie was it?"

Silence.

"I don't know, either," I say quickly, not wanting to ruin the moment with an entertainment brain teaser. "Anyway, all I want is for us to get married, and now that it's finally going to happen, I'm just so afraid something's going to go wrong, or I'm going to wake up tomorrow morning and find out I dreamed you, and all of this."

Silence.

"Jerry Maguire," I suddenly remember. "That was the movie. Jack?"

Snoring sound.

Oh, geez.

Did he really just sleep through my big romantic heartfelt speech?

I punch him in the arm, which jolts him awake.

"What? What's wrong?"

"You missed my big romantic heartfelt speech!"

"I did? Sorry. I'm sleeping. What was it?"

I sigh. "Never mind. Forget it."

"No, tell me."

"I love you," I say simply. "That was pretty much the gist of it."

"Oh." He yawns, his warm breath stirring my hair. "I love you, too."

And it's almost like it used to be—me and Jack, cozy, content, drifting off to sleep in each other's arms.

My plane doesn't crash.

That's the good news.

The bad news: thanks to a hometown bridal registry mix-up, I'm now the proud owner of, among other things: twenty-seven place settings, four food processors and eight identical sets of striped twin sheets.

"Good for you," my aunt Aggie called from her table when I opened the first set. "Your uncle Mario and I have slept in twin beds for forty-three years of marriage."

"Actually, we don't—I mean, we aren't going to—have twin beds," I told her as Cousin Joanie commandeered the package bow and started fastening it to the paper-plate bonnet she's making. "But," I added hastily, "these sheets will be great for our guest room!"

Yes. The imaginary guest room with twin beds that's just off the imaginary formal dining room where we're going to store all this china.

Now, ninety minutes and almost as many boxes and bows into this age-old bridal-shower gift ritual, the paper-plate bonnet is towering higher than the stacks of boxes on the table to my right—and I'm trying to figure out what to say to the third domed cake stand I've received—none of which were on my registry. Funny, the items people assume are crucial to establishing a household.

"Thank you, Mrs. Antonelli," I call graciously, holding it up so that everyone can see it and my mother can snap a picture, which she's been doing for every gift. "Jack and I just love cake!"

Yes, so I make three at a time. And have been so longing to display them on elaborate pedestal plates under etched glass!

"Oh, and you included a recipe for your tomato-soup-may-onnaise chocolate cake," I notice, blinking from the flashbulb.

"Use it in good health," Mrs. Antonelli calls back to me, and I assure her that I will. Tomato-soup-mayonnaise chocolate cake. Mmm, mmm healthy!

To my left, Mary Beth is dutifully adding *Cake Plate & recipe—Mrs. Antonelli* to the massive list of gifts she's keeping. That will come in handy when I sit down to write a hundred thank-you notes in my endless hours of spare time.

To my right, my sisters-in-law are unwrapping the next box like a well-oiled assembly line. What, you thought the bride opens her own presents? Not here in Brookside, where local rituals abound.

Here's one: over my head is the clubhouse's mounted beaver head—and it's wearing a little white veil in honor of my shower.

Here's another: in front of me is a sea of expectant faces.

No, not just because they're dying to get a look at the next place setting or cake plate. They're expectant because they're playing bridal bingo, and they want to win, dammit.

That was my cousin Donna's idea. She handed out cards to all eighty guests, along with packets of M&Ms to use as markers. On each square is a random item a bride might typically receive for her shower: blender, toaster, towel set, etc.

"They do it at all the showers now. It'll be fun—you'll see," Donna said earlier, in response to my dubious expression.

Not with this crowd. These women—many of whom are Most Precious Mother parishioners—take their bingo very seriously. At this point, most of the guests have only a couple of squares covered, and the plastic laundry basket full of fabulous wrapped prizes—which my sister picked up down at the dollar store—sits unclaimed.

I lift the lid of the next box and peek inside.

"Ooh," I say, mustering excitement, "a food processor."

"Did you say garbage can?" Aunt Aggie calls hopefully, an M&M poised over her bingo card.

"No—" I hold it up and smile for the camera "—food processor."

"What are you going to do with that?" Grandma asks with her usual tact. "That's the third one you got!"

Fourth, but who's counting?

"Thank you, Aunt Mary," I say cheerfully, ever the courteous guest of honor. "Jack and I love…"

To process food.

Or something like that.

My face hurts from this idiot-gaping grin, and I'm appreciative but really hope all this stuff can be exchanged.

Mary Beth writes down *Food Processor—Aunt Mary.*

Michaela hands me another box.

I open the lid. "Ooh," I say, "sheets!"

"Did she say garbage can?" Aunt Aggie asks.

No. Sheets. More sheets. Sheets galore.

And another cake plate.

One more place setting.

Then, just to shake things up a little:

A garbage *disposal?*

"Bingo!" Aunt Aggie bellows.

"That's a garbage disposal, Aggie," Grandma says, "not a garbage can."

"Well, who ever heard of a garbage can at a wedding shower?" Aunt Aggie replies. "That's what I want to know."

Who ever heard of a garbage disposal at a wedding shower? That's what *I* want to know. Did we register for this? No! I bet somebody's regifting it. I can only hope it's not used.

"Give Aunt Aggie a prize," I tell my niece Kelsey, whose job is to man the plastic laundry basket.

"But it's not a garbage can, Aunt Tracey."

"It's close enough," I mutter, and hold up the box. "Thank you, Snooky and Marie. Jack and I…"

Love to dispose of our garbage?

I mean, what am I supposed to say to this?

I'm saved as I smile obligingly when Ma aims her camera in my direction.

What I wouldn't give to be back home on my couch in sweats right now, with a big box of Choc-Chewy-O's and a good movie on TV. Better yet, a bad movie on TV.

There's really something to be said for the mundane rhythm of daily life.

And this bride stuff is not all it's cracked up to be, that's for sure. It was fun in the beginning, but at this point I almost wish the wedding would hurry up and get here—and get over with.

Almost?

When the last gift has been opened and I'm posing in my paper-plate bonnet amid dozens of flashbulbs, I realize I'm more than ready to stop being the bride.

I just want…

I don't know. Some serious Couch Time would be good. A conversation with Jack about something other than the wedding would be good. A meal I don't have to gobble on my feet, a Saturday morning to sleep in late, a day without a checklist…all good.

I desperately want my life to get back to normal.

But we still have a few more weeks left to go before normal can even become a speck on the Spadolini-Candell horizon.

Have you ever tried to fit 267 assorted family and friends into twenty-five tables of eight?

I'm no math whiz, but let me assure you, it cannot be done.

As it turns out, the famous 2/3 *Modern Bride* rule does not apply in Brookside, New York. In Brookside, we seem to have the ⁴/₃ rule, where not only does everyone accept the invitation, but they RSVP with added-on dates and/or children. The words *Adult Reception*—or the absence of the words *And Guest*—means absolutely nothing to these people.

"Ma, I didn't invite Joanie with a date," I explain for the gazillionth time when my mother calls to say, "Great news! Cousin Joanie has a new boyfriend and he's going to come to the wedding!"

"Tracey, she's family!" Ma protests. "And this is her first love. We're all so relieved she's found someone. You're going to tell her she can't bring him?"

Her tone makes it clear that I've already inflicted enough pain on poor Joanie, who is crushed that she doesn't get to be the junior bridesmaid and only grudgingly agreed to hand out programs before the ceremony.

"What's one more guest?" Ma wants to know.

"Ma, everyone is bringing at least one more guest. Bruce and Angie Cardolino are bringing their two kids and Michaela's brother and his wife are bringing four."

"You were always invited to weddings when you were little. Don't you remember waltzing balanced on Grandpa's feet?"

Yes. I do remember that, and I even grow momentarily misty at the recollection.

Then I get over it and say, "I have no idea where we're going to put all these people."

"Kids don't take up much room and they eat like birds. It'll be fine."

Yeah, but each of those birds still requires a chair and, according to the caterer, a fifty-dollar plate of food.

What would Jesus do?

Suck it up and spring for the extra guests, I suppose.

Jesus probably wouldn't get revenge by seating Cousin Joanie and her first love at a table with little Joey and the twins from hell, but what can I say? I'm a mere mortal.

I have to get Charles the banquet manager to add on a bunch of extra tables, which helps...a little.

I spend every night for a week moving three hundred Post-It notes around in a vast diagram on a poster board taped to our living-room wall, as Jack makes helpful comments like, "Don't seat Fat Naso next to Kate—he might crush her," and "Don't seat Raphael and Donatello near the church ladies."

It's like working a giant puzzle that refuses to fit together, but in the end I almost get it.

I say almost because there's one table strictly comprised of various strays—my parents' neighbors the Gilberts, Rev Dev, Aldo and Bud, Aunt Aggie and Jimmy the doorman with his date (I gave him a legitimate *And Guest* because he's coming so far and doesn't know a soul).

Relieved to have that monumental task completed, I send the final head count and seating plan off to Charles—who calls a few days later to tell me that I made a mistake and each of the tables seat ten, not eight.

I'm sure Jesus wouldn't hang up the phone, scream the F-word and sob into a bottle of cheap Pinot Noir.

But I'd like to see Jesus plan a wedding. I really would.

Jack and I are spending dawn to dusk on this gorgeous October Saturday in a dank basement of a Catholic church on the Lower East Side. Joining us are twenty or so other engaged couples and two middle-aged pairs of husbands and wives who are leading this marriage boot camp: aka Pre Cana class.

What a bummer. I'd rather be anywhere other than here this morning. Couch would be great. Bed would be better.

I got two hours of sleep last night—I was in Des Moines on Client business and my flight home was ridiculously late because of thunderstorms. To make matters worse, so is my period. Ridiculously late, that is. Not because of thunderstorms.

No, I don't think I'm pregnant. Jack and I are too busy and tired for much of a sex life lately, so that's not very likely. It's probably just stress.

Needless to say, I'm feeling a little short-tempered today. And these Pre Cana people are making it worse.

The leaders, of course, are oh-so-happily married. Like, freakishly happily married. Their job is to enlighten us all to the joys and responsibilities of a Catholic marriage. But frankly, I'm finding it hard to relate to these Stepford spouses on any level.

It would help if they were even the slightest bit hip, but they're buttoned up and preternaturally upbeat. It's hard to imagine any of them ever having had a good healthy argument with their spouse, let alone sex. I mean, sexual re-lations. Which we discussed earlier in the day, during a seminar called—ick—The Marital Bed. Considering that the class doctrine was handed down by a group of men who are forbidden to ever *have* sexual relations, I guess it shouldn't be surprising that I learned nothing whatsoever, other than that artificial means of contraception are sinful.

Both of the head Stepford husbands here are named Bob,

and one of the women—the one who never talks—is Kelly. Jack and I have no idea what the other one's name is; she does nothing but talk, so she's getting on our nerves.

So are most of the other engaged couples, for that matter.

The most entertaining part of the day, so far, has been the half hour Jack and I were supposed to be spending reflecting on what makes a marriage successful based on couples we know in real life. Instead, we spent the time figuring out where we're going to go for brunch tomorrow, and discussing which couples among the soon-to-be-marrieds here are obviously doomed, and why.

At the moment, the class has been broken up into smaller groups to share our answers to a series of questions about our partners.

It's actually surprisingly kind of fun—like a quiz you'd take in *Cosmopolitan* magazine, only it's fill in the blank, not multiple choice. The questions pertain to your relationship with your spouse, and presumably, your answers are meant to tell you whether you're ready to take this big important step together.

One of the Bobs is our group's moderator. His wife is the one who never shuts up. I can't help but notice he's relieved to have a little space from her, because he seems even more verbal and upbeat here in our little circle of folding chairs in the far corner of the room.

"All right," Bob says, rubbing his hands together eagerly. "Question number one—What do you love most about your spouse-to-be?"

He points to the first guy, who reads a little woodenly from the paper in his hand, "Jill has great teeth. That is my favorite thing about her."

"Peter! Thank you!" His fiancée is thrilled.

"Jill? Your turn."

"I wrote that Peter has a nice smile! I love your smile, Peter." He flashes it and yeah, it's nice.

Still, Jack and I exchange a glance, and I can tell we're thinking the same thing: shallow.

"My turn!" announces the next bride. "The thing I love most about you, John, is your eyes."

And John loves her eyes, too—what a coincidence! A match made in heaven! They are beaming at each other! Bob is beaming with approval!

Again, I catch Jack's eye. Again, I marvel at how much more enlightened we are as a couple compared to these people, Bobs and wives included.

I can't help but wonder what Jack wrote about me. I mean, it's not like we openly discuss what we love about each other, much as I would like to. I'm used to Jack being a man of few words, but that's not allowed here at Pre Cana. I can hardly wait until it's our turn to share our answers, but there's another couple before us. Ho hum.

She loves him because he's always wanted children, yet he stayed by her even after a bout with cancer left her sterile.

Wow.

Visibly moved, Bob motions for her groom to go ahead.

"What I love most about you, Eva," he begins, reading from the questionnaire that's trembling in his hands, "is the way you stared your cancer in the face and fought it with everything you have, and you beat it, honey." He's sobbing, tears running down his face.

"We beat it together, Royce," she replies, her voice choked with emotion.

"I love you because you're the bravest, strongest woman I've ever known, and you're my hero, the wind beneath my wings."

Now the rest of us are teary-eyed, too—especially Eva. And Bob.

"I love your spirit, your heart, your soul, Eva," Royce concludes, "and I promise to spend every day for the rest of my life making you happy."

They fall into each other's arms, violins play and little cupids fly around their heads.

Okay, I made that up about the violins.

And cupids.

But, despite being moved, I have to say it's a little much. I mean, we're not reciting vows here. We're supposed to be telling each other one thing we love about each other. Just one.

"Next," Bob prompts me.

Reluctantly, I read what I wrote to Jack, wishing I had broken the rules like Eva and Royce, or that we could have followed the eye, smile and teeth people instead.

"The thing I love most about you, Jack, is that you can make me laugh even when I want to cry. You have this way of putting a positive, funny spin on even the most depressing day, and I know that with you by my side, making me laugh even when I think that's the last thing I can possibly do, I can get through anything life throws our way."

Jack is obviously touched. "Thanks, Trace," he says a little shyly.

"You're welcome," I return, not feeling so inadequate after all.

And now…

The moment of truth.

He unfolds his paper. Hesitates.

I feel sorry for him, knowing he doesn't feel comfortable sharing heartfelt, romantic stuff like this in front of all these strangers.

"Go ahead, Jack," Bob says. "What do you love most about your fiancée?"

Jack looks down at his paper.

I brace myself in anticipation.

He mumbles something.

"What?" I say, straining to hear him, not wanting to miss a word of it.

"Speak up, Jack," Bob urges, "so that we can all hear you."

Jack clears his throat. "I love her hair."

My hair?

"That's it." Jack nods and sets his paper aside.

Wait—

"Next," says Bob.

What?

That's it?

That's what Jack loves most about me? My hair?

Were we or were we not just minutes ago exchanging glances, thinking about how shallow these first few couples are with the eyes, the teeth, the smiles?

I guess *we* weren't. Jack's concordance must have been my imagination.

Even more troubling than that: he just wasted a perfect opportunity to tell me how he feels about me.

I'd say I have a right to be pissed.

Or maybe I don't, but I can't help it.

Blame it on PMS.

Blame it on lack of sleep.

Blame it on wedding nerves.

Whatever. I'll drop it for now—but I'm not going to just let it go.

On, and on, and on we go, round the circle, sharing answers.

It turns out Jack and I are perfectly compatible—at least, according to our responses to the rest of the questions. How we'll spend our money and our time, how many children we'll have, where we'll go for holidays—blah, blah, blah.

Meanwhile, all I can think is, he loves my hair? That's all he has to say? He couldn't come up with anything better, more original, more romantic? Something like…

You're clever and big-hearted and gentle and crazy and magnetic…

No.

I can't go there. I don't dare go there.

This is about me and Jack. It has nothing to do with Buckley.

It has to do with Jack not stepping up when I wanted him to.

Naturally, I don't bring it up again until Pre Cana is safely over and we're on our way home, certificate in hand.

"That was actually almost fun," Jack comments, sitting beside me as the number six train rumbles uptown.

"Mmm, hmm."

"I learned a lot, didn't you?"

"Oh, yes."

He squirms a little.

"I learned that the only thing you love about me is my

hair, Jack." My voice wavers and suddenly there's a monstrous lump in my throat.

"What? I didn't say that."

"Yes, you did. You said 'I love her hair.' That's a direct quote. See?" I wave his questionnaire—which I kept as evidence—in the air.

"I do love your hair. But that's not the only thing."

"That's all you wrote."

"Because we were supposed to say what we love most. One thing. I thought you'd be happy because you're always complaining about your hair."

"No, *Eva* was happy. She got to hear all this great stuff."

"Who?"

"Eva! With the cancer."

"*Pfft*," is Jack's response. "That guy Roy was so sappy."

"Sappy? What he wrote was beautiful. And his name was Royce."

"What? Beautiful? He pretty much ripped off some old Bette Midler song. Anyone could do that."

"Yeah, well, I wish you had," I mutter.

"What?"

"Nothing." I fold my arms and turn to look sullenly out the window behind me at the dark tunnel flying past.

"You wanted me to quote some old song?" Jack asks incredulously.

"No, Jack. That's not what I wanted."

But quoting an old movie—like *Jerry Maguire*—would have been nice. I'd love to hear that I complete him. So it's not the most original sentiment in the world. At least it's deeper and more meaningful than *I love your hair.*

"Well, what did you want, then?" Jack asks.

I want you to tell me that *I'm* clever and big-hearted and gentle and crazy and magnetic. That sometimes when we're together, just hanging out talking and joking around, you're thinking about grabbing me and kissing me.

"Nothing," I say glumly—and a little guilty. "Never mind."

14

"He just doesn't get it," I tell Raphael the next day as we ride the elevator up to the neonatal floor at the hospital, where Kate delivered a seven-pound baby girl at around 3:00 a.m.

I was the first one she called, which means I got about two hours' sleep for the second night in a row. I couldn't fall asleep again after we hung up. In part because I was excited about the baby, and in part because I was still upset about Jack liking my hair. Period.

"What do you want from him, Tracey? He's a man," Raphael says with a shrug, barely visible behind the enormous teddy bear we picked out at Toys "R" Us in Times Square.

"You're a man," I point out. "If you had to tell Donatello what your favorite thing about him is, I bet you wouldn't say his hair."

"I bet I wouldn't," he agrees with a lascivious bob of his brow.

"That's not what I meant." I toy with the ribbon on the bouquet of pink roses in my hand. "I just can't believe I'm about to spend the rest of my life with someone who doesn't get it."

Come to think of it, I can't believe that I'm actually poised on the rest of my life. It seems so final. Like an ending instead of a beginning.

Yes, it's a happy one.

But like I said, I'm not good at endings.

"What doesn't Jack get, exactly?" Raphael wants to know.

"That sometimes I don't want to be taken for granted. I need to *hear* things."

The elevator stops and the doors open.

"Do you want to back out of the wedding, Tracey?" Raphael asks, a little breathless from lugging the bear around as we emerge on Kate's floor.

"No! Of course I don't want to back out. I just…I wish he was a little more…"

"Verbal."

"Yes, that, but also…"

"Poetic?"

I nod.

"Romantic?"

I nod again…

And, rounding a corner, walk straight into someone.

"Oh, sorry!" I say, then realize who it is.

Irony of ironies…

It's Buckley.

"Tracey! Hi!"

"Hi."

Dare I say he looks great? He's wearing a tan shearling coat, jeans, boots.

But no, I don't dare say it, because he might get the wrong idea.

Then again, it's been weeks since he told me he was in love with me. Maybe he fell out of love when I told him I wanted to marry Jack anyway.

What if he didn't, though?

What if Buckley is still in love with me? What if he's still holding out hope that somehow we might get together?

A few times lately, I've found myself wanting to call him and get this all out into the open, but I haven't. I guess I don't know what I'd want to say.

I just miss him. As a friend. I miss the way we used to be.

Not as much as I miss the way Jack and I used to be, of course.

It's as if this wedding has turned all my relationships upside down lately. I haven't had time for my friends, and I've spent more time than I'd ever want to with people like Kathleen and the twins. Who, to be fair, have all been behaving themselves. At least when it comes to the wedding. The girls really are excited about being flower girls, and so is my niece Kelsey.

"Hi, Buckley—I'm here, too." Raphael pokes his head out from behind the giant stuffed bear.

"Oh! I thought you were just a big escaped grizzly hanging out with Tracey."

"You're so funny, Buckley!" Raphael screams with laughter.

"And you're such a good audience for my lame jokes," Buckley says in return. "Listen, I hate to break it to you guys, but Billy hates stuffed animals. And that is no joke."

"We know," I tell him with a shrug.

"We don't care," Raphael adds. "Why should that poor baby suffer just because its father is a cold-hearted bastard? That's no joke, either, Buckley."

"No kidding. Have you guys seen the baby yet?"

"No, we just got here. Have you?"

"No. I'm going down to the nursery now. Want to come? The nurse is in there with Kate right now. She just put on some rubber gloves and kicked me out—not that I wanted to stay! She told me to come back in fifteen minutes."

"Then let's go with Buckley and see the baby," I tell Raphael.

I'm in no hurry to see Kate anyway. When she called earlier to tell me she'd had the baby, she described every gory, nightmarish detail of her labor and delivery and informed me that there's more—but she has to tell me in person. She also mentioned that I'd be out of my freaking mind to ever consider having a baby.

Raphael and I set off down the hall with Buckley. A few seconds in, Raphael sets the bear down in a huff and announces, "I can't lug this thing another step."

"Leave it here," Buckley suggests.

"Buckley! I can't do that. Someone will steal it!"

"How? By smuggling it out in a body bag?" I ask.

"Or they can dress it in a robe and push it out in a wheelchair," Buckley suggests.

Raphael scowls. "Laugh if you must—"

"We must," Buckley inserts.

"—but I'm staying with Big Ted. You two go ahead. I'll see the baby later."

I hesitate.

"Coming?" Buckley asks me.

I nod. I do want to see the baby, even if it means being more or less alone with Buckley for the first time since that day on the beach.

We head off down the hall together.

I wish I could just grab your hand and run away with you.

No! I can't start thinking about that again.

I've made my peace with the Buckley issue—even if I haven't seen much of him since that fateful Sunday. I know he was at Jack's bachelor party the night I was up in Brookside for my shower. I also know that Kate tried to fix him up with her sister-in-law Amanda, which didn't work out.

Turns out down-to-earth Amanda only likes guys who have real estate, 401Ks and five-figure bonuses. Freelancers who rent aren't her style. Imagine that.

Kate said Buckley didn't seem very into Amanda, either.

"No chemistry," Kate declared. "I could tell right away."

Chemistry.

"Hey, where's Jack today?" Buckley asks me as we turn down the corridor toward the nursery.

"He's at the Mets playoff game with Mitch." We were supposed to go to brunch, but then Kate had the baby, and Mitch called first thing about the game, so we went our separate ways for the day.

"I thought Jack was a Yankees fan and hates the Mets."

"He is and he does," I tell Buckley. "But Mitch got great seats through some guy at work at the last minute..."

And Jack probably couldn't wait to get out of the apartment and away from me after I gave him the silent treatment all last night and most of this morning.

I couldn't seem to help it.

I was overtired and cranky and I still haven't gotten my period. Plus, I keep dwelling on how he had the perfect opportunity to say something really romantic and blew it.

Is this how it's going to be from now on? Am I doomed to spend forever with someone who can't be bothered to come up with something more compelling than "I love your hair"?

All right, maybe I'm being childish and unfair.

I mean, it could have been worse.

He could have said his favorite thing about me is my bullet boobs.

Maybe I'm trying to pick a fight because...

Well, I have no idea why I would want to do that.

"So are you getting excited about the wedding?" Buckley wants to know.

"Of course!" I say too quickly.

"Yeah...it should be fun."

He's right about that. It *should* be fun.

But lately, it's just intense. The wedding machine has taken on a life of its own. And in the myriad details that are involved, nothing seems to really have much to do with who Jack and I were—or will be—as a couple.

It's like our lives are hanging in limbo, and everything around us is changing. I don't recognize us, and I don't recognize anyone else lately, either. Buckley is distant, Kate is a mother, Kathleen's twins are angelic...

What happened to my old life?

I don't want it back necessarily. I just want to ease out of it a little more gradually.

Too late for that, though.

Buckley and I have reached the newborn nursery, where rows of babies lie beyond the glass.

"Which one is she?" Buckley squints at the pink and blue name cards attached to the glass boxlike cribs that hold the babies.

"There," I say, and point at a pink bundle. "That's little Kate."

Yes, Kate named the baby after herself, surprising no one other than perhaps Auntie Amanda, who favored Cleopatra for a girl.

Buckley and I stare reverently at the infant for a few minutes, marveling at her tiny hands, her tiny head and her incessant wailing, which can be heard loud and clear through the glass.

"She's her mother's daughter, all right," I say, watching a team of nurses scurry over to tend to mini-Kate's needs. "Billy's going to have his hands full."

"He already does. But he's glowing. He obviously loves his girls."

"Wait, Billy's glowing?" I ask Buckley.

"Yeah, I think fatherhood has tamed him. He almost seems human all of a sudden, and he's fawning over Kate and the baby."

Billy might be an ass sometimes—all right, most of the time—but you can't say he isn't crazy about Kate.

"Well, I guess there's someone for everyone," I say—and I'm talking about Billy and Kate, of course.

But as soon as the words are out of my mouth, and I see the expression on Buckley's face, I wish I could take them back.

"I know what you're thinking," he says right away. "Listen, I'm okay."

"About...?" I decide to play dumb.

"About you and Jack getting married."

"Oh." I nod. "Good. That makes one of us."

Dammit. Why did I have to say that? I didn't even mean it. Did I?

Buckley's eyes widen. *"What?"*

"No, it's just...I guess I'm having...prewedding jitters." There. It's out. It's official.

"Cold feet?"

"No. I don't want to back out. I just... I guess I'm second-guessing everything all of a sudden."

"Yeah. I've been there."

Yeah. He has.

But he backed out.

"Do you want to talk about it?" Buckley asks. "I'm a good listener. And a good friend."

"No, thanks," I tell him, and check my watch. "We should go and see if we can get back into Kate's room yet. I want to give her these flowers before they wilt."

"I already saw her," Buckley says, "so I think I'll get going home. I've got a copywriting project to finish by tomorrow morning."

We walk slowly and silently down the busy corridor again and part ways at the elevators.

"Tracey, if you ever need to talk..." Buckley tells me, stepping into one.

"Thanks." I wave.

The doors slide closed and he's gone.

If only, I think wistfully, turning away, letting go of Buckley were as simple as letting go of Will McCraw.

★ ★ ★

Jack is home when I get back.

"Hey," I say in surprise, dropping my jacket and keys on the nearest chair.

"How's the new little family?"

"The baby is adorable, Billy gave me a cigar for you and Kate has blossomed into a mother hen, if you can believe that."

"I can't."

"You have to see it to believe it," I tell Jack, smiling at the memory of Kate making a loving fuss over another human being. "The center of her universe has shifted."

"Good. It's about time."

"So what are you doing home? Is the game over already?"

"Nah. I left."

"Well, you hate the Mets," I say as he gets off the couch, where he was sitting with his feet up—and the television off, I notice in surprise.

"I do hate the Mets," he agrees, "but that's not why I left."

"Are you sick or something?"

He shakes his head.

"Then what?" I kick off my shoes and leave them by the door.

"I missed you. I wanted to be here."

It isn't just the words—it's his tone that makes me look at him in surprise.

"But—I wasn't even gone that long."

"No, not that. I mean...I *have* missed you. Lately. I've missed *us*."

I find myself looking at him through tear-filled eyes. "I've missed us, too."

He comes over and takes me into his arms, hugging me hard.

So maybe he does get it after all, I realize.

Maybe he's just as scared—and tense—as I am about all the changes we're facing.

There's a measure of comfort in that…but not as much as you might expect.

I just wish I didn't keep worrying that every minor moment of tension between us might herald bigger problems down the road.

I just wish there hadn't been so many minor moments of tension lately.

I wish there could be more…joy.

I want Jack to tell me that we're doing the right thing, getting married. Of course we are. But he doesn't say that.

Because he isn't any more sure of that than I am, I realize. We love each other—there's no question about that. But are we really going to make it together forever?

We hold on tightly to each other, for a long time.

I want to ask Jack if he thinks we'll ever be *us* again…

But I don't.

Because I'm too afraid of the answer.

"Do you realize that in a matter of days Tracey Spadolini will cease to exist?" I ask Kate edgily in her apartment a few nights after she gets home from the hospital.

"Well, you can always keep your own last name if that bothers you." She hands over mini-Kate and a bottle of formula the nanny just warmed.

No, she's not breast-feeding.

Yes, she knows it's better for the baby.

No, she's not a terrible mother.

You have to give her credit for knowing her limits. This way, the nanny can get up with the baby in the wee hours.

By day, the well-rested Kate is downright doting.

It's as strange to see her cooing and fussing over her tiny daughter as it is to realize that Tracey Spadolini is fading fast.

I ease the rubber nipple into little Kate's hungry mouth and tell Kate, "I don't want to keep my name. It isn't about that. It's about…the end of an era, I guess. I don't know. Forget I said anything."

"It's prewedding jitters," she tells me. "Look, everyone has second thoughts. I did."

But she was marrying Billy. That's to be expected. I mean, who wouldn't have second thoughts about that?

I'm marrying Jack, though. Jack, who is as close to perfect—for me—as anyone ever could be.

Jack, whom I love more than anything, flaws and all.

I just wish I could relax and stop worrying.

"I'm not having second thoughts," I tell Kate. "I want to marry Jack. There's just a lot of stress and we've just been bickering a lot, about stupid things that don't matter."

"Like?"

"Like what he's wearing to the rehearsal dinner, and which bags to pack our stuff in for our honeymoon, and why his mother can't sit at a different table from his father at the reception and whose turn it is to wash the dishes."

"Billy and I fight about stuff like that all the time, if it's any comfort."

It's not. I don't want to compare me and Jack to her and Billy.

"This just isn't like us, though," I say, stroking little Kate's downy head with my freshly manicured fingertips. "We normally get along great, but these last few months—especially the last few weeks—"

"Everyone fights," Kate says logically, "especially before they make a lifelong commitment. You're about to take the biggest step in your life. It would be strange if you weren't a nervous wreck, don't you think?"

"I guess."

I wish Jack were here. I could use a reassuring hug right now.

But he left this afternoon on a business trip to Knoxville, and he won't be back until tomorrow night.

The next morning, I e-mail Buckley:

Hey, I would like to talk, after all. Can you meet me for lunch?

It takes awhile for the response to come back.

Which is unusual, because he's always online on weekday mornings.

I'm busy running around preparing for a presentation, but I keep checking my BlackBerry.

Finally, I hear from Buckley.

Sushi Lucy's, 1:00 p.m. B.

That's all it says.

My reply is even shorter:

OK.

I'm fifteen minutes late, thanks to Carol and Adrian and a series of unreasonable Client demands. Nothing unusual about that.

Buckley is waiting for me in the vestibule, unshaven and wearing jeans, sneakers and an untucked flannel shirt.

Nothing unusual about that, either: he works from home, and Sushi Lucy's is casual.

Still—I'm not a big fan of the rumpled, stubbly look.

Which is good. I'm really glad he didn't show up clean-shaven and bare-chested.

At a fairly secluded table, we order.

Then the waiter leaves and I wonder, uneasily, what to say.

I suppose you're wondering why I've asked you here today would probably be a good start, but I'm not sure of the answer myself.

It was pure impulse, and now that we're here, I wish I hadn't done it.

Buckley rests his chin on his fist and looks at me. "You okay?"

"Pretty much." I sip my ice water, which leaves a funny aftertaste.

"Meaning…?"

"Meaning…I don't know. I'm just stressed, I guess." I gesture at my water glass. "I hate tap water. We should have asked for bottled."

"Is that why you're stressed?" he asks, smirking a little.

"That, and the fact that I'm getting married any second now."

He nods. "That'll do it. Look, Tracey, for what it's worth, coming from me—I don't think you're making a mistake. I think you should marry Jack. I think you'd be crazy not to."

Wow.

"That's worth a lot, coming from you," I say softly.

"You guys are good together. And you're both ready for this. I mean, in an ideal world, you and I would have gotten each other out of our systems first, but..." He shrugs.

Okay, I have to ask. That, after all, is why I'm here. To get him out of my system. But not, I suspect, in the way he has in mind.

"What do you mean, Buckley?"

"You know...we would have had our fling and moved on, instead of being left feeling like there's some kind of...unfinished business between us."

Unfinished business.

That's actually how I've been feeling about it, too...

But I wasn't thinking fling.

I was thinking more...

I don't know, that maybe if I hadn't met Jack, Buckley and I would have ended up together. Long-term.

"If I didn't think Jack was such a great guy," Buckley says, "I might actually be suggesting that we...you know."

"What?"

"Have that fling before you move on and marry Jack and I move on and...well, don't marry anyone. Not for a good long time, anyway. If ever."

"You honestly don't want to get married?"

"Not in this millennium. Just kidding," he adds with a wry grin. "Sort of."

"That surprises me. You don't have any desire to get married?"

"It surprises me, too. I mean, it would make my life a lot less complicated, because most women are into monogamy."

For the first time, I'm seeing Buckley for who he really is—and isn't.

All these years, I was thinking he might be right for me, because of chemistry, and because we have so much in common, both being creative types and coming from large Catholic families.

But now I realize it takes more than that.

A lot more.

"So if you weren't friends with Jack," I say, just to clarify what he's getting at here, "you'd be suggesting that you and I…"

Sleep together?

I can't say it.

I don't have to.

We both know that's what he means.

And there's a graphic—make that pornographic—visual in my head right now that I'm a little uncomfortable with. Then I remember Brenda and Tony, and Kate and Gabriel, and I forgive myself. After all, I'm only human.

"I think that would be a really bad idea," Buckley informs me.

"Because of Jack."

"Right. And because it's definitely not your style."

"No. It's not."

Is it Buckley's?

He smiles—wryly—again. "You know, even though I knew that all along about you…I guess I was kind of hoping you were going to contradict me."

I raise my eyebrows at him. "Sorry."

"It's okay." He sighs. "We'll just move on, and it'll be fine."

"Yeah? You think we can put this behind us now and get

back to being friends?" I, for one, would relish at least one relationship in my life getting back to familiar footing again.

"I never wanted any of this to come between us, Tracey," Buckley says. "It was really selfish of me to tell you that I loved you in the first place—even though I meant it."

"I thought it was really unselfish, actually," I tell him. "Especially since you knew all along that nothing could ever come of it."

"Yeah, well, I'm a great, unselfish guy."

"You are."

"No, I'm not. Jack is a great, unselfish guy. That's why you guys are getting married. Me—I'm too selfish to marry anyone."

"Maybe someday you won't be. If you find the right person."

"Maybe."

He doesn't look very sure about that, though.

"You've found the right person, though," he tells me. "You do know that, right?"

I nod and reach for my icky tap water again. I do know that. It's just…well, sometimes I'm scared shitless of the future. That's all.

"Good," Buckley says. "Because the way Jack was talking about you at his bachelor party last week…"

"What did he say?"

"Oh, he was trashed. I can't repeat it."

"Buckley! You have to!"

He grins. "No way. My lips are sealed. Just know that the guy is head over heels in love with you. Okay?"

"No. You have to tell me what he said. At least one thing he said. Come on, Buckley. Throw me a bone here."

"All right. I'll tell you one thing he said. He said he loves your hair."

Oh, God. Here we go.

Why did I insist?

"Why would he bring that up?" I ask, wondering if Jack told the guys the whole Pre Cana tale.

"Oh, because Mitch was hitting on some bleached-blonde stripper with bad roots. And Jack started talking about hair, and how it reflects a person's true character."

"He said that?"

"Believe me, it didn't make a whole lot of sense, but he meant well. He was going on and on about how soft your hair is, and how he loves the color—how he's so glad that you don't dye it or use a load of gunk in it. He kept saying how great it smells, and he loves when you fall asleep on his chest because he can breathe into it all night. And he said that sometimes when you're away on business he opens your shampoo bottle in the shower so he can smell it and not miss you so much."

Wow.

"Jack said that? At his bachelor party?"

"I told you he was trashed." Buckley shrugs. "The guys gave him a hell of a time about it. And if you tell him I said any of that, I will be dead to him, so keep your mouth shut, please."

"I will. But…thanks for telling me, Buckley."

Jack loves my hair.

I think that's the sweetest thing I've ever heard in my life.

That night, riding up to our floor in the elevator after another long day at work, I imagine what it would be like to find Jack waiting for me with a homemade dinner, candlelight, champagne, a dozen roses.

It would be like walking into somebody else's apartment—that's what it would be like.

Because I can predict what's going to happen in ours: there's going to be clutter, television, beer and takeout—at best. Jack is going to be there on the couch in jeans or sweatpants, watching the Yankees playoff game.

But that's what counts. Out of all those details, I now realize that I don't really care about the clutter or the beer or the sweatpants.

I missed him last night when he was gone.

And tonight, I care about one thing only: Jack is going to be there.

Jack is going to be there, for the rest of my life.

He's willing to stand and make that promise—that *vow*—in front of a few hundred people, Father Stefan and God.

There are no guarantees.

Plenty of people make that same vow, and break it.

His parents did.

Yet somehow, despite that—despite seeing firsthand the evidence of a marriage that failed miserably—Jack is willing to take a chance on us.

So am I.

And plenty of people do make it.

My parents did.

Okay, maybe there's no candlelight and romance in the Spadolini house back in Brookside these days—maybe there never was—but there's a dishwasher. And there's always been a lot of love.

I step over the threshold into our apartment.

There's Jack, on the couch. Sweatpants. Pizza box. Yankees game.

"You're home," I say.

"Yeah," he says, looking up. "So are you."

"Yes," I say around a heavy, happy lump in my throat as he pats the empty spot on the couch beside him in silent invitation.

We're home.

15

The rehearsal dinner is held in the private party room at the Greenway Inn, which is where all the Candells are staying, along with Kate, her nanny and the baby, Raphael and Donatello, and, yes, Buckley.

He made it.

He's on the opposite side of the candlelit dining room, sitting with the other guys in the wedding party. He's been flirting with Jack's cousin Anne, and guess what? That's fine with me.

It's wedding eve and I'm the bride. I've only got eyes for Jack.

But it's not like the groom and I have had a moment alone together since we got up to Brookside a few days ago—and that's not likely to change tonight. There's a big crowd at the dinner, of course. Both our immediate families and some out-of-town relatives, plus all of our attendants and their spouses, Father Stefan and even Rev Dev.

Jack's parents are hosting this party together, and I can't help but notice that they seem to have called a truce for the occasion.

"They seem almost happy together," I whisper to Jack, watching Wilma—elegantly dressed in a black velvet sheath—laughing with her ex over sips of cocktail-hour champagne. "Do you think there's any chance they'll get back together again?"

Jack shudders. "God, I hope not."

"Why?"

"Because two people can never be more wrong for each other than they are."

"Why do you think they got married in the first place, then? Did they change that drastically? Or were they just blind?"

"Who knows? I'm just glad they did, or you and I wouldn't be here."

Father Stefan steps in with a, "Well? How are you two feeling tonight? Are you ready to take this big step?"

Naturally, Jack and I nod vigorously.

"Any questions about what's going to happen tomorrow?" Father Stefan wants to know.

I assume he's definitely not talking about later, at the hotel near the airport where we're spending our wedding night. I really hope he figures we've got that part covered, and that all is forgiven at this point. I did go to confession the other day, before we left New York, so I'm starting marriage with a nice clean soul.

Jack and I tell Father Stefan that we have no questions about the ceremony. Earlier, at the church, we went through the motions for tomorrow's mass—stuff like who stands where, and who says what. Things were a little chaotic, but Father Stefan assured us that it's always that way.

"All right, then," he says now. "Just let me know if you have any questions."

He pats Jack on the back and gives me a hug before wandering off to say hello to my Aunt Aggie.

"He never did ask you whether you actually followed through and moved out," Jack comments. "Or did he?"

I shake my head and wonder—for the first time—if maybe I should have moved out. Would we have taken each other less for granted these last few months? Would I have found some kind of spiritual enlightenment?

Who knows?

But now is not the time to start second-guessing myself.

Jack and I separate to mingle. I go first to the table where Raphael is cuddling Kate's newborn under the watchful gazes of her doting mother and the nanny who now accompanies Kate everywhere. Billy couldn't get away for the wedding. No surprise there.

"Donatello has decided he wants to start a family, Tracey!"

"Are you serious? That's great!"

"I know! Can you just see me with a baby carriage?"

"I just can."

"Now we only need to find a surrogate." He gives me a meaningful look.

"No," I say. "But hey, good luck with that."

"Tracey! We're willing to pay."

"Then you shouldn't have a problem finding someone," I say briskly.

"Leave her alone, Raphael," Kate drawls. "Tracey's going to be popping out her own babies after the honeymoon."

I have to laugh at that visual. "Not right after. I've got other things on the agenda." Like house-hunting. And career-changing. And a whole lot of Couch Time with my husband. "Anyway, Kate, aren't you the one who told me I'd be out of my freaking mind to even consider childbirth?"

"Did I?" she asks mildly, and reaches out to adjust little Kate's pink bootie.

Raphael and I exchange a glance.

"Maybe," he suggests in a low voice, "Billy had them give her a lobotomy while she was in the delivery room."

"That would explain a lot."

I plant a kiss on mini-Kate's head and move on to Brenda and Paulie, Latisha and Derek, Yvonne and Thor.

"Tracey! This is the most go-aw-jus place I've ever seen!" Brenda informs me.

"The inn?"

"And the town! Right on the lake, and all these big old houses…"

"We picked up a real estate book when we stopped for coffee earlier, and now she wants to move here," Paulie explains.

"We could afford a mansion here!"

"Yeah, but Bren, what would you do here?"

"She'd be a stay-at-home mom," Latisha tells me.

"Just like she's going to be back in New York," Thor puts in.

"Shh!" Yvonne elbows him.

"*What?*" I raise an eyebrow at Brenda.

"I was going to wait to tell you until after the wedding...but I gave notice yesterday, Tracey. Paulie made sergeant."

"That's great! Congratulations!" I tell Paulie, but even I can hear the hollow tone in my voice. "And Bren...good for you! You always said you were going to quit as soon as Paulie made sergeant."

"Yeah, I've always wanted to be a desperate housewife. But I'm going to miss you guys."

"We'll still do happy hour," I tell her.

"God knows you're going to need it," Yvonne comments.

"Just don't you start talking about retiring again," Latisha tells her.

"What? Yvonne, you can't retire!" I protest.

"Technically, she could have retired a few years ago." Thor's comment is met with a dark look from his wife.

"If you retired, baby," Derek tells Latisha, "just think of all the energy you'd have for other things."

"Yeah, well, too bad for you that I'm a spring chicken," Latisha retorts.

Unfazed, he nuzzles her neck, saying, "No kids with us this weekend—this ol' rooster will take what he can get."

"I can't believe you guys are leaving Blaire Barnett," I tell Brenda and Yvonne.

"I didn't retire yet."

"Maybe not," I tell Yvonne, "but just the fact that you're talking about it..."

She's going to be out of there. I can tell.

Another end to another era.

But I don't dare think about that now. One ending era at a time is about all I can handle...and somebody is clinking a glass.

"Tracey," Jack says, grabbing my hand. "Come on. They want to get started."

For presumably the last time in my life, I wake up alone in my girlhood bed.

From now on, whenever I visit my parents in Brookside, Jack will be sharing my bed with me. That will seem strange, won't it? Sleeping with a guy under my parents' roof?

Not just any guy.

My husband.

My stomach erupts in a thousand butterflies.

Yup, today is the end of an era and I feel like I'm about to freak out.

Jack, I think. *I need to talk to Jack. That would help to keep me grounded.*

I reach for my cell phone on the bedside table and dial Jack's cell phone. Last night after the rehearsal dinner, he spent the night at the Greenway Inn with his family and some of our friends.

He was going to share a room with Mitch and I wonder if it's too early to call, but Jack picks up the phone instantly. "Hey. I was just going to call you."

"You were?"

"Yeah. I miss you. I feel like I'm going through this huge thing alone."

"I feel the same way. I feel like there's so much we have to get through before we can be back to our normal selves."

I just hope we can find our normal selves—our normal lives—again, when this is all over.

"Why don't you meet me at Bob Evans for breakfast?"

Jack suggests, as if that's the perfectly logical next thing to say. "We can have zau-zage gravy."

I laugh.

We love Bob Evans sausage gravy.

Zau-zage.

Just like that, I feel like we're really going to be able to become us again. That after today—well, after today, and Tahiti, anyway—we'll be able to think about ordinary things like sausage gravy again.

"That sounds so good," I tell Jack wistfully. "But you're not supposed to see me on our wedding day."

"I thought that was just in the dress. Don't wear the dress."

"You're not supposed to see me at all. It's bad luck."

"Are you sure?"

"No. But why take chances?"

He sighs. "Then I guess I'll just see you later, at the church."

"Okay. Are you nervous, Jack?"

"A little. Are you?"

"A little," I admit. "But only because there are a million details that have to fall into place between now and two-thirty. I almost wish we were eloping to Tahiti."

"Not me," Jack says unexpectedly. "This is going to be great, Trace. You'll see."

"The wedding?"

"Everything."

I smile. "I love you."

"I love you, too."

In less than an hour, I will no longer be me.

It's the end of an era.

Tracey Spadolini is about to drop into the past, replaced by Tracey Candell.

I suppose that's fitting, considering that I no longer even look like Tracey Spadolini. The woman in the mirror of my girlhood bedroom is a solemn stranger in white.

All that's recognizable is her hair—worn long and loose, the way Jack likes it.

"You look beautiful," my mother, in blue satin, teased ringlets and a corsage, chokes out. She's been crying into her embroidered hankie all morning.

"Cut it out, Ma," Mary Beth says, adjusting the fall of my lace veil. "You'll smear your eye makeup."

"I can't help it. My baby is getting married."

"All your babies have gotten married, Ma," I point out.

"Don't remind me!"

"Well, I'm not married," Mary Beth points out, stepping back to survey the veil. "Maybe someday, though…again."

I smile at my sister in the mirror. I really hope so. Nobody deserves what Vinnie put her through.

I'm so lucky.

And so scared.

"Ma?" I say in a small voice. "On your wedding day… how did you feel?"

"Nervous."

"But were you sure you were doing the right thing?"

"I was positive." She looks worriedly at me. "Aren't you?"

"Yes!" I say as the doorbell rings.

My mother hurries out of the room to answer it.

"I wasn't positive," Mary Beth offers. "I knew, even on my wedding day, that I was probably making a big mistake."

"Why did you go through with it?"

"Because I was afraid to be alone. I needed someone to take care of me because I couldn't take care of myself. I wasn't like you, Tracey."

Well, there was a time when I was just like her.

Afraid to be alone. Uncertain that I could take care of myself. Willing to be with the wrong person—Will—because he was all I had. Or thought I had.

Turned out I never did.

And when he left me alone, there was nothing I could do but learn how to take care of myself.

That was a lifetime ago.

Look at me now.

For the first time today, I smile a smile that actually reaches my eyes.

Then my mother comes bustling in saying, "Look who's here!"

If it isn't the wedding photographer…

Followed by Grandma, who is wearing a low-cut dress that is oddly evocative of a shower curtain.

"*Dolce mia!*" she exclaims, catching sight of me. "You're a *bellissima* bride!"

She comes rushing over.

"Grandma," I say as she envelops me in a hug, "that's some dress. Did you make it?"

She nods proudly.

"Wow, where did you get that fabric?" Mary Beth asks. "It's so…unique."

"I found it at Bed, Bath and Beyond when I was shopping for Tracey's wedding gift."

"Did you say Bed, Bath and Beyond?"

"Shh—it's a shower curtain," she says with a conspiratorial wink. "But no one at the wedding will ever know."

God, I hope not.

Grandma spins around to model for us, and I check the back of her hemline to make sure there are no ring holes showing.

"Hold that shot," the photographer commands.

Grandma poses and preens as he snaps her alone, then a few shots of the two of us. Then he has to get me and Mary Beth and Grandma, then just me and Mary Beth, then Ma and me...mother and daughters...three generations...

You get the picture.

And the photographer gets the pictures; hundreds, it seems, and I can't wait to see Jack.

Then Ma says, "It's time to get to the church."

"Already?" I ask, and my stomach flip-flops nervously.

Then I remember that Jack is going to be there, waiting for me.

"Okay," I say, picking up my bouquet and taking a deep breath. "Let's go."

Standing at the end of a white satin runner in the vestibule at Most Precious Mother, I realize that this is it.

Goodbye, single life.

Hello, married life.

The organ is playing, my mother's been seated and most of the bridesmaids have made their way down the aisle—which, of course, has taken a good long while. Now the twins and Kelsey are on their way, scattering rose petals as they go, leaving me, my sister, my father and the photographer's assistant in the back of the church.

"Can you see Jack?" I ask Mary Beth in a whisper as she moves forward, poised to start toward the altar.

"No. But he's up there somewhere," she says with a smile, and then she's gone.

Moments later, the organist shifts to the opening chords of the wedding march, and I hear a massive creaking sound as three hundred people stand in anticipation of the bride.

"Are you ready?" my father asks.

I cling to his arm tightly.

Am I ready?

Panic sweeps through me.

No.

I'm not ready.

I finally figured out how to be Tracey Spadolini! I figured out who she was, and what she needed and wanted, and how to take care of her.

Now I'm going to start all over again from scratch, learning how to be Tracey Candell. Jack's wife.

I swallow painfully hard and look straight ahead.

For a moment, all I can see is the glare of the photographer's spotlights.

I can't do this, I think.

I'm just not comfortable with endings. Not even happy ones.

Then the lights shift and I blink, and look again, and suddenly, I catch a glimpse of Jack.

There he is, in a dark tux, stepping forward at the opposite end of the runner.

All the faces seem to fall away, and all I can see is Jack. He's smiling.

This is going to be great, Trace, he's thinking. *You'll see.*

"Tracey?" That's my father again. "Are you ready?"

This time, I nod.

I'm ready.

I could go on to tell you that my father walks me down the aisle past a sea of faces: everyone we love—everyone who loves us, believes in us.

I could tell you that before all of those people, and Father Stefan, and God, Jack Candell and I promise to love and honor each other all the days of our lives.

I could even tell you that the highlight of the reception is Raphael doing a wild tarantella with Grandma in her shower-curtain dress, or that Jack surprises me by renting a honeymoon hut-on-stilts in Tahiti after all, or that Jack's father's wedding gift is the better part of a down payment on a condo—maybe even a house.

But you know what?

I'm not sure which part would be the happy ending.

So I think I'll end it right here, in this moment, with me taking my first steps toward my husband, full of hope and trust and love, with no idea what's going to happen next.

That way, it's not an ending after all.

It's a happy beginning instead.

And those are even better.

Mystery writer Sophie Katz is back in the
sequel to SEX, MURDER AND A DOUBLE LATTE!

Passion, Betrayal
and Killer Highlights

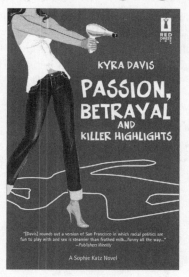

Only this time, she's trying to clear her sister's name
after her brother-in-law is found murdered.

With no help from the San Francisco police department,
who refuse to take Sophie seriously, she finds herself
partnering with sexy P.I. Anatoly Darinsky.

But will Anatoly be able to protect Sophie from her crazy plans
to lure the killer out of hiding? And most importantly, will she be
able to solve the case before her next book-signing tour?

**Available wherever
trade paperbacks
are sold!**

RED
DRESS
INK
TM

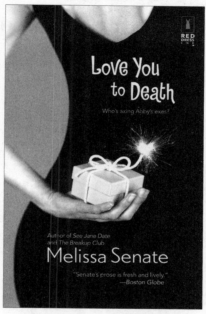